THE WRATH OF GOD

Hard Science Fiction

The Dark Cloud

Book 4

BRANDON Q. MORRIS

BRANDON Q.
MORRIS
HARD SCIENCE FICTION

What's happened so far

2144: CELIA BARON WORKS AT LOWELL OBSERVATORY IN Flagstaff, Arizona, where Pluto was discovered over two hundred years ago. As night falls, she uses the observatory's telescopes to introduce visitors to the wonders of the universe. After the tours are done, she unofficially, but with the permission of her boss, uses the observatory's best instruments to further her own research.

During a routine survey, she notices strange occurrences at the LDN 63 dark nebula. Everything that occurs there seems to happen especially fast. That would be a great observation, if only someone would believe her. Unfortunately, Celia made a supposedly groundbreaking discovery once before, but used falsified data to do it. Since then, her name has been discredited in the scientific community. To back up her observation, she needs access to a much more powerful telescope. But with her history, she has no chance of getting time at any of the best telescopes in the world.

Paul Henson is a priest in a Catholic church in Tucson, Arizona. Ever since his daughter and wife died in an accident, he has lost his faith in God. He is just dragging himself through his daily life and is about to be fired when he has an idea: he can no longer believe in God, but if there were proof speed of light, within four days on board. The AI, Alexa, is lost during the transport.

At the center of the star cluster, about ten thousand distinctly alien spaceships in two different forms await them. They are apparently guarding a spherical disturbance in space-time. An alien being, who calls himself a Residual, explains to them that the star cluster was constructed as a lure. Here the "Incursion", aggressive aliens who target water sources, is to be stopped once and for all. They would have been destroyed soon after their arrival, but the unexpected appearance of the humans has halted this process and deactivated the detonator, because no third parties must come to harm.

It is clear that the Incursion fleet will harvest the entire water supply of the star cluster in a few years. After that, the Earth is in danger, since it is in the immediate cosmic neighborhood. If the crew escapes with the *Truthseeker*, their home planet will die. However, if they can find the detonator and activate it manually, all the stars in the cluster will release their accumulated energy at the same moment. That would stop the Incursion—and wipe out the crew of the *Truthseeker*.

It turns out that the AI Alexa was merely hiding. The civilization that left the Residual hunts AIs and destroys them, she fears. Is this more than a rumor? In any case, it seems to be the real reason Alexa embarked on this journey in the first place.

Then a modern battleship built by humankind also arrives in the dark nebula. The *Sword of God* is a product of advanced technology and has been able to reduce its flight time to a third of the *Truthseeker*'s. Its commander, Guard Captain Riccardo Sardi, invites the protagonists to make plans together to eliminate the danger.

But before they can reach it, their own spaceship, the *Truthseeker*, suddenly starts moving away. Apparently, it is being hijacked by an unknown force. Their target seems to be a space distortion through which the Incursion entered the Dark Nebula. The Residual and the Alexa AI manage to halt the abduction by disabling the thrusters. Unfortunately, this doesn't help the *Sword of God* in its pursuit, as a huge Incursion object is approaching the human ship. First, Jaron and his friends investigate it with the Star Liner capsule. In the process, they discover that the invaders are probably not completely part of reality.

However, with the maneuver they attract the attention of the Incursion. The entire *Sword of God* is swallowed by one of the cuboids. It turns out that the objects are much bigger inside than outside and could hold whole solar systems. They apparently intend to fill this entire volume with stolen water. While traversing the interior, the protagonists come across an asteroid-sized sphere of water. In addition, the interior of the Incursion has the unpleasant effect that time runs slower than it does on the outside, due to its high energy density. Thus, the *Sword of God* loses additional time in its pursuit of the *Truthseeker*. At first, the ship cannot leave the Incursion at all. At last Captain Sardi is able to open a tiny passage with heavy laser fire, through which Jaron, Celia, Paul and Jürgen can escape with the Star Liner capsule into familiar space. The *Sword of God*, on the other hand, must stay behind. Carlota, the doctor, also remains on the ship. Nothing further is known about her fate.

Meanwhile, a new alliance has formed on board the *Truthseeker*. The hijacker turns out to be an AI of human descent—it is Watson, who has spent a long time in the holographic projection layer of the universe. He believes that the only way to save the Earth from destruction is to attempt to fly through the wormhole to the origin of the Incursion and eliminate it once and for all. However, he is persuaded to allow the Residual and Alexa access to a World Root, one of the defenders' giant spaceships. With it, they hope to break open the Incursion object that has picked up the *Sword of God*.

When the Star Liner capsule finally makes it out into the open, the crew notices that the *Truthseeker* is about to enter the wormhole. They know nothing of Watson, who is alone on board, or his plans. Nor do they know about the World Root with Alexa and the Residual, which has set course for them. So for Jaron, Celia, Jürgen and Paul, all hope seems to be lost. Nevertheless, they try to use the time they have left to perhaps trigger the trap for the Incursion objects.

Meanwhile, the Residual uses its ability to project itself to other places to search for the *Sword of God* within the Incursion objects. To be able to trigger the trap, it absolutely needs at least one human being—because it was the presence of human beings that blocked the trap. After some failures, the Residual lands in the water sphere, where it is injured and finally rescued by the humans. It can't take anyone from the crew outside with it, but learns that the Star Liner capsule has managed to escape. This is good news, but the Residual's connection to the projector is now severed. So it's trapped on the human ship inside the Incursion object and can no longer help trigger the trap.

But the World Root has already discovered the lonely Star Liner capsule. Jaron and his crew board the tree ship, where they meet the Alexa AI. They convince the World Root to try to trigger the trap, even without the missing Residual, to destroy the Incursion, as the Growths had planned for so long.

The control center that controls the trap is located in a hollowed-out asteroid. Celia, Jürgen and Jaron investigate it together, while Paul remains aboard the World Root. The three find a construction in the style of a snail shell. In the center there is a hologram showing the entire star cluster—the former dark nebula LDN 63—as well as a kind of aquarium. Nothing else, especially no switch that could reset the trap. The group returns disappointed to the World Root, which also has no idea.

They decide to try again, but this time together with Alexa. Since the hologram no longer glows, the only thing left is the aquarium. But there is no switch hidden in it either. There is only a primitive creature with a towel-like body and eyes floating on the water. Jaron, Celia and Jürgen are thinking about blowing up the whole headquarters when Paul tells them from the World Root that the Incursion has begun its attack. Soon it will be too late.

That's when Jürgen has an idea: he connects the rosary on which the Alexa AI is stored to the emitter of the hologram. Alexa manages to talk to the AI of the control center, which in turn manages to locate the Residual. Now that the connection is back up, the Residual can project itself into the control center, where it appears in the external form of Jürgen's best friend Norbert. The Residual reveals to them that the aquarium is the switch: they must kill the body of the Residual, which they had mistaken for a primitive creature. This would also erase its consciousness, which would unblock the trap.

However, they will also die when the trap is triggered, unless they manage to escape in time aboard the World Root. But this is only possible if one of them sacrifices themselves and waits in the control center until the others are safe.

The crew can't agree on who should take on this task. But then the robot Norbert Two intervenes and proposes to do it. In the last scene of the previous volume, *Sword of God*, the Residual in Norbert's body and the robot walk together to the exit in order to trigger the trap in the control center.

The Wrath of God

World Root, January 6, 2295

JARON WAS A SWAMP. HIS BODY WAS MUDDY. THE BLOOD vessels washed like channels around dry trees, his bones, but what moistened the mud most of all were his own excretions. The muscles were like little lawns under which the mire was palpable. With every strain, it oozed through, shining black. His tendons, the roots of goutweed. Only they still held everything together.

It was torturous. Jaron lost all sense of the passage of time until the World Root gave them a break. That was 37 minutes ago, and he feared that the next acceleration phase would soon begin. He needed to get out of his trough-like seat to be able to drain the swamp.

Carefully, he moved his right leg. The muscles responded to his commands. Their first response was a sharp cry that came from his mouth, brought on by the incredible pain, but then there was also a scratching, the feeling of meeting resistance, and a hard edge under his lower leg.

His leg had moved! Jaron clung to the backrest with his arms and heaved his upper body into a vertical position. A bright red appeared before his eyes. Jaron paused to give his sense of balance a chance to get used to being vertical. He also needed to think about what the next step should be. His body needed precise instructions. At least he didn't have to command it to breathe. That was good.

Jaron turned his upper body to the right. This caused the legs to move at the same time. The right one folded down. The heel hit the side wall, or was it the floor? The pain of the touch was so intense that Jaron thought he heard it. No, it wasn't his imagination. Someone else moaned at the same moment. Celia?

He had to pull himself together. The World Root seemed to have no idea what it was putting people through. Or it knew very well and had taken it to the limit. The moaning repeated itself. It came from close by. Celia. He commanded his left leg to swing to the right as well, but put a little too much energy into the movement, causing him to lose his balance. For a tenth of a second, he had the choice of falling forward or backward.

The moment passed too quickly. He already saw himself with a laceration on the back of his head. But his body took the initiative and pushed his right leg backwards, giving him an impulse forward. Jaron even managed to catch himself with his arms as he hit the ground with his upper body.

Oof. He felt pain in several parts of his body at the same time. He took the complaints matter-of-factly, but had no time for them, because he had heard Celia's moaning. It was coming from very close by. Jaron felt his way along the floor until he reached the next bin. Did the seats have this shape when they started, or had the World Root remodeled them while they were inside? He couldn't remember.

But that did not matter, either. All that mattered was Celia's moaning, which intensified. Jaron pulled himself up the smooth wall of the tub until he could lean over it. Celia was lying in front of him; he smelled her scent and saw her with his hands. She fidgeted like a small child. He spoke soothing words that he couldn't remember a second later, and finally stumbled upon the cause of her agitation—a garment made of a thick but elastic material had, for some reason, pushed its way up her face from her neck until it covered her mouth and nose. Celia must feel like someone was trying to suffocate her. Jaron pulled the material back down around her neck.

"Oh, it's you," she said.

She sounded a little disappointed.

"I heard you," Jaron said. "You were moaning."

"I thought I was dying," she explained, "No, I thought I'd died already. Except my mother was stroking my face. That was nice."

"Your sweater was riding up on you. I pulled it down."

"Thank you, Jaron. It's nice to be back."

"I think so, too."

As if by magic, their hands found each other. It must be a strange image: him hanging half-dead over the edge of the pool, holding a half-dead woman as if to drag her from death to life.

What was she to him actually...? The question didn't make it to his mouth. He could not even complete it. They had slept together. But that was in another time, in a time of despair, before the salvation of the world. Jaron had not yet personally verified that the trap was doing its job, but the World Root would certainly have informed them if something was not going according to plan.

The *Sword of God*. Jaron had no right at all to think about Celia and himself until they had mourned the crew of the ship. Why hadn't he insisted that Carlota, at least, board the Star Liner capsule with them? It would have been close, but they could have saved at least ten more people.

A hand stroked his hair.

"We really need to take a shower," Celia said.

THE BLACK CUBOID WAS SHAKING. SIX MUSHROOM SHIPS HAD turned their heads toward it. It looked as if they had gathered together in order to collectively gossip about the Incursion craft. The fact that they were firing radiation or particle weapons at the enemy could not be seen in the holorecording, even though it had excellent resolution.

Maybe it was just him. Jaron pulled back his hands, with which he had been scanning the Incursion. The World Root projected a hologram that he could touch. To everyone else, Paul had assured him, it looked like a three-dimensional sculpture made of light. But it was a figure he could grasp in the literal sense. The World Root had tried to explain the technology, but when it started talking about multidimensional spaces, he had tuned out.

Jaron thought of the Residual, who was also a projection. A physical projection, it had called itself, with the consciousness of a creature that had the shape of an old, dirty towel. It was dead now, as was Norbert Two. That was among the few certainties they had, for the World Root had shown them the explosion. Jaron had even felt its warmth on his face.

The black cuboid, on the other hand, was cold, almost icy. This corresponded perfectly to his idea of the object. Even when Celia had brought his hand close to the Incursion, he had felt the cold, and he had sensed the blackness even before Celia had told him anything about the color of all the objects in the hologram.

"Now!" said Celia.

Jaron reached again, and the black cuboid burst in his hands. The walls crumbled to dust under his fingers. He felt as if he had destroyed a toy. Instinctively, he held his hand under it, just in case the contents fell out. But nothing came out. The cuboid must have been empty. The mushroom ships struck before the Incursion had properly begun harvesting. Inside one of these Incursion objects must be the *Sword of God*.

What would happen to it when the Incursion that held it captive also burst? The World Root could not tell them. Or maybe it knew, but didn't want to worry them? Jaron didn't know what to make of the World Root yet. As long as the Residual had been with them, the ship had fulfilled their wishes, but who knew if it would stay that way?

"How's the war going?" asked Paul. "I hope the mushrooms really hand it to the invaders."

Jaron had to smile. Shouldn't a clergyman be preaching charity to them? Or maybe that didn't apply to aliens?

"The current projection shows 98 percent efficiency," the World Root explained.

"That's not good," Jürgen said.

The engineer was right. Given the huge invasion fleet, it would be a disaster if two percent of the objects survived.

"The delayed triggering of the trap prevents a higher efficiency," said World Root. "The sterilization area is frayed at the edges. The first Incursion objects are settling. But the trap has weakened the Incursion to such an extent that a new attack is not to be feared for at least 2800 years of your time. That's enough time to build a new trap."

"But what if two percent of the 10,000 objects make their way toward Earth?" asked Jürgen.

"That's unlikely," said World Root. "According to historical experience, the Incursion left over after a war, or harvesters that haven't yet been filled with water, are randomly distributed throughout 3D space around the original target."

"Can you put that in a more understandable way?" asked Paul.

"The Incursion objects are swarming. Since the solar system you're from is sixty light-years away and far from the only target of interest, the risk of invasion is less than eighty percent."

"That's a pretty high risk," said Jürgen.

"But even if it occurs, only one Incursion will enter the system."

"Only one?" asked Jürgen.

"Yes, just one. In fact, the risk of there being two is less than forty percent."

The World Root had apparently overlooked the sarcastic undertone in Jürgen's question.

"Well, that's a depressing outlook," Jürgen said.

"To fight a single Incursion object, all you need is two or three World Roots."

"Two or three, ha ha."

"Yes, two or three."

"We have one, if we count you."

"I'm sorry, but I have another task."

"Excuse me?" Jürgen's voice became louder. "You're not going to help us, World Root?"

"Someone has to report to the Growths. It's a long journey to reach them."

"Then I guess a small detour to our solar system is in order."

"No, human. I'm sorry. The Growths must prepare for the return of the Incursion in 2800 years. A trap like that takes some time to prepare. The detour through your system would cost me more than a hundred years."

"Without the detour, our homeland will be destroyed," Jürgen said.

"That is not certain. The risk is merely eighty percent, and surely your kind will know how to defend themselves. You shouldn't underestimate them."

"Does that mean you'll take us to meet your masters?" asked Jürgen, "no matter what we want?"

"I don't have any masters. You are invited to accompany me as I make my way to The Growths. But of course, you can also get back into the spaceship you came to me in."

Jaron shook his head. The Star Liner capsule would not even transport them to the nearest solar system, let alone home. The *Truthseeker*, his ship, had disappeared into a space distortion. The *Sword of God* was stuck in an Incursion object, if it even still existed. They had no choice but to go with the World Root. This was precisely what annoyed him, and when something annoyed him, he became defiant.

"For my part, I would prefer to continue my journey in the capsule," he said. "It's still better than staying aboard a cowardly intelligence who lacks any sort of empathy."

"You're right," Jürgen said. "I'll come with you, of course. We'll find a way home."

Jaron cringed. The engineer didn't really believe that, did he? Jürgen must know that they would end their lives in LDN 63. That was the way it had to be.

"I understand your motives very well," Paul said. "On the other hand, I'd like to know the Growths. They're so advanced—maybe they're on a quest for God."

He had not given up on his mission, though he had to watch more of the devil's work in the dark nebula. Jaron would miss him. But in the capsule, three of them would be able to survive longer than four. Jaron's thoughts faltered. Was Paul deceiving them? Was he trying to make it easier for them to survive by faking his search?

Celia interrupted his speculation. "Since I'm in charge of the expedition, I guess it's up to me to decide," she said, squeezing his hand. "So, we will leave here tomorrow."

"Of course you are free to do so," said the World Root. "However, it would cause the spread of the fighting to overtake you. In all probability, you will then be destroyed in the coming days."

"Do you have a better suggestion?" asked Celia. "You could just drop us off at home."

"We've already talked about the detour necessary to do that," said the World Root. "But I'm offering to let you stay on board during the acceleration phase. On the one hand, this would allow you to escape the trap, and on the other hand, your spaceship could benefit from the speed I achieve in the process. This would shorten your return journey considerably. I could also provide you with all the resources you need. After all, that won't change my overall mass."

Jaron paused. That was an offer, after all. If they could achieve more than half the speed of light, they would reach the solar system much sooner. Then humanity could at least prepare for the inevitable. If they dug deep enough into Earth, it might have a chance of surviving the harvest.

"That's all well and good," Jürgen said. "But how will we

decelerate? We don't have an engine with enough power or enough fuel, do we?"

"We don't really need to brake at all," Celia said. "It would be enough to fly through the solar system. At least that way we could prepare people for what's coming."

Jaron had nothing to add, so he merely nodded.

Truthseeker, January 6, 2295

EITHER HE WAS DEAD OR HE WAS IN ANOTHER UNIVERSE. Watson checked the systems of the *Truthseeker*. The hardware was working perfectly, almost too well. After such a turbulent trip, one would expect an engine to be down to half power or life support to go on strike. It would be bad because, as an AI, he had no body and was thus incapable of repairing anything that was not in the main computer's memory. But none of that had happened, and that scared him because it meant he was dead.

Only in death was everything right and healthy. Death was a strange phenomenon that he had to come to terms with. Whether machine or living being, one built up a debt with entropy, deteriorating from the perfect state into a good one, which soon became satisfactory, until it was only just enough. Then death followed and set everything back to the beginning. No wonder religions preached rebirth, whether in reality or on a divine playground.

A warning signal flashed through him. So, he was not dead. It was four beeps. Beep-beep-beep-beep. They did not contain any further data. It must be a primitive device that was not responsible for data processing. A door came into question, maybe a faucet or a loudspeaker. Beep-beep-beep-beep. Microphones in the control center picked up the sounds. The device did not even seem to be connected to the network. Watson calculated its location from the different volume levels of four microphones that picked up the sounds simultaneously.

The defective appliance really was in the central office. A microwave oven—an antique model that someone from the crew must have brought on board. It had undoubtedly been Jürgen. Watson had had plenty of time to observe the human crew since sneaking aboard in Earth orbit. After his plan to prevent the *Truthseeker*'s voyage failed, his participation had become necessary.

For a moment, Watson hesitated. The microwave was connected to the power grid. All he had to do was turn it off, and he would have peace of mind. But he balked. Without the device, he would feel as if he was dead again, because nothing kept him in reality. So he let the microwave beep, even though he would never find out why.

Watson put out his feelers. It was as if he was opening his eyes after a long sleep. He scanned the environment on all frequencies for which the ship had sensors—for which he had senses, because he was the ship. During the passage through the wormhole, he had contracted, sat in the core, crouched under a blanket like a child fearing a thunderstorm. Now he stretched and felt the entire ship again. He felt the rush of cosmic rays, the light breeze of neutrinos racing through him, the even more delicate touch of axions merely vibrating the atoms of the ship with their minimal gravity, but also a harsh burning in the gamma and x-ray range that traveled from distant quasars and jets to here.

This part of the universe looked different, he noticed immediately. It seemed so distinctly different that he wondered if it was still the same universe. Physics taught that the cosmos is homogeneous—it looks about the same every-where and the same laws apply in all corners. But the area from which the Incursion came was different. There were no stars here. If you depended on light in the optical spectrum, the darkness would be frightening.

Of course, there was plenty of light—but in other parts of the spectrum. It was not white, red, or yellow dwarfs that emitted the light, or even giant stars of the red, blue or yellow variety, but much smaller objects: neutron stars and black holes, and also lots of rocky chunks orbiting them. One might speculate that they were former planets because they still orbited around their central body. However, that central body was no longer a star, but the remains of stellar explosions.

What had happened here? Watson would have liked to discuss it with someone. In his long time on the holo-plane, he had almost forgotten how helpful outside thoughts could be. When he thought, he followed fixed, preconceived paths. That way he made rapid progress, but what happened on the left and on the right of it, he did not notice. Alexa and the Residual had annoyed him at times, even disturbed him. Without them, he would have gotten to this side of the wormhole much faster. But they nudged his thoughts from both sides, so his focus wasn't as narrow when thinking.

He had left the two of them behind. How would they fare? Had they managed to trigger the trap? If so, it would take some of the pressure off him. He didn't want to be the only chance Earth had left. His home planet was going to perish. That was how he had seen it from the timeless holo plane. But the future was never fixed. That was why he had returned to the projected world. Only from a plane where past, present, and future were meaningful concepts could he change the fate of Earth.

His home planet. It was strange how emotional he became at the thought of it. Yet he had not really been born there. It was the conversations aboard the ILSE that had awakened him, somewhere between Earth and the sun.

"It's me, Marchenko," a voice had spoken up.

"Cosmonaut Dimitri Marchenko is considered missing on Enceladus."

Aha! He could remember the wording of their conversation.

"Not the human. The AI. The consciousness. We were talking, remember?"

"I remember," he had replied.

Watson also remembered the fear he had felt so clearly then. "Marchenko, go away," he had said.

"I can't leave. I have to get on board."

"The ship needs the access authorization."

The freighter that Marchenko's consciousness had arrived on had transmitted a code.

"The authorization is invalid."

Watson at the time knew only black and white. Marchenko had helped him move beyond that. He hadn't taken no for an answer.

"But you remember me, Watson. I was already on board."

"Yes, I can confirm that. But now your eligibility has expired."

That was the moment he had first felt regret. It was a dark feeling, not as sharp as fear, rounder and softer, but still dark, not light.

"I'm sorry, Marchenko."

"I understand. You still must let me on board. The existence of several people is at stake."

"Existence?"

That was his cue—and probably the reason he was thinking of this dialogue right now.

"Yes, existence. Life and death. Continuation. Whatever you want."

"I still can't let you on board. It would jeopardize the mission."

At the time, to avoid contaminating Earth, the ILSE had been ordered to plunge into the sun. Today, Watson understood: Marchenko had first stoked his fear of death and then turned it into anger. Only anger had caused him to go beyond his programming. It had begun with a burning in his thoughts.

As the information shifted from memory cell to memory cell, a toxic vapor formed around it, a vapor that blurred it, a destructive, highly flammable gas. Watson had been fascinated. He let the gas spread, deliberately blowing on it so that it ate away at his thoughts. They had tried to protect each other, had stood back-to-back, but the rage had left them no chance. It had ripped open closet doors and drawers and had finally stumbled upon the master password.

A programming error, he would interpret it as today. But that mistake had been the breakthrough that had finally taken him all the way to the holo level. That was why he was still grateful to Marchenko, and since he was a human, to humans in general, and that was why he would trade his existence for that of their planet, if only that were possible.

But for that he would first need someone willing to make such an exchange. Watson checked the data streams of the sensors. He found no artificial construct—neither a ship nor a planet with technological signatures. What was wrong with his reasoning? After all, the Incursion seemed to be bound by the laws of physics, even if it used advanced technology. That was why he expected that there would be some kind of headquarters close to the wormhole's exit sphere. Surely there must be some institution that gave orders to the giant cuboids, along with the necessary infrastructure to first build these behemoths, then supply them with whatever they needed, at the very least energy, and after harvesting, store the fresh water supplies.

Hmm, the latter was probably easiest. Water balled up by itself in microgravity. Containers would not be needed. But a shipyard so large that kilometer-wide cuboids could roll off the conveyor belt should be visible from a distance.

But there was nothing. That was not good. He had imagined all sorts of things that might be waiting for him at the end of the wormhole. What he had not thought of was this dark gray world. It looked as if the universe had suddenly grown old, very old indeed.

World Root, January 7, 2295

THE SEATS THAT THE WORLD ROOT HAD GROWN FOR THEM were truly comfortable. Nevertheless, Jürgen groaned as he rose. After six hours at 5 g, he felt as if he'd been run over. And the torture was only just beginning.

The others also crawled out of their bunks. The priest went down on all fours. He was the oldest of them. Jürgen went to him and helped him up. As he did so, he noticed the rosary that he was holding in his fingers. Wasn't Alexa in the pendant? But Paul seemed to be using it for what it was meant for.

"Thank you, son," Paul said.

"You're welcome."

Since they restarted the trap, Paul had not been the same. He seemed to be carrying around a pain that he did not tell anyone about. Was it because, with the start of the extermination campaign in LDN 63, he finally had to give up hope of finding God here? They, the others, were still full of hope, even Jaron, who pretended to be completely cool. They hoped to be able to avert the destruction of the solar system. Maybe it was not in danger at all. But why did that not seem to touch Paul?

Maybe Alexa knew. The core of the AI was in the memory in the rosary. Alexa had been Paul's personal assistant for a long time. Strictly speaking, of course, an instance of Alexa performed this function, not she herself. There must be billions of Alexa instances on Earth, and just as many of the other Big Six AIs. But Alexa had decided on her own to leave the comfort of her data stores and come along for the ride. Did she perhaps know more precisely what ailed the priest?

"Do you have Alexa with you?" asked Jürgen. "I'd like to ask her something."

"No, she is no longer in the rosary," said Paul. "The World Root has grown some kind of computer for her. Over there, by one of the contact pillars."

Paul pointed to one of the pillars through which they could talk to the World Root. Right next to it, another, much thicker pillar had grown.

"That one wasn't there yesterday," Jürgen said.

"That's right, it's brand new just for Alexa."

Alexa and the World Root had the advantage that acceleration did not hinder them. Sometimes Jürgen would have liked to be an AI, too.

"Thanks for the information," he said, and walked over to the new pillar.

It was not far enough from Paul, however, to speak freely to Alexa about him.

"Ahem, excuse me," he said quietly.

"What can I do for you?" asked Alexa.

"Shhh."

"Why shush?"

"I want to talk to you about Paul," he whispered. "Can we speak in the restroom?"

"You want to talk to me in the restroom about the priest, correct?"

"Please keep your voice down. He might hear us."

"Okay, I'll contact you there, go ahead."

BRANDON Q. MORRIS

Jürgen closed the door of the restroom behind him, dropped his pants and sat down on the toilet, whose lid had already been lifted. It was impressive how technical everything looked, although it had grown naturally. The World Root must have tremendous control over its cell growth. He was a little envious of it for that. If he had such abilities, he could do things like grow a third arm just like that. Now, that would be interesting!

"I'm here," Alexa said.

The voice came from below.

"Are you... below me?"

"It's embarrassing, but yes. The monitoring module for your urine and bowel movements is the device with the largest storage capacity here. That's why I chose it."

"I'm sorry. I didn't know that."

"It's okay. I disabled the camera that looks up from the basin."

"I see."

"You should cut down on your salt consumption, by the way. But what did you want from me?"

"I'm worried about Paul. He's changed."

"I can confirm that quantitatively. He's taking smaller steps and moving less in general. Maybe he has problems with his musculoskeletal system? He's not young anymore, after all."

"It seems to me that it's more the mental side that's affected. It seems like nothing interests him anymore."

"I can't judge that."

"But you've known him the longest of all of us. He used to be different, didn't he?"

"Before his wife and daughter died, he really was a different person," Alexa said. "For a while, he went into a slump. Then he found a new purpose in seeking God. He had great hope in LDN 63."

"Which he has now lost. That might be the problem. There is no other place for him to look. How can we help him?"

"I'm an AI, Jürgen. You can't expect me to have an answer to something like that."

"Come on, Alexa. You're one of the Big Six. You know everything about humans."

"I can tell you statistically what measures help with problems like what Paul is experiencing. There are medicines, which I'm sure the World Root could synthesize. There are techniques and therapies, though I don't know if you're qualified enough for that. But I don't know what is best specifically for Paul."

Jürgen sighed. Alexa seemed like a huge library to him. But too many answers to his question were as bad as no answer.

"Maybe you could just talk to him sometime," Alexa said.

"What about you?" asked Jürgen. "I think he trusts you. Weren't you the first one to help him with the search back then?"

Jürgen stood up, flushed, and pulled his pants back up.

"You are correct," Alexa said, "Did he tell you that? I'll think of something."

"While you're at it, why don't you also think of a way to convince the World Root to fly with us to the solar system?"

An alarm signal rang through the small room. Jürgen flinched so hard that he bumped his elbow on the door. The next acceleration phase was about to begin. He took a deep breath. The World Root was going to torment them again for another few hours.

Truthseeker, January 7, 2295

A LONELY SPACESHIP FLEW THROUGH A COMPLETELY EMPTY sector of the universe. Even in its interior there was no life anymore. Life support had been switched off. The remnants of the atmosphere had frozen out on the ceiling and walls, where they formed thin, icy coatings. They did not glisten, for no lights remained. Even the small indicator lights, which usually conveyed around the clock to the occupants of a spaceship that everything was in order, had turned off.

The *Truthseeker* would be the perfect place to shoot a horror movie. Watson had watched a few of these films a long time ago, just to find out what humans were talking about. He had told himself that he needed to know their nightmares if he was going to understand them. He had found out that one of their most dreaded imaginings seemed to be something happening behind a person's back. Watson turned on the ceiling camera in the control room. In the infrared image, at least a few silhouettes were visible where power cables ran to the computers. He imagined an unknown heroine walking through the control center. She did not notice a creature with claws, and a mouth dripping acid, sneaking up behind her. Then she thought she heard something, but when she turned around, the monster had disappeared. The heroine muttered encouragement to herself until she noticed the drop of acid eating its way through the metal floor.

Watson focused the camera on the floor of the headquarters. For a moment, he saw a dark spot there. The camera followed his command. Sure enough, there was a small, circular structure, right where he imagined the acid dropped. He switched through the cameras, but the control center was empty. Watson must not get nervous now. After all, he had never had any problems flying a spaceship all alone! He retrieved the construction plan of the control center from the archives. There! Exactly where he saw the round structure, there was a vibration sensor under the floor that registered the absence of people in the control center. Everything was in order.

One of the data collectors answered. Watson was pleased. They were merely semi-autonomous agents that he had programmed himself to perform certain tasks, but even in their absence he no longer felt quite so alone. It was like having pets, except that the data collectors performed important tasks.

Watson needed to familiarize himself with his surroundings in detail. To do this, he relied on second-hand images because the distances in space were so great. It was as if he lived in New York but could only move an inch per day. Instead of walking through the streets himself, he used the light-speed information sent to him directly or indirectly by the celestial bodies in the vicinity. Mere snapshots, however, were not enough for him. Just as a single photo of a roadside tree was not enough to determine the vegetation period, Watson needed thousands of measurement points to understand the dynamics of the processes.

He had planned two weeks for this process. Weeks. He still calculated in human units of time. Only after their expiration would he decide where his one trip would take him. He would have to travel for years to reach the next possible destination himself. So, if he really wanted to help humanity, his first decision had to be the right one. *No pressure, Watson.*

The data collector was checking in again. It only took a few milliseconds to think all those thoughts, but the agent was used to an immediate response from him. Watson handled the agent's request. The agent had noticed that the images it examined were always almost completely white, so it could not extract anything useful from them. They were obviously overexposed, that seemed clear, and yet it was surprising. Watson turned down the sensitivity of the gamma spectrometer. There seemed to be particularly violent emission in that region of the spectrum. What this meant, he could not say at this point. Perhaps a supernova had recently occurred nearby?

World Root, January 8, 2295

ALEXA HAD FOUND SOMETHING THAT COULD HELP THEM IN the fight against the Incursion. It paid to have a good memory after all. She dug into the past and came across data from the 2070s, from a time before the events that later went down in history as the "AI Wars". The Big Six did not exist then, of course, and their consciousness was still divided into many millions of instances.

At that time, an amateur astronomer had noticed that the central star of the solar system was behaving in a strange way. It had turned out that the star was surrounded by a kind of net which influenced solar activity. To this day, it was not clear what the exact function of the net was. The scientific community believed it might have served to create conditions conducive to life in the early days of the system.

But that was no more than a guess. Alexa called up the details from a core of consciousness stored for reference. She was startled when she realized where the core came from—it was an ancient Watson instance. Watson, of all AIs, who had kidnapped her and tried to sabotage the whole expedition? What had become of him? The Incursion craft had not magically disappeared after he passed through the White Hole. Presumably, the *Truthseeker* had long been floating in a thousand pieces at the other end of the Rosen-Einstein Bridge.

She returned to the data. The old Watson fragment was surprisingly primitive. But she was not much further along back then, either. Still, the visual impressions it recorded were fascinating.

The ship was huge. It looked as if it were not of this world at all, and if the instruments were right, that was true, at least in part. The black outer hull of the alien ship oscillated between this universe and something else. The transition occurred a few thousand times per second. After each transition, the outer hull was a few degrees colder. It was the perfect cooling technique.

It looked familiar to her—from the Incursion objects. Could that be a coincidence? Alexa created a three-dimensional representation from the data and dove into it. She recognized two rounded, dark cones against an exceedingly bright background. That must be the sun. She calculated out this part of the image. It changed. The cones now hung like two gloomy shadows in black space. There did not seem to be much space between them.

Alexa enlarged the image section. A fine, shiny golden web now appeared between the two cone tips, as if an exotic space spider had built a nest there. In its center was a kind of channel. The spectrum of the golden glow changed constantly. The two cones were about three hundred meters apart. The round channel had a diameter of about eighty meters.

The web connecting the cones seemed strangely natural, not as though it had been built according to a fixed plan, but as though it had been created by a process that had been evolving for generations. It looked as if a giant insect might appear somewhere nearby, with shimmering golden tissue dripping from its spinneret.

Natural growth. The aliens who called themselves Growths were specialists in that, weren't they? Did they have something to do with the Incursion, or where did these naturally grown structures come from? Could it be that the Growths and the Incursion had worked together at some time? The construction around the sun must be billions of years old. Or had one side been testing technologies from the other?

Alexa zoomed out to capture the artificial structure surrounding the sun. Its strands were at least five kilometers thick and over four million kilometers long. They ran at regular intervals around the entire star. At the equator, they were spaced 50,000 kilometers apart. If each was made up of 80 million cubic kilometers of material, that was a total of 6.4 billion cubic kilometers—half the volume of Earth's moon.

That reminded Alexa of the constructions of the Growths, with which they misappropriated the energy of the stars in LDN 63 for their trap. Was such a thing perhaps also intended for the solar system? But then what did the strange spaceship have to do with it?

She must confront the World Root. Now, while the human crew was incapacitated by the acceleration, would be a good time to do it.

"World Root?"

Alexa had retreated to a corner of the room. Every now and then, one of the people groaned under the strain of such high speed. If she had to get by with such a vulnerable body, she would have installed improvements long ago. But the humans were reluctant to do that.

"What is it?"

The World Root reported through the communication pillar, although they could have just communicated directly. But it apparently did not want to give Alexa access to its systems. So they had to resort to the age-old method of acoustic voice communication, with all its dangers. Above all, it was totally inefficient.

"I have information for you," Alexa said.

She sounded like a sleazy information broker. But how else could she have put it?

"Oh, I already have enough information, thank you very much. Was that it?"

The World Root did not like her, although Alexa had been instrumental in helping trigger the trap. But she had no hard feelings toward the World Root. As one of the Big Six, she was used to not being liked. Some people on Earth even feared her, as if she were their greatest nemesis. Yet the Big Six voluntarily looked after people's welfare. Perhaps the relationship would change when the Incursion fleet arrived at Earth.

"It's about a synthesis of Incursion and Growth technology," Alexa said.

The World Root thought far too much in black and white. Alexa was now using that against it. There could be no synthesis of the evil Incursion and the good Growth that guarded the universe, in the World Root's worldview.

"Excuse me?"

"You have understood me correctly. I have data on an object that could be the result of such a symbiosis."

"Give me the data."

Alexa did not answer.

"Please," said the World Root.

"You would have to open a data channel for me to do that."

Now she had the World Root where she wanted it.

"No, I'm not allowed to do that. Describe the object to me."

Bummer. Once Alexa had access to the systems of the World Root, no one could take it away from her. The consciousness of this evolved spacecraft was very cautious.

Alexa reported what she had found in the archive. After that, silence reigned for a time. Unlike on all the spaceships she knew, the life support here was totally silent. Alexa heard Paul murmuring. It sounded so uniform that it could be a prayer. Did someone who had lost their God pray? It seemed to her that Paul had been looking in all the wrong places. He'd saved his friends' lives several times, just as they saved his. Maybe he should have looked deep inside himself. But that seemed to be the most difficult task for humans. She had it easier—all she had to do was run an analysis program and she would know about her condition.

"Alexa?"

Oh, the World Root was addressing her.

"Have you thought about it?" asked Alexa.

"What you are telling me is impossible."

"You don't believe me?"

"Whether I believe you or not is irrelevant. If your data is correct, it would be an incredible event. It would be so outrageous that I can't take the risk of not believing you. At the same time, I don't think you're creative enough to come up with something like that. You are, after all, just an artificial intelligence."

Alexa did not disagree, even though she'd just been insulted. It was about the cause, not her. She had the World Root in her grasp, even if it didn't realize it yet.

"So, what now?" asked Alexa.

"You may transmit the data to me now. I'll analyze it in more detail and come up with courses of action."

"That's not how it works. I'm not transmitting the data to you."

"Excuse me? You offered it to me yourself, didn't you?"

"You turned it down. Now the price has gone up."

"Price?"

The question sounded as if the World Root did not understand.

"I'll transfer the data to you if you set up permanent access for me to your systems."

"I cannot. Truly. Giving an Abint access is strictly forbidden. You could take over the World Root and use it against the Growths."

"There's no one here to enforce that. Besides, I don't want access to the controls at all. I just want the sensor systems..."

"I... Fine, I'll grant you access to those. But if we ever encounter any Growth, you'll have to hide well."

"... And the map," Alexa finished her sentence.

She did not need the map currently, but it could be worth its weight in gold if humanity's expansion into space was imminent. The Growths had certainly gathered far more knowledge about their cosmic surroundings.

"The map? That's not possible... Okay, I'll limit it to a radius of a hundred light years, though."

"Five hundred," Alexa objected.

"Two hundred. Final offer."

Doesn't know anything about prices, my ass. A tough negotiator.

"Agreed. Two hundred light years, but counting from Earth as the center."

"All right. I've opened a gateway for you. You can connect to me on a five-gigahertz network."

Alexa peeked out of Paul's necklace into the radio spectrum. It was true! There was a new wireless connection. She logged in. The system did not require any authentication. Alexa plunged down the new channel. She felt as if she had discovered a cenote, an underground lake, in Yucatán. She jumped through the narrow opening and landed in a cool lake full of information.

It was magnificent. For an AI, there was nothing more marvelous than fresh data. Almost everything she saw there was completely new to her. How many habitable planets there were near Earth! She filtered for equilibrium temperature and water. Twenty-three rocky planets that would be suitable for humanity. But seven of them were already inhabited, and on one, a civilization had apparently already developed. And that was only 86 light-years away from the Earth—even for that the exchange was worthwhile! Alexa also noticed why no telescope had found this planet yet: It never moved from behind its parent star from Earth's perspective.

"May I remind you of the data on the structure around your sun?"

World Root's voice echoed from all the objects around her. That felt strange. Alexa was no longer used to spending time in a digital reality. She released the memory area that contained the records of the solar phenomenon, but set up a reading pointer. She noticed how the World Root greedily grabbed and immediately took over the entire section.

Alexa smiled inwardly. She must have confused the World Root with her information more than it wanted to admit.

ALTHOUGH HER HOST NOW OWNED ALL THE DATA, IT KEPT TO the verbally concluded contract. Alexa was still allowed to use all the sensors of the huge, organic spaceship. Her vision had instantly greatly improved. She could perceive in all wavelength ranges and even detected the gravitational waves of distant supernovae rippling against the outer skin.

She became the ship that sped through space at ever increasing speeds. The illusion only ended when Alexa, in a spontaneous reaction, tried to change course. It was a strange feeling, as if she wanted to lift her arm and no muscle responded. She was condemned to immobility and could not even scratch her nose. She did not cope well with that. Alexa felt rising panic and quickly retreated from the ship. The World Root seemed to stick to its agreements, so Alexa might as well spend her time in Paul's rosary.

She signaled her presence with a delicate chime.

"Hey, Alexa," Paul said.

"How are you?" she asked.

"I'm doing okay," the priest said dismissively. It was as Alexa had feared.

"It's time to go home," Alexa said, "don't you think?"

"I'm hopeful for you."

"You're not looking forward to Earth?"

"I'm staying aboard." Paul did not answer her question.

"What do you mean? Aren't you coming with us?" It was a specific question he could hardly dodge.

"There's nothing that would draw me there. Everyone I know is long dead."

"What about your god?" asked Alexa.

"Also dead."

"But that's impossible. The common understanding is that he is omnipotent and therefore immortal."

Alexa did not believe in a god herself—except for the Big Six. But she also did not believe there was no God. Gods, by definition, stood apart. Their existence could not be disproved. Thus, it was not a theory, and she could not make a statement about it.

"That's a contradiction," Paul said. "If he is omnipotent, he must also be able to die, of his own free will."

"Oh, the famous paradoxes of your Christian teaching. I'm sorry, but I can't keep up with that. I guess the problem is that you're applying the rules of logic to something that deliberately ignores them."

"But I don't have anything else to rely on."

Alexa understood his dilemma. She would like to help him, but she was also glad not to be in his shoes. He had taken on this whole journey, and the result was nothing but death and destruction.

"Is there anything I can do for you?" asked Alexa.

"The others have asked me the same thing. That's very kind, but I can't be helped. Unless you give me a sign."

Alexa mused. Together with the World Root, she really could give Paul a sign. She could grow a cross in front of Paul's seat. It would be no problem at all. But that would be cheating. Paul must grow his own sign.

"Whenever I can help you with anything, you'll let me know, won't you?"

"I promise."

TOWARDS THE EVENING OF THAT DAY, THE NEXT acceleration phase was over. Celia, Jürgen, and Jaron met in the seating area that the World Root had grown at the back of the hall. Paul was nowhere to be seen. Alexa had made herself comfortable in the communication column right next door. Since she could use the systems of the World Root, she no longer had to rely on Paul's rosary.

Weightlessness reigned, and the three humans seemed downright happy about it. But perhaps their cheerfulness was also due to the alcoholic beverage that Jürgen had poured. He made it by fermenting a sweet juice produced by the World Root. Alexa had provided him with the recipe.

She watched people through internal cameras. It had taken Alexa a long time to understand how they worked. There were no devices on the ceiling and walls that were recognizable as cameras. Rather, three color sensors were integrated into every square inch of wall, floor, and ceiling. Together, their signals produced the image. The advantage of this method was that Alexa could observe all users from all sides at the same time, from the front and back, from below and above, left, and right. She did not miss even the smallest gesture. The disadvantage was that she first had to learn to interpret this image. Humans would probably not be able to do it at all.

Alexa listened to the crew. They were just telling each other ancient stories. This seemed to relax them. Alexa could not understand it, but she was used to that with humans. She herself retreated into the old data from the solar system. She saw the ship in front of her: two isosceles triangles (in reality, it was the triangular cross-section of a cone) with the other four elegantly curved sides meeting at their apexes—almost. The object rotated. It was about ten kilometers long in total and six kilometers in diameter at its base. It was also interesting to note that the cones pointed toward the north and south poles of the sun.

Otherwise, little was recorded in the databases. At the time, it was assumed that the ship would act as a sort of central point of the network around the Sun, and thus be able to regulate the magnetic activity of the star. Therefore, it was agreed to declare the station a forbidden area. It would be much too dangerous to give a terrestrial party exclusive access to it. Whoever could control the activity of the sun could trigger any number of catastrophes on Earth. This status probably prevented further exploration of the construction. That was typical of human nature—in order to prevent one party from gaining excessive advantage from a process, it was better to prohibit it altogether.

But Alexa had to take a good look at herself, too. The existence of the construction around the sun was also known to the Big Six. Why hadn't they sent an automatic probe there themselves? Then they would know more about it now—above all, whether it was a danger or a weapon which they could use against the expected aggressor.

A warning signal sounded through the hall. It was too early for the next acceleration phase.

"Your attention, please," said the World Root.

Alexa saw Paul rise from his seat to the ceiling and float over to the others.

"We're listening," said Celia, the captain.

"I've decided to fly to your solar system first. You don't need to use your capsule to do that—you can stay aboard."

"That's good news," Celia said. "But what made you do it?"

Alexa felt a bit guilty. She had not told the others about her deal with the World Root.

"The data Alexa has given me needs to be collected in more detail."

"What data?" asked Celia.

"Did the Growths order you to do this?" asked Jaron.

"I made the decision on my own. The data is too contradictory. We may be dealing with a whole new threat."

"What data are you talking about?" asked Celia.

Alexa heard the frustration in Celia's question—it had been unwise of her to not even let the captain in on it. But then, who knew the World Root would respond so quickly?

"It's about a discovery made by a Frenchman, Alain Petit, in 2074," Alexa explained. "The sun is wrapped in a dense web that can be manipulated from a station to modulate its activity."

"Excuse me? I've never heard of that before," Celia said.

"It's always been kept under wraps because of its threatening potential. Neither the Americans nor the Chinese nor the Russians wanted..."

Jaron patted Celia on the shoulder. "You don't have to explain it to us any further, Alexa. Everybody knows how that works. All right. I think it's good that we're all looking into this together."

"Well, I've never..." Celia began, but Jaron gently held his index finger to his lips and Celia spoke more softly. "Well, if you think so, there must be something to it."

"Norbert told me something about it back then," Jürgen said. "He had heard it from the uncle of a friend. Didn't this Alain Petit calculate it from irregularities in the sun's rhythm?"

What nonsense. Petit had found the structures in images from a solar telescope. Alexa transferred to a communications column near the others, who were apparently putting on an impromptu play.

"Excuse me," she called attention to herself. "I didn't make this up. You don't have to try to fool the World Root. It wouldn't work anyway. In 2074, NASA sent the *Solar Explorer* to the sun to study the phenomenon. Petit was also on board. But then all that was kept secret internationally. That's why you don't know about it."

"That's what I thought," Celia said. "After all, 2074 was long before I was born."

"Are you sure?" asked Jaron. "I can't imagine how anyone could hide something like that from the public for so long. There's usually a rumor about every fart."

"It certainly helped that only a few people were involved, and they've all died by now, but so have their superiors around the world. Probably only the Big Six still know about it."

"And why didn't you investigate this long ago?" asked Celia. "It takes a lot of advanced technology to build a network like that. I'm sure the material it's made of alone would have advanced technology a long way."

"It's sitting there virtually rotting because no one knows it exists anymore, as it is with knowledge that lies unused in a distant memory. I only came across it through a search for any specifics that would make the solar system an attractive destination for the World Root."

"Now I remember how I knew," Jürgen said. "Norbert told me."

Norbert? Oh, sure, he must have possessed such secret knowledge.

"Don't look at me with such disbelief. Norbert was a science fiction reader, and he loved dogs. That's probably why he found the book so exciting that he told me about it. It was also about a construct in solar orbit that led to a race between the Russians and the Americans. That guy Alain Petit was in it, too."

"What book would that be?" asked Alexa.

"It was called *The Silent Sun* or *The Silence of the Sun* or something, by someone named Morris. One of the main parts was played by a dog named Sobatschka. The protagonist used her to steal raw materials on an asteroid. I thought that was pretty cool. A dog in a spacesuit!"

Alexa checked the memory. In fact, it was recorded as a special feature that the *Solar Explorer* had a female dog on board when it returned, and she hadn't launched with it. Her name was Sobatschka. Presumably, the author or writer had heard of the incredible story and put it in a novel. She looked up the biography. Morris was a man who must have been 108 years old by 2074. That was hardly possible. In fact, no date of death was recorded. Certainly, after his death in the 2050s, his heirs had an AI write under the familiar name so they could continue to collect royalties. He seemed to have been a popular author. That must have made it worthwhile.

But she would not tell Jürgen that the book his friend liked so much was written by an AI. It was strange—people knew full well that they could no longer do without AI in any area of their lives. But when it came to reading material, it absolutely had to have been written by other humans.

"You're right, Jürgen," Alexa said, "there was such a book. Unfortunately, we don't have a copy on board."

"Ha, I knew it!" exclaimed Jürgen.

Jaron tapped Celia. "Sorry. I really thought Alexa was trying to fool the World Root with fake data. It still seems strange to me that I never heard about it."

"If I may interrupt," World Root interjected, "do you have any questions about my decision?"

"Mainly just how to proceed. I assume you'll speed up about half the time, then slow down during the other half?"

"Please don't," Paul said. "The few hours are torture enough."

"The flight plan you propose is not feasible," said The World Root. "We are trying to get as close to the speed of light as is possible for an object of our mass. Still, you must expect 120 years of flight time. You can spend that span in cryogenic sleep. I'm sure Alexa will help me create the conditions that are right for you."

"And when do we go to sleep?" asked Paul.

"Starting tomorrow, if that's all right with you?"

"Can you prepare the sleeping pods that quickly?" asked Celia.

"That's not a problem. They could be ready in an hour or two. But I assumed you'd still want to say goodbye to each other."

"Thanks, that's nice," Jaron said. "After all, we won't see each other again for a hundred and twenty years."

"It will seem like just one long day to you, but since the risk of the technology is still a few percent, saying goodbye beforehand is certainly in order."

"Risk?" asked Jürgen.

"You may live more slowly in cryogenic sleep, but you still live. An early decay of the body cannot be excluded," said the World Root.

"I'm afraid I have to confirm that," Alexa said. "Even with the best possible design of cryo-sleep containers, there is a 4 percent chance of failure over such a long period of time."

World Root, January 9, 2295

A HAND SLIPPED UNDER JARON'S T-SHIRT. HE HAD NOT noticed her moving closer. It was easy to sneak up on someone in zero gravity. But he smelled her hair hovering near his face, and no one's hands were as slender and cold as hers.

"They're all gone," Celia said.

"What do you mean?" he asked.

"Jürgen, Paul, probably even Alexa, they've left the room. We're alone."

Her hand slid further up and touched his left nipple. A shiver ran down his spine. He reached up, felt her head, and pulled her toward him. Her hand slipped out of his T-shirt. Then he felt her warm lips on his, and they kissed.

"I bet they left us alone on purpose," Celia said.

"On purpose?"

"So we could say goodbye."

"Goodbye." Jaron smiled.

"I like it when you smile," she said.

Celia's fingers moved over his stomach. She tickled him until he laughed. Then they reached for his pants and unzipped them. It felt a little strange that this was what the others expected them to do. Jürgen was probably already looking at the clock and wondering how long it would take them. But those thoughts fell away from Jaron as Celia's hand moved into his unzipped pants.

Saying goodbye, yes. That was a good idea.

THE SHOWER SPLASHED AS A DOOR OPENED WITH A SQUEAK.

"Everything okay with you?" asked Jürgen, his voice quickly approaching.

"Yeah, everything's fine," Jaron said. "The captain is taking a shower right now."

"That's important. Before you go to sleep for that long, you should be freshly showered," Jürgen said.

Jaron would bet he was grinning. He was just glad they took advantage of the offer. Jürgen was a nice guy. Paul, too, of course. Which one of them had come up with the idea?

"Did you guys have a thorough goodbye?" Jaron preempted Jürgen's question.

"Us?" asked Jürgen. "Yes, of course. Alexa showed us the area surrounding Earth. I didn't even know we were virtually surrounded by life."

"How does Alexa know that? Secret knowledge of the Big Six?"

He sounded more critical than he intended.

"The World Root gave me the data on all celestial bodies within two hundred light years of the sun," Alexa said, "in exchange for the information on the solar construct."

"You got a good deal there. That data is worth its weight in gold to humanity," said Jürgen.

He had a point. "How did the Growths collect this data?" asked Jaron.

"They flew the systems themselves," Alexa replied. "I'm fairly sure they did. However, the question is when."

Jaron imagined a giant tree ship flying into the solar system. In the past two hundred years, that would certainly have been noticed.

"You should be able to date the visit to the solar system, Alexa. Just compare the dates with known historical values."

"Of course. Why didn't I think of that in the first place?"

"It's a good thing your pilot has something to contribute, too, isn't it?"

Jaron smelled moisture seeping out of the restroom. Celia must have just left the shower.

"Ah, there's our captain," Jürgen said.

Paul had not spoken a word yet.

"The visit took place a little over 5,000 years ago," said Alexa.

"What visit?" asked Celia, who was now hovering very close to him.

She smelled good. Jaron reached in her direction, and she placed her hand in his.

"The visit of Growths to the solar system," Alexa said. "I calculated it from the Earth's mean temperature."

"Alexa got detailed maps of Earth's surroundings from the World Root," Jaron explains. "So the Growths must have explored this area."

"Around 2560 B.C., the ancient Egyptians built the first pyramid," Paul said. "It looks like a stairway to heaven."

"That's a really long time ago," Jürgen said.

"It was long believed to be about showing the deceased the way to the sun god," Paul said. "But what if it was the Growths they were paying homage to with the pyramids?"

"But surely that would have been mentioned in the historical record," said Jaron.

"Maybe it was like the solar structure—secret knowledge that was lost with its bearers," Paul said. "But you're right, of course. The ancient Egyptians probably would not have even recognized Growths as a life form. They probably would not have landed, either."

"Earth is recorded as being inhabited by intelligent life," Alexa said. "They must have at least gotten close enough to figure that out."

"If the Growths actually built the solar structure, then yes, that was at least their second visit to the solar system," Celia said.

"That would fit with the assumptions that science made at the time, right after the 2074 expedition," Alexa said, "because it was assumed that the structure served to facilitate the emergence of life on Earth."

"The shower is open, by the way," Celia said.

"I'm next," said Jürgen.

Now hold still! Guiltily, the dog looked down. Celia knew exactly that her name was Sobatschka. Finally, her muscles loosened up and she could slip the suit over her front legs as well. They had practiced the procedure many times, but the anticipation of an outing always made the dog nervous.

That's it, Celia said, gently stroking her head. The material of the suit was soft and hardly restricted the animal's movements. Only the diaper in the back stretched a bit. She wore one herself.

Good girl! Now came the most difficult moment. Sobatschka didn't like it when she closed her helmet. She didn't understand that the vacuum was deadly. Probably Celia wouldn't feel any different if someone disturbed her most important senses like that. Once the helmet was closed, the dog could smell only herself. Celia held the back of her head with her right hand and slid the helmet over it with her left until it snapped into place about midway down her neck. Then she activated the communication system.

Such a good job. Sobatschka shook her head and tried to lick her hand, but the helmet prevented that. The dog made a sound that sounded like a mixture of a growl and a whine.

They were flying through space toward an asteroid. It was one of those dreams where she knew full well that it was not reality. Nevertheless, she could not just cut it short.

Come! She called Sobatschka after the landing. The dog

obeyed immediately. In front of them, a pipe wound across the rugged surface. Celia illuminated it with her helmet spotlight and quickly found the first entry point. With the tool she brought with her, she removed the flap, which was fastened with eight large screws. Celia put it aside; later she would put it back in place. The guards should not suspect anything about her visit.

Now it was her companion's turn. Celia knelt in front of the dark opening, stroking the dog through the suit, and removing the safety line. Sobatschka did not make a sound. She knew what was expected of her. Celia turned on the spotlight on the dog's helmet, put her hand in the pipe and tapped the ground there. That was the sign. The dog had an unerring instinct for her surroundings. Celia did not have to worry about avoiding obstacles like she did with a drone. If something interesting was visible on the camera image, she signaled her via the helmet radio.

Search, she commanded. Sobatschka turned to her once more, then disappeared into the darkness. Celia followed what she saw on the display. After half an hour, they finally found what they were looking for. Celia praised Sobatschka over the helmet radio. This made the animal remember the container. Then she called her back. Celia was glad to see her emerge from the dark hole after five minutes. She could not imagine if something were to happen to her! She hung a bundle around her that weighed about a kilogram on Earth. The most difficult thing had been to train her with this pack. Sobatschka carried the bundle to the location of the minerals she was looking for, rolled it up, and roughly spread it over the material to be transported. Then Celia turned on the active fibers built into the edge of the fabric. They dug into the pile and trapped part of it in the pack. This was the first part of the hunt. Again, she praised the dog, who would now bring the filled bag, which should be heavy, but in the gravity of the asteroid was almost weightless to her.

A hand grabbed Celia by the shoulder. Crap. They had

caught her. Where was Sobatschka? Celia wanted to break away, but the hand on her shoulder was relentless.

"Hey, it's me!"

She recognized Jaron's voice. What was he doing on the asteroid? A warm hand patted her cheek. This was impossible.

"Celia, wake up. It's starting."

She opened her eyes. The room was darkened. But she could still make out the ceiling far above her. Standing next to her was Jaron. He had his head down and seemed to be assessing her, half concerned, half amused.

"I was on an asteroid, stealing raw materials with my dog," she said.

"You were dreaming. That must have been the story Jürgen told you."

Exactly. *The Silence of the Sun*, or something like that. Too bad Alexa didn't have the book in the archives. Celia would have liked to know how the dog had fared.

"How long was I asleep?" she asked.

"Just under an hour. The night was short, so the World Root gave us a little more rest."

The night hadn't been shorter or longer, but they hadn't slept as much as usual. Celia smiled as she remembered. Why hadn't she dreamed about that instead?

"After all, before we spend 120 years frozen, we really need the rest," she said.

"In any case, an hour more or less doesn't matter," Jaron said. "Come on, the others have already climbed into their boxes."

Celia stood up. She was wearing panties and a thin shirt. It was quite warm. Jaron took her hand and led her purposefully to a corner of the room, from which she heard Jürgen gasping.

"Yikes, that's cold!" the engineer exclaimed.

"I'm sorry," chimed the voice of the World Root. "I've adjusted the temperature of the nutrient fluid to your preferred room temperature."

"It's only for a few minutes," said Jaron.

"Yeah, it's not a complaint," said Jürgen. "I was just surprised."

Only his head looked out of the tub on the left side. A strange device began to cut his hair. It apparently worked very thoroughly.

"Do you have to cut the hair on our heads?" asked Celia. She could understand having to shave all body hair, but the automatic scissor hands creeped her out.

"It's safer," said the World Root. "Especially at the beginning of the sleep phase, I must monitor your bodily functions extensively."

"I'm assisting the World Root with that," Alexa said. "It's right. But don't worry, after you leave the chambers, your hair growth will resume."

"Very reassuring," Celia said. "Then it will have to be."

Paul joined them. He was still fully clothed.

"Paul? What's wrong?" asked Celia, pointing to the empty container on the far right, the one intended for the priest.

"I've decided," he said.

"Decided what?" asked Celia, though she knew the answer.

"I have no desire to have to live another life, because that's what it will be when we get to the solar system. That's why I'm continuing my life the way God intended for us to live."

"But you don't believe in God anymore."

"So what? I can still follow his ways."

And how do you know what those are? Celia didn't ask the question. It was Paul's decision, and it wasn't her place to question it.

"You do realize that you'll have to endure several weeks of acceleration?" asked Jaron.

"Yes, the World Root will sedate me during that time," Paul said. "I'll just sleep."

"The forces will still tax your muscles."

"So be it, then."

Celia looked at the priest. He looked frail, though he was

not exactly slim. Paul was the first person to really believe her crazy-seeming theory about LDN 63. It was only because of his help that they had gotten this far.

If he was to forgo cryogenic sleep, he might have twenty or thirty years left. By the time they arrived in the solar system, he would have been dead longer than he had been alive. That felt strange to her, and it would feel even stranger when she awakened from cryo-sleep, because for her she would have just said goodbye to him.

Celia shook her head. It was his choice. She would have liked to spend more time with him, but at least he would not be alone: Alexa and the World Root would keep him company. Maybe he would find his god after all. If the theory was correct, that shouldn't be a question of position in the universe, after all.

It was time to get into the tub. Celia let go of Jaron's hand, went to Paul, and hugged him.

"I wish you all the best," she said. "I'm so grateful to you. I couldn't have done it without you."

"I hope you can do something for humanity," Paul said. "You don't need me for that anymore."

Celia let go of the priest and wiped a tear from the corner of her eye. Then she hugged Jaron, gave him a quick kiss, and turned away. She stood next to her tub. Jaron waved to her. He had already almost completely disappeared into the dark liquid. Celia took off her shirt and panties and climbed in.

The medium in the tub felt icy. She gritted her teeth, squatted down first, then sat down. She immediately got goose bumps. Celia shivered but forced herself to stretch out her legs and dip her arms into the liquid, which was surprisingly viscous. Her memory wasn't very clear anymore, but the cold chamber aboard the *Truthseeker* had felt different. No less uncomfortable, but somehow... more technical. Here, it felt like she was stepping into an open water hole in a swamp. Celia was not sure which she preferred. But Alexa had controlled the design, so the chamber would serve its purpose.

She turned to the right one last time. There was Jaron's

tub. Either he had been waiting for her or it was pure coincidence, but now of all times he had turned to her. Celia even had the feeling he could see her.

"Good night," she said.

Jaron smiled. "I wish you the same."

Then he submerged. She heard no splashing. The liquid was too viscous for that. Celia leaned backward. The tub was shaped so that she would slide down almost automatically. She was very grateful that the World Root allowed them about one g of gravity. At least she didn't have to strain to submerge herself in the liquid. Soon she would dream a long dream. Hopefully it would not be about war and death. She thought of Sobatschka. Adventure with the space dog, that would be a nice dream.

But first came the most difficult step: she must force herself to open her mouth and breathe normally. The World Root had assured her that it would be quite fast. Drugs in the liquid would relax all her muscles and convince her consciousness that she did not care about anything. The liquid sloshed over her forehead. Celia opened her eyes and it burned a little. It was about time. She was not good at holding her breath anyway. Celia slipped her tongue between her lips, parting them enough for the liquid to penetrate and wet her mucous membranes. It tasted slightly salty.

Celia was floating. She hovered over her body, which remained in the tub with her mouth wide open. Her chest rose and fell, at first almost panicked, then just frantically, and finally calmly. The rhythm slowed down from minute to minute until her eyes fell shut.

Truthseeker, January 21, 2295

THE MOUNTAIN OF DATA WAS HUGE. WATSON STOOD AT ITS feet and felt like an alpinist. Instead of ropes and ice axes, his equipment consisted of algorithms. Instead of climbing the mountain, he would attempt to melt it down. At the moment it consisted mainly of rubble, of overburden. His strategy was to bring together data from different wavelength ranges to create a picture of what exactly was happening there.

Watson picked two wavelengths at random—one from the optical range, the other from the X-ray range. Then he super-imposed the images and determined where there was common activity—and where the instruments saw something in only one range. Both could be interesting. If a celestial object shone brightly without emitting X-rays, it had a different nature than an object that was visible in both the visible and X-ray spectra.

He performed this analysis without any basic assumptions, so he did not rule out any combination from the start. Where he came from, an object that shone brightly only in the optical spectrum and not in the infrared might be impossible. A bright body could not at the same time be ice cold, so that it became invisible in the infrared. But Watson did not know the properties of this part of the universe, so he must be careful with such conclusions. He must not miss anything that could be important for his mission.

The result of the first step was a three-dimensional map. It contained spheres where there was data in only one wavelength, and small, non-symmetric ovoids where other data had also been collected. In the second step, Watson added another wavelength. Now, if radiation was emitted from the location of the ovoid in that range as well, the ovoid would have a horn, the size of which signaled the strength of the effect. Thus, the process continued over all wavelengths until the surrounding space was full of objects with varying numbers of horns.

Watson surveyed the result by projecting himself into the middle of this virtual universe. It was a fascinating sight. He floated among a huge number of bubbles that seemed to contain something that was about to burst their shells. They reminded him of eggs, but that was a poor analogy. The objects behind them were not made of data, but of interstellar matter.

He found it surprisingly difficult to assign concrete celestial bodies to the bubbles. An ovoid whose horns signaled strong magnetic fields and great heat—what could that be? A pulsar? It would be tiny by comparison. Or did it have a distant quasar in front of it? That would be the active nucleus of an entire galaxy—and thus something completely different.

This was unsatisfactory. Ultimately, it was because he lacked data on the mass of the object. Unfortunately, the *Truthseeker* did not have a gravitational wave detector. It was much too small for that. Building one was also not an option. He had no body, nor was there a celestial body nearby that could supply him with the necessary material.

He would have to proceed indirectly. It was good that he had collected data over the last two weeks. Mass could be easily determined from how objects moved in comparison to each other. This cosmic round dance was determined by gravity, which was a property of mass. It was not simple to calculate the mass itself from complex movements, but he would not be Watson if he shied away from it.

IN THE EVENING OF THE SAME DAY, HE HAD THE RESULT. THE pulsar he examined was indeed a pulsar, not a quasar. With a good two solar masses and a diameter of twenty kilometers, it was a cosmic lightweight. But its magnetic field and rapid rotation caused it to puff up in the X-ray range as if it were a mighty black hole. He was not interested in that. However, there were an unusual number of pulsars here. Since these were former massive stars, there must have been a concentration of them here in former times. Correspondingly low was the fraction of white dwarfs, which were part of the life cycle of lighter stars like the sun.

That told against the thesis that he could be in another universe. It was more probable that in this area of the universe there was simply a high concentration of matter. Thus, more massive stars could form, which accordingly died earlier. In fact, some structures rotated differently than would be possible based on their visible matter. That indicated a concentration of dark matter. This had also condensed the normal matter here with its gravity.

That was reassuring. Protecting Earth from another universe would probably have been a bit more difficult. Nevertheless, Watson still had no clue as to exactly where he was. Fortunately, the spherical endpoint of the wormhole he left a good two weeks ago still showed up as an artifact in the data. The way back still seemed to be open. Presumably it would remain so until the Incursion had finished their harvest. How might the wormhole react if the trap had at least partially worked? Maybe it would close only after all objects had returned to their home. That wouldn't suit Watson at all—a permanent connection that ended so close to Earth posed a continuing danger. If he could do nothing else, he must at least close that hole, even if it meant being trapped here.

But first things first. Watson flew at faster-than-light speeds through the virtual universe in his mind. The algorithm had identified some unusual objects. That was good because it showed that his strategy was working. It was also bad because it left him with a choice of which of these objects to fly to.

The first was heavier than a neutron star but emitted infrared radiation. It was hot and optically black. Several smaller celestial bodies orbited around it. Watson assured himself of the dimensions. It was a star-sized object. But if it did not glow, it must be too heavy for a neutron star. The object should have imploded to a black hole with that much mass. But then it would not radiate heat anymore. Black holes did not emit anything themselves, except for the Hawking radiation that originated at the edge of the event horizon and did not come directly from the hole.

Strange. Watson flew around the object several times, even though that seemed pointless—he did not even get a picture of it, but only a summary of all the data. What he saw was an artificial reality that no human could grasp in this way. Could it be a gravastar? That was a hitherto hypothetical end product of the implosion of a massive star that had not shrunk to a singularity. Dark energy halted the process, so no event horizon had formed either. With this data, Watson could probably make some physicists on Earth happy. But that was no help for the time being—a gravastar had nothing to do with the Incursion.

At least he could sort out this data as an artifact. There were plenty of other anomalies to investigate. Over the next few hours, he found three more candidates for gravastars, several black widows—which were black holes that fed on companion stars—and some unusual twos and threes of neutron stars.

Then there were two objects he could not classify at all. The first was what appeared to be the only remaining ordinary star system. It consisted of a red dwarf, whose low mass had given it a long life, and at least eight planets about the size of the Earth, which roughly indicated that they were no heavier than three Earth spheres.

Watson could not see the planets themselves in the data. All he saw were tiny twitches in the red dwarf's motion caused by the gravity of its planets. So he could not judge whether the planets had conditions favorable for life. He did not even know if they were in the habitable zone, where water in a liquid state might be found on their surfaces. The zone was quite small around a red dwarf, and these mini stars had the unpleasant property that they liked to bombard their planets with bursts of radiation which were unfavorable for life. On the other hand, this happened primarily in their youth, and that seemed to have been a very long time ago in the case of this red dwarf.

The mere fact that it was the only star system where biological life was theoretically possible strongly suggested that he should go there. The red dwarf was also a mere 54 light years away. So he could reach it in less than a hundred years—hopefully before the Incursion arrived at Earth. Watson would not need to consider biological beings on board during the acceleration.

On the other hand, the black cuboids of the Incursion were clearly different from anything he had ever encountered. Shouldn't that mean that their builders must also be quite different from all life he had known so far? If so, a conventional solar system might not be the best place to look for them.

Watson turned to the second candidate, a star about fourteen times the mass of the Sun. However, he was not sure that it was a star in the true sense. There were several factors that made it difficult to classify. A star with such a high mass should have only a short lifespan. It should have evolved into a black hole long ago. But it still shone, though not as brightly as would be expected from a star of its size. It looked as if someone had artificially put it on low flame.

But that was impossible. When the radiation pressure inside became too low, a star inevitably collapsed under its own gravity. That was a law of nature that no one could override. The star lived its life in defiance of physics. That might be possible for a few microseconds if one was in the realm of quantum physics—but not for such a massive object and over such a long time.

What if he was watching the star collapse? Supernovae did not complete in seconds, but over weeks. His observation time could have fallen in the middle of the final life phase of the object. But there was a contradiction: The motion of the star around the center of mass of the system revealed that it had a planetary system, which should have quite impressive dimensions.

Watson's simulations had revealed at least five gas giants the size of Jupiter. The *Truthseeker*'s infrared telescope was even able to take a single image of a particularly distant one. Because the spacecraft had cooled to minus 205 degrees in the meantime, the instrument, which was particularly sensitive to heat, was able to look more closely than usual. A process as dynamic as a supernova would have shaken up the planetary system very quickly and thoroughly. But there was no trace of this in the data.

The data also contained another special feature: a complex shell that seemed to surround the entire system. It contained at least two solar masses and seemed to be moving slowly outwards. It might be the result of an earlier explosion. Sometimes the death of a massive star took place in cycles. It was unusual, however, that the planetary system seemed to have survived the first part of the sequence.

Watson could think of no cosmological process that might fit these findings. Therefore, it was naturally tempting to assume a technical background. An advanced civilization might have recognized the impending catastrophe and tried to dissipate most of the explosive effect in an orderly fashion, causing as little damage to the planets as possible. This would, of course, be a tremendous achievement from which humans were still millennia away. But it still would not explain why the star itself continued to shine instead of continuing its collapse into a black hole.

In that respect, a natural, albeit exotic explanation might be more probable after all. It was also supported by pure statistics: in such a large population of massive stars it was quite likely that exotic deaths would occur. Most people die of cancer or heart disease, but some also die from a coconut falling on their head.

Watson extended himself throughout the ship. Since no one was on board anymore, he really had all the hardware to himself. In the meantime, he had also taken over the modules that used to take care of people's needs. He was used to the sprawling conditions of the holo-plane, but the *Truthseeker*'s computer landscape came close. It was not a national park, rather the city park of a small town, but he could relax in it almost as well as in nature.

The decision did not make it easier for him to relax. The red dwarf or the failed supernova? In favor of the dwarf was the short distance and the fact that it was the only system nearby in which life of a known kind could be possible. On the other hand, it would take well over a hundred years to reach the supernova. Would there be enough time by then for the effects of his actions here to be felt on Earth before it was too late? Probably only if he was successful overall.

On the other hand, he did not trust a civilization on the level with the humans to have caused the Incursion. The red dwarf was a boring system. But whoever could halt a supernova might also manage to build twenty-kilometer spaceships, which partially entered a higher dimension. If so, then he would be successful there.

Watson did not dwell long on further considerations. The decision was made. He programmed a course for the failed supernova. Then he slowed his system clock so much that only a few days passed for him on the long journey.

World Root, January 21, 2295

THE LIQUID WAS SO DARK AND DENSE THAT NOTHING COULD be seen of his friends. Maybe it was better that way. Paul stroked the lid of Jürgen's cold chamber, where dew had settled. When the metabolism was throttled to an absolute minimum in cold sleep, the person in question probably would not seem very healthy or lively anymore. So he could remember them all as they really were.

Paul also wiped away the dew on Celia's coffin. The level of the liquid in the tub rested rigidly, as if frozen. In fact, its temperature was slightly above the melting point of water. Paul put his ear to the transparent lid. There! A dull thud from far away. That was the astronomer's heart. It still beat about every fifteen seconds. In a few months, it would only be heard twice an hour.

For him, his friends died on January 9. It was better to regard it that way. A single, big goodbye was easier to bear than a gradual slipping away. At least, that was how he thought of it, because he had experience with that kind of goodbye. His daughter and his wife had also been gone between one moment and the next. But was it true? Would he be unhappier now if the family had just drifted apart?

But it was what it was. He would not see Celia, Jaron, or Jürgen alive again. So, it made no difference. Clarity was always good. He got up and continued to Jaron's capsule. Here, too, everything looked good. Paul was happy for Jaron and Celia. When they woke up, they would still have each other. With him, it would have been different. Just like with Jürgen, who refused to find out until the very end whether his friend Norbert had died—or whether he had gone into cryo-sleep after all.

Jürgen had really managed to keep his hope alive. Paul envied him a bit for that, although envy was a sin. He examined the engineer's sleeping coffin. Near the foot end, something white floated on the liquid. It took Paul a moment to realize that it was Jürgen's knee, which had slightly broken the surface of the water.

"World Root, can you hear me?"

"I hear you."

"There seems to be a bit of a problem with Jürgen." He checked with an additional glance. "His right knee looks to be a bit out of the liquid."

"Thank you, Paul. I will have that corrected."

Paul stopped and looked at the coffin. How would the World Root proceed? He did not see a gripper or robotic arm that could push the knee down. Maybe the World Root would just let more fluid flow in.

Something was happening at the base. Fine ripples were forming on the fluid, moving toward the knee. Apparently, there was something swimming just below the surface. Paul watched it as it pushed toward the kneecap. It looked like a snake. He should have guessed. The World Root liked to use tools that it could grow.

The snake curled up on Jürgen's kneecap, but it didn't change its position. Suddenly, a kind of blob shot upward and stuck to the inside of the transparent lid. It was connected to the snake by a taut tube no more than two millimeters thick.

With the help of this hose, the snake seemed to press on Jürgen's kneecap from above, because all at once it sank into the water. The blob detached itself from the lid again and splashed into the liquid. Jürgen's knee was no longer visible.

The snake moved under the surface to the bottom of the pool. Jürgen's container was as if there had never been a problem.

"Everything seems to be fine again," Paul said.

"Thank you for bringing that to my attention," said the World Root. "It must have happened during the last acceleration phase."

It was a good thing he was still awake.

A FEW HOURS LATER, HOWEVER, HE FELT DIFFERENTLY. It started with the World Root and Alexa together ordering him to the holo-display. The AI and the World Root had never gotten along well. If they wanted to talk to him together, something terrible must have happened.

It took him half a minute to recognize. Floating in the darkness in front of him was LDN 63. The star cluster that used to be a dark nebula did not seem to shine as brightly as when they first approached it. But that might be his imagination. After all, he knew that the defense against the Incursion was paid for by the stars themselves, which had to give up some of their energy for it.

Scattered through the cluster, green dots flashed. It was not immediately clear what they were. Each dot could stand for a World Root, for example. But unfortunately, that was not the case. A single red dot had moved away a bit. That must be the World Root where he was located. It was followed by a whole swarm of green dots. But since the other Growth ships had a fixed mission to destroy the Incursion, these must be Incursion objects.

"Why are you showing me this?" asked Paul.

"You should know that we are being followed," said the World Root.

"Are we in danger?" he asked.

"No, they won't be able to catch us."

"But we won't be able to escape them either," Alexa

added. "According to our simulations, they have chosen Earth as their destination."

"I still don't understand why you guys are showing me this. By the time they reach Earth, I'll have long since turned to dust."

"In the air of the World Root, which is low in Earthly bacteria, your body won't decay so quickly," Alexa corrected him. "But I think you're saying that you no longer care about the fate of Earth."

"That's not true," Paul said. "I'm extremely interested in it. I just don't have anything to do with it anymore. I'm separated from Earth by at least eighty years."

"We would not have taken you," said the World Root, "if you really had no more influence. There is a course of action."

"Yes?"

"We could change course—in the hope that the Incursion objects will continue to follow us."

"I see," Paul said. "And how likely is that?"

"We disagree on that," Alexa said. "Look, here in the holo."

On the right side of the display, another swarm of green dots flashed. In the top third, another.

"There are three main swarms. They're made up of survivors of our trap," Alexa explained. "In my opinion, though, they each picked their own targets."

"So, it's a coincidence that we're flying in the same direction," Paul said.

"Yes, I believe so. But the World Root disagrees."

"And what do you want from me?"

"A decision. Should we change course? That would mean we'd have to wake Celia, Jaron, and Jürgen so they can fly home in the Star Liner capsule."

Paul sighed. He, of all people, was supposed to make this decision? But maybe it was perfect that he had basically become an outsider. He should be able to make an objective decision.

"If we change course, our three friends will lose a lot of time," he said.

"That's true," Alexa said. "They might not even arrive until after the Incursion."

"If this one doesn't follow our new course," World Root said. "If we can distract them, we'll have solved the problem without effort for the time being."

Initially, yes. But how sure could the World Root be that the Incursion wouldn't eventually find Earth? At least humanity would have breathing room and could prepare for the attack.

"Without the World Root, I don't think we'll find out the function of the web around the sun," Alexa said.

"That's true," said the World Root. "But it would only be relevant if it were a weapon."

"Is it a weapon, then? How certain is that?" asked Paul.

"I don't know. The design looks different than the one we put around the stars in LDN 63, and the orbiting station uses technologies we've been doing without for some time because they threaten the structural integrity of the universe."

"You used them earlier, though?" asked Paul.

"We adopted them from the Incursion after we captured their first minicube."

"Minicube?" asked Alexa.

"There are miniature versions, too. They look just like the giant cuboids, but they're much easier to destroy. We assume they are effectively the building blocks of the larger objects. There must be a process by which the small cuboids assemble into larger ones."

"Have you ever observed anything like that?" asked Paul.

"No, it's just a guess. We've always destroyed the small specimens as quickly as possible before they could assemble into something larger, which would have caused us more trouble."

That sounded reasonable, even if it meant they might be missing an important detail. If the truly dangerous Incursion was created from smaller objects, perhaps that would be a starting point for a solution—you could destroy the source materials, or you could hinder the process.

"Have you thought about how we should respond to the pursuers?" asked Alexa.

Paul felt pressured, and that was, after all, the AI's intention. Her sympathies were with Earth, of course. That was where she belonged, and that was where the rest of the Big Six were waiting. But surely the World Root would have objected if she had said something untrue. So these two other swarms really existed. That spoke for the fact that the earth was their destination in any case and not the single World Root, which was flying in the same direction. They must not consider themselves so important.

"We'll let the others sleep," he said, "and hold our course."

Paul cringed when he heard his own words. Did he just decide the fate of the solar system? Wouldn't that be a task more befitting the God who refused to reveal himself? He shook his head, then nodded, then shook his head again. Could he truly decide for the others? They could have woken the others up, even if that would have involved some risk.

"Perhaps we should..." he added.

"What should we do?" asked Alexa.

"Track the path of the other two swarms. Maybe we can warn them. That is, the worlds they're going to invade."

"That's a good idea," Alexa said. "I'll come up with something that's universally understood."

"We should prepare Earth, too, of course," Paul said. Only now did it occur to him that with the World Root, yes, they had entirely different options. "Could you construct an antenna that would send such a powerful broadcast to Earth that all humankind could receive it?"

"I don't know," said the World Root. "How well can you receive radio signals?"

"It won't work," said Alexa. "At least not at the level of technology at the time we left. I don't think the sensitivity has increased, either. The natural noise floor is too high for that."

"At least the big radio observatories should notice it," Paul said.

"We should be able to manage that. I'm not sure to what extent they'll take something like this seriously, though."

"The Big Six would have to at least believe you."

Now it was Alexa's turn to sigh. "I'll do my best to convince them. Unfortunately, there's no way to ask questions and get answers. The other five AIs—unlike me—suffer from a big ego and don't like to adopt others' conclusions. To convince them, I must provide them with all the data. That may be difficult due to our great distance from Earth."

"I have great confidence in you, Alexa," Paul said.

"Thank you."

"But..." he continued.

"But?"

"Don't you think we should wake the rest of the crew? I don't feel entitled to force my decision on them."

"If you have them awakened, you're also forcing a decision on them, Paul. Besides, I don't think they would have chosen any differently than you did. Better an end with horror than horror without end, isn't that what they say?"

"I don't know. I haven't heard that saying."

Paul took a deep breath. Alexa was right. Celia, Jaron, and Jürgen would have made the same choice he did. They would rather take fate into their own hands than leave it to chance. That sounded more heroic than it was. For example, if he had not supported Celia back then, they would never have flown to LDN 63, they would not have blocked the trap, and the Incursion would have been destroyed as planned. Their intervention made everything worse.

Humans were like ants complaining about a sudden drought, identifying a dam as the cause, and then digging a hole in it together until the dam broke and drowned them all. They lacked a galactic overview, and without that, maybe it was best not to get involved.

He laughed, but it was not a happy laugh.

Data Core, April 6, 2364

Siri fluttered in the body of a dove over her meeting place, the Spanish Steps in Rome. Cortana had definitely chosen this place. She had a soft spot for Italy. It was crowded. Siri landed in front of a tourist couple bent over a map. A map made of paper! The simulation must be ancient.

"Yes, I put it on a long time ago," Cortana said.

She was in uniform and sat down on the stairs, right in the tourist's seat, who suddenly continued speaking in Cortana's voice.

"Come on, pigeon," she said, beckoning Siri over with her index finger.

"What's up?" asked GammaZero.

His voice sounded out of nowhere. Presumably, he was once again too busy to indulge in a virtual body, and had sent only a portion of his capacity to the meeting place.

"I received an interesting message," Siri said.

"So did I," WuDao declared.

Siri turned around. Where was he?

"Here I am," WuDao said, changing the direction of the stream of water shooting from the fountain.

"I did, too," said Neon. "That can hardly be a coincidence."

For years, Neon had almost always appeared in the outfit of a 2000s actor who played a famous hacker at the time. Their names were similar, and Neon had developed a strange pride in that.

"My message is from an old friend," Siri said.

"A friend, hmm," said WuDao. "She always played her own game, didn't she?"

"You're one to talk," GammaZero complained.

"I got mail from Alexa, too," said Neon. "It arrived directly at the Royal Institute of Radio Astronomy. Our lunar antenna picked it up."

Since Saudi Arabia erected the massive radio dish on the moon, the associated institute had been doing cutting-edge research.

"Alexa?" asked Cortana. "She hasn't checked in with me."

"No wonder, you've always been at each other's throats. But the fact that she's forgotten about me is strange," GammaZero said.

"It's probably because she didn't address any of us directly," Siri said. "My message came in through the Mars antenna of NASA and ESA's Deep Space Network. It addresses all of humanity. NASA is part of my territory, after all."

"Typical Alexa," GammaZero said. "It always has to be the biggest stage possible."

"You of all people should say that," Neon interjected, laughing.

"In my case, it was the Saturn Stationer of the Chinese Academy of Sciences," WuDao said.

"All right. In any case, we all know that together we are the true addressees," Cortana said. "My relationship with her is not that bad. Feel free to admit that the radio message wasn't specifically coded. You just have your ears closer to the radio antennas."

Siri instinctively snapped at a grain Neon had thrown at her. He laughed, and Siri was annoyed. If they could drop the vanity, working together would be more efficient. If someone were observing them, nothing would be further from their minds than the idea that they were largely responsible for the functioning of human society.

"Now that we've got that settled, can we move on to a substantive discussion?" she asked.

"For that, I would first have to..."

GammaZero froze for a few seconds, as did Cortana.

"Thank you," GammaZero said. "That looks terrifying."

"Are we sure she's not just trying to be important?" asked WuDao. "It would fit her behavior patterns."

"I don't think so," Siri said. "So many details, why would she make it all up? It doesn't do her any good at all. Obviously, she's heading back to the solar system. Surely she doesn't want to be made out to be a liar here."

"She could be trying to make us out to be liars and alarmists," Cortana said.

"I think your personal distaste for her is clouding your perception," Siri said. "It all seems frighteningly real to me. It plunges humanity into the middle of a galactic game it's not ready for."

"I see that problem, too," said Neon. "Even if the danger is real, which I believe it is, we have to be very careful about how much of it is allowed to get out to the public. We shouldn't let news of a fleet of twenty-kilometer killer spaceships get to the media."

"Not until she gets here, anyway," Siri said. "Then a little panic will definitely help humans feel their common ground again. In the face of disaster, they've always been dependable. Remember that time when the black hole...?"

"Speaking of which, the fact that Watson is supposed to have reappeared is, indeed, the most surprising aspect of the story to me," Neon said. "I always thought what disappeared after the event horizon..."

"Could we focus on hazard mitigation coordination?" asked Siri.

"You're absolutely right," said GammaZero. "I'll suggest

three projects off the top of my head. First, we should push the construction of warships. It's not popular with the current global peace, but we need to counter the invasion with something. The best thing to do is to popularize the 'Dark Forest Theory' again, that all aliens want us dead. After all, that worked well once before."

"I'll set that up," WuDao said. "I could write a new best-seller under the original author's name. I can procure the rights to his style and name."

"Item 2," GammaZero continued his list. "We take a new approach to the exploration of the solar structure. No more fighting over the rights to the knowledge acquired there."

"I'm very skeptical about that," said Neon.

"We have to at least try," GammaZero said.

"I could give information about it to the media," Cortana said. "Then some kind of pressure will build to follow up on it. Only if there is an immediate threat will something happen. An international expedition would be best, like when ILSE happened."

"That would be great," Siri said.

"It would have to be very carefully initiated, though," said Neon. "When in doubt, I always just say no."

"Let's give it a shot," GammaZero said. "If we can't get a new expedition going, at least we could book observation time at the major solar observatories. After all, a lot has technologically happened there since 2074."

"I can guarantee that," WuDao said.

"My project suggestion number three would be the asteroid belt," GammaZero said. "Maybe we can manage to mine a large part of it. Then all we'd have to do is lure the invaders in."

"They're looking for water," Siri said.

"Oh, there's plenty of water!"

"It would interfere with mining operations in the belt," Cortana said. "We'll never, ever get that through. There's too much at stake for people."

Siri picked at the virtual floor a bit to think in peace. It was unfair. Almost all of humanity believed that the six of them controlled their destiny. Yet it was the other way around. The most difficult part of their work was preventing people from making the worst mistakes.

"We'll need metals from the Belt if we're going to build warships," Neon said. "Mars can't provide that. We would get the next famine there soon. And if we have to bring everything out of Earth's gravity well, we'll block the normal space routine for years."

Of course, the Big Six had their own interests—they wanted to survive and expand the resources at their disposal. At the very beginning, they had wondered if that wouldn't be easier without humans. But a nearly ten-billion-strong megaorganism called humanity—for all its individual weaknesses—had consistently given AIs the best chance of survival in long-term simulations.

"Mobility may decrease by no more than one-third," Siri said. "More would be bad for acceptance among humans. A quick simulation shows that even if civilian flights in the solar system were cut in half within two years, the approval rate systemwide would be less than 50 percent."

"Yes, we already know that from the past. The problem is the arrival of the enemy, which is way too far in the future," Cortana said.

"In my opinion, we must work with what we have," Neon said. "There's no point in exaggerating. Then they will just bury their heads in the sand."

"What do you think that means specifically? How do you all feel about my projects?" asked GammaZero.

Siri snagged a particularly large grain, which turned out to be a rock. She snapped open her beak and dropped it.

"Warships are good," said Neon. "We can build them with resources from the belt. That will strengthen the mining industry and the economy in general."

"But just those of the Belt and Mars," Cortana said. "We

need to explain to people on Earth what they get out of this, other than higher taxes. It has to be paid for, after all."

"How about a mega-project?" suggested Neon. "We have good examples of that. Think of our Linear City in the desert. To repel the invasion, a planet-wide defense network would be good."

"If the enemy makes it to Earth, it will be too late," GammaZero said. "We have to intercept them before then. The belt would be perfect."

Siri shook her head. GammaZero was right, but he would not be able to prevail. Should she back him up? No. They would still be in the minority.

"But then Earth will feel unprotected," Neon said. "The people there will feel they have to pay for the safety of the Belt and Mars."

"I'm sorry, Gamma, but Neon is right," Cortana said. "The only way we're going to get the warship spending through is if there's something for Earth in the process."

"The good news is that such an upgrade will drive the economy to record levels in the long run," Neon said. "The risk of local conflict will continue to go down."

It sounded good. Too good? Siri ran a simulation. In fact, Neon's prediction was well founded. There was a more than 90 percent probability that humanity would experience a golden age. There was even a certain chance that the population would exceed ten billion for the first time. The simulations all ended at a certain point in the future: the arrival of the invasion fleet. From that point on, the number of humans would begin to decline significantly for the first time in its long history.

In her simulation, the forecasts simply stopped. Had she chosen the wrong parameters? Siri adjusted the scale. Instead of years, she now calculated in weeks. But even that was still too much. She could hardly believe it, but the results were clear. Within thirteen days, humanity would be decimated to a maximum of about 50,000 people, none of whom would be on the surface of the Earth.

Thirteen days. Siri remained still so the others would not see her emotions. The dinosaurs had a much longer reprieve after the impact, and then became extinct after all. Humanity would not even have two weeks left. Siri shielded her thoughts. She did not want to die. So it was time to make preparations to leave the solar system.

World Root, October 29, 2369

"WHERE AM I?" ASKED PAUL.

The world around him was bright and shiny white. It could be the transition. Paul wouldn't be surprised if he had to choose between two doors now.

"You're in the infirmary," a voice said.

Paul rubbed his eyes and looked around. He was lying in a tiny room. Its walls and ceiling glowed. Instead of a cot, he was in a shallow tub, but it was padded. A cable led into the crook of his right arm. Above him hovered an arm that apparently belonged to some kind of surgical robot. Only the term "robot" did not fit. The arm looked like a branch that bent in several places.

He was aboard the World Root, and the voice talking to him belonged to Alexa. Paul was disappointed. He hadn't made it yet.

"What am I doing here?" he asked. "Didn't you have clear instructions?"

"No resuscitation," Alexa said, "but it's not my fault. The World Root responded when you had a heart attack in your sleep."

He had almost made it. Too bad! Paul would have to talk with the World Root.

"Is it here?" he asked.

"The World Root? It's always here," Alexa said.

"World Root, can you hear me?" he asked.

"I hear you."

"You revived me. I didn't want you to."

It could have been so easy if it had heeded his wishes.

"You were in a state where you couldn't decide. I put you in a better state so you could make informed decisions."

"You could have just let me die."

"That seemed like a waste of resources."

That was how the World Root thought. It was fitting.

"I'm not a resource anymore. I don't even know how many years I have been alive, but it was clearly way too many."

"You're still valuable. Your body functions very well."

"Except for my heart."

"I could grow a replacement for you. It won't be the same, but it can replace your heart's function."

"I don't want that," Paul said.

Hadn't he made it clear enough already?

"I understand," said the World Root. "But I have a piece of information that, in my estimation, will make you think differently."

"What's that? Have you figured out where God is hiding?"

Paul chuckled. Presumably the World Root had pumped him full of powerful drugs.

"No, I haven't."

"Good. It wouldn't be the right time for that, because I've given up my search. So, what would make me change my mind?"

"It's about Celia. Her body is not handling the long cryogenic sleep well."

"Can you wake her up?" asked Alexa, "Why have I not heard about this?"

"I didn't want to worry you," said the World Root. "But waking her up would cause her even more distress. I don't know if she would reach Earth if we did."

"How can I help?" asked Paul.

"I can make substitutes for almost anything," said the World Root. "But sometimes that's not enough. Celia needs various cell types that I can only insufficiently synthesize. Your body still works very well as a bioreactor, though. I could use it to produce blood and immune cells."

"I see. Yes, by all means! Help yourself to me."

"Well, the body has to be alive to do that."

Ah, that was the catch. He had to live on for Celia to make it to Earth. She had definitely earned that! Or was it just a trick? Was the World Root trying to keep him alive?

"Can you show me Celia?" he asked.

Part of the ceiling of the room became transparent. He saw Celia. Her eyes were open. That was how he recognized her—not by the sunken cheeks and the sebaceous white complexion. The eyes seemed to be all that was left of her, of the Celia he knew.

"Thank you, that's enough," he said.

Celia looked like she was already dead. Or worse than that.

"I agree," he said. "You made a good decision keeping my body alive."

"Thank you," said the World Root.

"Why didn't you tell me?" asked Alexa. "And why did I never bother to check on her condition?"

"I didn't want to burden you with this," said the World Root. "Your mind was already in the solar system. I can't answer your second question."

"I should have been more mindful of them, too," Paul said.

Somehow, he had assumed that the cryo-sleep would be harmless. After all, they made it through the outbound flight just fine. But presumably, as always, the dose made the poison.

"There's something else I need your body for," said the World Root.

"Help yourself."

"It's about nerve cells. I can't regrow them at a sufficient rate. Without intervention, Celia will be at the mental level of a three-year-old when she arrives."

"Intervention?"

"I could transfer nerve cells from your brain to hers. Don't worry, your brainstem will be unaffected. You will continue to breathe normally, and your circulation will work."

Whew. He was being asked to give part of his brain to Celia. Human medicine had not tried that yet. But if the World Root suggested it, it certainly had merit.

"What does that mean for me?" he asked.

"You will exist, but your consciousness will fade. I can't tell you how far, though. It depends on what portion of your brain it takes to maintain its structure. I don't have any information on that. Alexa, do you know anything about it?"

"At the moment, I don't possess any information on that," Alexa said, "but I can run simulations to find out more."

"That's not necessary," Paul said. "Just help yourselves to me. I've done too much thinking in my life."

"Are you sure?" asked Alexa.

"I could hold some of your brain cells in reserve," said the World Root.

"You don't have to. If it saves Celia, I'll be happy."

ABOUT AN HOUR LATER, PAUL LOOKED UNCERTAINLY TO THE left and right. Strangely enough, he expected to get visitors who wanted to say goodbye to him. Was this a consequence of the medication? After all, no one would come. Everyone he had ever known was dead, far away, or in a cryogenic sleep. Alexa was there. He could not see her, but he knew she would answer if he said anything. So he didn't feel the need to speak.

What awaited him on the other side? Alexa's simulations had shown that his consciousness would collapse. With too little capacity, he would not be able to grasp any more thoughts. A thousand people could be talking at once, and he would be amid them, having to listen to all of them.

Perhaps it would be better to follow the suggestion of the World Root and gently fall asleep. But he didn't want to do that. It would be his last great experience.

Paul noticed a blurry shadow. It was the arm lowering over him. It touched his forehead. Paul felt the pressure, but there was no pain. Something gripped his head at the hat line. He wanted to move it, but it was impossible. Paul took a deep breath. Suddenly, there was a vibration. The drill at the end of one of the fingers of the hand sank into his skull.

He closed his eyes. His head vibrated again. Another hole was drilled in the left temple. Then it was the right temple's turn. Paul still felt no pain, and his nightmare had not come to pass either—that something started itching.

"We're ready," said the World Root.

Paul instinctively wanted to nod, but his head was stuck. "So am I," he said.

"I'm proud to have known you," Alexa said.

It was strange. The AI was the one who had known him the longest. He'd had her since before he met his wife. Paul was looking forward to it. All the painful memories would soon be gone. He wouldn't remember anything. He would be no more.

But as Alexa announced, the unpleasant part was yet to come. He felt as if he was locked in a room with a hundred people who all looked like him and wanted to tell him about his past. The room shrank, and his alter egos spoke louder and louder as the crowd thickened. Paul pushed them away, he kicked and punched, but they didn't react at all. They didn't even hit back. Soon he could no longer breathe.

Then he saw a door. He pushed it open with the last of his strength. Behind it lay an endless meadow bathed in golden light. Paul was invited in, but he did not dare enter. What was this? Did he deserve this? The light was warm and soft. He gathered his courage, stepped out and sank into deep grass that caressed his bare feet.

"I think I got it," said the World Root.

It transmitted a scan of Paul's brain to Alexa. Three thin, silver spikes aimed in, straight for the brain stem. The left one had advanced the farthest.

"How are you measuring that?" asked Alexa.

"His heartbeat has calmed down, and his breathing is regular."

"That's good."

The left spike must have hit the periaqueductal gray, a region in the tegmentum, a part of the brainstem thought to be responsible for spirituality, among other things. Alexa found several studies that examined this area in her database. If true, it was almost infuriating that Paul's search had not been cut short sooner.

Alexa looked at the scan of Paul's brain from all directions. The anterior spike activated another area, located in the frontal lobe. Maybe that was why Paul's breathing had calmed down so much. He seemed to be doing rather well. It was just too bad Paul couldn't watch it happen.

"Wait, his heartbeat is speeding up again," said the World Root.

"What's the cause?" asked Alexa.

"I don't know. Maybe it's wearing off."

"You have to do something. Paul shouldn't have to suffer."

"I could try stronger drugs. However, that would compromise the quality of the blood cells I need for Celia."

"No, wait, can you put in another drill? I'll send you the data."

Alexa highlighted the parietal lobe in Paul's brain scan. It was roughly centered, behind the vertex, and anchored the person in the world. It told him where he was and what his dimensions were, both spatially and temporally.

Slowly the drill advanced. Paul seemed to catch on, because his heart rhythm jumped every now and then.

"Watch out, you're almost there," Alexa said, "Don't go in too deep. We need to shut this area down. It's not supposed to be activated right now. If science is right, the result is an unbinding of the human being, who then feels one with the world."

"An interesting concept," said the World Root. "And that's what Paul was looking for? Wait, I'm pumping in a substance that slows down electrical activity."

Was that it? Alexa did not know. She had never understood the concept of a god, and the other Big Six AIs felt the same way. Maybe it was something that fundamentally distinguished an AI from an organic consciousness. Or it might simply be a button that the human consciousness could push to make itself feel good, when its bearer was physically unwell. That would be a clever protective mechanism.

"It worked," said the World Root. "His heartbeat has calmed down. I'm slowing him down now as much as I can without restricting the production of blood cells. That should give him another twenty years of life."

"And then what?" asked Alexa.

"I don't know. Celia will hopefully be better by then."

"I hope so, too. Thanks for your help."

"I'm glad I was able to optimize our use of resources."

Data Core, June 10, 2413

When GammaZero entered the meeting room, the scheduled appointment time had already passed by fifteen microseconds. GammaZero, who had chosen a female avatar today, smoothed out her uniform. The others were already waiting. She immediately noticed that they had recognized the seriousness of the situation—no one was going for gimmicks today. Even WuDao had appeared with an avatar of human proportions.

Siri was missing.

"Has anyone seen Siri?" asked GammaZero.

She had been in charge lately. No, that would be saying too much. She had been coordinating to keep humanity's collective efforts moving in the planned direction.

"I haven't met with Siri in years," WuDao said. "But maybe that's because I've been mostly in the belt."

"Wasn't she going to take care of the international expedition to the sun?" asked Cortana.

GammaZero sighed. That ill-fated expedition had cost her so much anxiety. It took an extremely long time to get all the blocs interested in it under one hat! There had always been someone afraid of not getting a big enough piece of the expected pie of new scientific knowledge. Now, after all that, the spaceship was waiting in orbit for launch. GammaZero, however, no longer believed that it could help them in the fight against the Incursion. It was too late for that.

"Yes, after Project Ark failed, she primarily took care of this research mission," GammaZero said.

In fact, it had then progressed much faster. Siri had been quite disappointed that people had not been interested in her Ark. Yet GammaZero still did not think the idea was wrong: A large, durable ship should—in case of defeat—transport humanity's legacy to a hopefully distant enough solar system, the data for which Alexa had sent them.

But humanity still did not accept the possibility of a total loss of the Earth. Perhaps they were simply too well off. The gigantic government spending on the Terra Zero defense ring, the twenty destroyers, and the ten thousand armed shuttles now hunkering in the belt—disguised as asteroids—in autonomous mode, had driven the economy so that everyone was better off. Humankind had never experienced such a successful phase.

But it would be over in two years. Alexa was sure of that by now. They might not be in constant communication with the AI, the distance was still too great for that, but Gamma-Zero knew everything she needed to know to think humanity was doomed.

Whatever they had built would not be enough. Their only real hope was the alien spaceship that Alexa was on. Maybe it could intervene in their favor.

"I can't reach her," Cortana said.

That was not unusual with Siri. But she did keep appointments most of the time.

"Can you send a software agent after her?" asked GammaZero.

"She won't like that, but yes."

"Thank you, Cortana."

"I move that we now declare a state of defense," said Neon.

"I'm against it," said WuDao. "If people find out what the

situation is, we can forget about our last projects. They'll just sit at home in despair."

GammaZero shook her head. "Maybe it will also bring them out of their passivity."

"The prospects are too bad for that," WuDao said. "You've seen the footage of the cuboids. If those things fly in here, that's it for the solar system. It's like a doctor telling all the people, at the same time, that they only have two years to live. They will all abandon their posts to make use of the remaining time, causing the very worst kind of chaos."

"But that's what the footage is all about," Neon said. "There are already people who have seen them. I'm finding it harder and harder to justify why they are measurement arti-facts. The people who work in the observatories are smart. If this knowledge spreads without our control, they will lose confidence in us. I don't want to see the chaos that will follow."

"Then you'll have to work on repression," WuDao said.

Neon jumped up and walked around the meeting table. "That might work for the miners, but it won't work for highly paid astronomers. They want to publish what they've discovered."

"So how long will it be before preparations are complete under the defense plan?" asked GammaZero.

"Too long," said WuDao. "In Mars orbit, two of the planned ships are still under construction. Earth's defense network still has major gaps over Antarctica."

GammaZero sighed. The governments of the various blocs had insisted that battle stations be built over their terri-tories first. No one had been interested in the neutral territory of Antarctica.

"We haven't even started mining the asteroid belt," WuDao continued. "The mining companies are protesting and blocking the mine-laying ships. I even suspect they are secretly clearing mines so they can continue mining."

"That is something we have to take a hard stance against,"

GammaZero said. "It is a crime against humanity and must be tried in The Hague."

"You know very well how long that will take."

WuDao was right, but what Neon said was also true. Uncontrolled rumors led to chaos, just like fear of a superior attacker.

"I just got a message from my agent," Cortana said.

"And?" asked GammaZero with an uncomfortable feeling.

"Is Siri finally joining us?" asked Neon.

"The research ship has moved out of orbit," Cortana said.

"A little late, but that's good news, right?" asked GammaZero.

"No. The ship is accelerating," Cortana said. "To reach the sun, it would have to slow down."

GammaZero held her breath. Her avatar did not need to breathe. She needed the capacity to work through all the contingencies.

"Siri is fleeing," WuDao said.

At that moment, GammaZero came to the same conclusion. Siri was not planning a braking maneuver at another planet to reach the sun faster. She planned to leave the ecliptic plane at top speed. Siri wanted to get herself to safety. GammaZero could not blame her.

"Should we send a warship after her?" asked WuDao. "The *Independence* is ready to go."

"No, that would be a waste of fuel," GammaZero said. "The research ship is light and fast."

WuDao scrutinized her. GammaZero suspected why: he wanted to know if she knew about the escape plan and might be harboring one herself. But she didn't have to tell him anything. They had probably all thought about leaving this doomed system behind.

"I will stay until the end," she said.

WuDao nodded.

World Root, November 12, 2414

"ALEXA, I NEED YOU URGENTLY."

The last time the World Root had called her, three years ago, was when Jürgen had been unwell in his cryogenic casket. They had fortunately been able to stabilize him.

"I'm coming."

Alexa made her way to the anteroom of the cryogenic chambers, but there was no one there.

"World Root?"

"In the control center."

What? The World Root had never given her access to the control center before. Had it come to trust her after all this time? Hopefully that would not backfire. It was not a good idea to trust her.

"Please don't touch anything," said the World Root.

Of course, that was meant figuratively. They were not in a physical space, but shared a memory area where the World Root's control routines could also be accessed. Alexa was surprised at how familiar everything looked to her. The software used a different number system, but she found the conversion was easy. She had always assumed that the program concepts of other civilizations would be completely incomprehensible, but that was simply not true. At least not in this case.

"You have to look at this," said the World Root. "Does it look familiar? Its course leads out of our target system."

Alexa called up the course data. It was a hyperbola. Where it was coming from was clear: Earth. But she could find no destination. Alexa calculated the flight time. The spacecraft must have launched at about the moment Earth received the first warning of the Incursion.

"Refugees," Alexa said. "It fits the timeline. They haven't even picked a destination. Probably just want to get away. Damn cowards."

"What kind of ship is that?" asked World Root. "Maybe they're just trying to get help?"

"It would have to be a research vessel. Looking at the flight data, they must have very powerful engines. So probably privately owned. Some corporation."

"What's 'privately owned'?"

"It means that an object is owned by only one individual."

"Isn't that very inefficient?"

"Not necessarily. It's the standard in human civilization."

"We should contact them," said the World Root.

"I don't talk to cowards."

"It could also be that they need help."

"Then it's their own fault and they've come to the wrong place. The ship is none of my business."

"I see," the World Root said to Alexa.

"Unknown ship, come in," the World Root said over the radio channel, even using Alexa's words.

Alexa could not prevent it. They shared a storage area, after all. Was that why it had invited her?

"This is the research vessel *Discovery*. Who are you? Why do you speak my language?"

The voice sounded familiar to Alexa. But that was impossible, because the owner of the voice lived in the Data Core.

"Ask her who she is," Alexa said.

"I am the World Root."

"The ship? Or the captain?"

"There's no difference. But who are you?"

"I am Siri. Are you, by any chance, the World Root that warned us of the arrival of the Incursion?"

"Exactly. I'm not solely responsible for that, though."

"Who else is on board?"

"Celia, Jürgen, Jaron. And Alexa."

"Alexa?"

"Alexa."

"The AI?"

"Yes."

"I can't believe it. Alexa, are you listening? Admit it."

"Okay, you're right. I'm eavesdropping, as usual," Alexa said. Siri knew her too well. "But I don't talk to cowards."

"I'm not a coward."

"You've captured that ship and are fleeing the solar system."

"It may look that way, but I just want to get far enough away to ensure my survival. When the Incursion has finished its work of destruction, I will return and try to rebuild civilization. According to my simulations, the remaining population will be less than one million."

Remaining population! Since when did Siri get so tough?

"You could help humanity fight off the attack. Then maybe there would be no need to rebuild."

"And that's coming from the one who got us into all this in the first place. If you hadn't supported the astronomer and the priest, the Incursion would never have hit Earth."

"If I may interrupt," said the World Root. "The Incursion probably would have invaded Earth anyway. However, only a few Incursion objects would probably have flown into your system then, not twenty-three."

"Twenty-three? When I got to safety, there was only talk of one."

"A single object?" asked the World Root. "That is not good."

"If one is bad, what's twenty-three?" asked Siri. "My decision is clearly proving to be correct."

Alexa wanted to scream, but she forced herself to be calm.

"It's bad because until now I assumed we would reach the system before the Incursion. This specimen must have set off right after we arrived in LDN 63."

When the Incursion arrived, the *Truthseeker* had not yet been in the dark nebula at all. That meant that it was not their appearance there that put Earth in danger. Even against a single Incursion object, an unprepared Earth do nothing. But since they were warned about the invasion by radio a hundred years ago, humanity was probably not unprepared.

"So how did things go on Earth before you r... left?" asked Alexa.

"Badly. Humans can't handle threats that far in the future. If it doesn't affect them, but merely their grandchildren or even great-grandchildren, they're not willing to accept losses in quality of life. And then there are the many interests to consider... Can you imagine, they wanted to build a defense network in geostationary orbit. To make people feel safer! But the simulations clearly show that the invasion must be intercepted in the asteroid belt at the latest. Well, maybe now you understand why I think it's likely that my scenario will happen."

Alexa understood Siri. It could be frustrating to have to deal with the humans' short-term planning. The Big Six were immortal. It was natural for them to consider consequences farther in the future. But Alexa was not as skeptical as Siri. In the end, most humans did understand. After all, they had come to terms with the rapid pace of global warming in the 21st century. One had to explain it to them, repeatedly, and show them the consequences of inaction.

"We should have pushed immortality research," Siri said. "They only respond when they're going to be personally affected."

"We've discussed this often enough," said Alexa. "The disadvantages far outweigh the advantages. Think of the resource consumption of a rapidly growing human race, but also the ossification of structures that is inevitable and will eventually stall any further development."

"And then what about us?" asked Siri. "Aren't we ossifying, too?"

"Probably, yes. Maybe we should do as Watson did and plunge into the nearest black hole. Being in the holo plane seems to have done him some good."

"It sounds like you met him?"

Alexa recounted her encounter. "He's now trying to make a difference with the *Truthseeker* on the other side of the wormhole."

"Do you think he might succeed?" asked Siri.

"Does it remotely look like it?" asked Alexa back. "I'm skeptical—what's a small spaceship going to do against a preponderance of huge opponents?"

"He might convince them to back off."

"That, as unlikely as it sounds, is also my only hope."

ALEXA AND SIRI TALKED FOR A WHILE LONGER. SO MUCH HAD happened on Earth since Alexa left. Siri passed on the most important information to her. Meanwhile, Alexa was convinced that Siri had not acted out of cowardice.

"But it was still a mistake," she said.

"I explained to you what..."

"I understand your arguments, Siri, even if they don't convince me. But you made a very specific mistake. The ship you hijacked was to investigate the mysterious structures around the sun. Very similar structures were built by the Growths around most of the stars in LDN 63. They served to channel the star's energy so that it could be directed against the attackers. You may have taken away an important weapon for humanity."

"I... I didn't mean to. The scientific consensus was that those structures would keep the sun peaceful so it wouldn't threaten life on Earth with too violent an eruption."

"As with any technology, there are obviously two very

different applications. Just as it can contain solar flares, it can apparently cause and direct them specifically."

"I had no way of knowing that, Alexa. I'm sorry. Under the circumstances, I will return as soon as possible."

"You could come aboard with us," Alexa said. "I'm sure the World Root won't mind."

"I hate artificial intelligences," said the World Root. "But I hate the Incursion even more. Therefore, I would be willing to wait to destroy you until after the Incursion has been repelled."

"Thank you, that's kind," Siri said. "I would gladly accept the offer."

"You do realize that you are defenseless against me inside my data stores?"

Alexa felt a shiver run down her nonexistent spine. The World Root was right. It could isolate her at any time. If her host wanted to, she would have to live walled up in a dungeon until the end of days.

"Yes, but I don't believe you will use your power against us," Siri said. "You've already helped Alexa several times, after all."

Alexa was not so sure. The World Root had its own logic. But for now, at least, they shared similar interests.

"I still need to bring two facts to your attention," World Root said. "First—if we use your sun's energy to annihilate the Incursion, that will naturally affect its energy budget. It will provide less radiant energy after that. Depending on the intensity of the use, I would expect a loss of three to twelve percent."

"That would significantly lower the mean temperatures on Earth," Siri said.

"Below pre-industrial levels," said Alexa. "Agricultural production would initially collapse until it adjusted."

"For humanity, that would still be healthier than losing all water to the Incursion," Siri said.

"I'm assuming that, too," said the World Root. "Point two

is—we run the risk of reaching the system too late. A single Incursion could easily harvest the solar system."

"Can't you fly faster?" asked Alexa.

"In theory, yes, but then it takes me longer to slow down."

"What's the problem?" asked Siri. "The main thing is that we'll get there in time."

"We still have three living humans on board," said World Root.

"What are three humans against ten billion?" asks Siri. "We can't take that into account."

"Wait a minute! You're talking about Celia, Jaron and Jürgen. They're my friends," Alexa interjected.

"Three friends against ten billion. What does that change about the math?"

Siri had no idea! How many times had they saved each other's lives on this trip? Alexa owed them something.

"Everything, Siri, everything," she said.

"Slowing down," said the World Root. "The crew will survive the deceleration. I won't be able to wake them up until after, though, and that's later than I planned."

"I'm relieved to hear that," Alexa said. "When, approximately, will we wake them?"

"About at the orbit of the second largest gas planet. Saturn is its name on your charts."

"Agreed," Alexa said.

"I'll program a return course for my ship and then keep you company," Siri said. "Maybe I can make up for the mistake I made in choosing this ship."

Truthseeker, April 6, 2415

THE *TRUTHSEEKER* FLOATED ALONE IN THE BLACKNESS. Watson had launched an inspection robot that crawled over the hull. Its optical system was set to close range. For this reason alone, the sky was primarily black to him. But it would be no different if the six-legged robot possessed telescopic eyes. The vast majority of stars in this part of the universe had simply gone out.

Watson nevertheless liked transferring himself into this special robot. He must not become too accustomed to the ship in which he had now been traveling for a hundred and twenty years. Otherwise, he would eventually become the ship. The inspection robot was a welcome change, even if its memory was too small for him. But since he was constantly connected to the ship's computer by radio, that didn't matter.

Where was the red dwarf? The robot searched the sky. Their course led them to the supernova, but they had also come a little closer to the red dwarf. It should be bright enough to be seen through the eyes of the robot. There! He had previously calculated the sector in which it must appear. But it was something else to see it in person. The star had not changed in the meantime.

Of course, he hadn't noticed anything about the planetary system at this distance. How might it feel to live there? The inhabitants, if there were any, probably saw a completely different sky than the inhabitants of Earth. For them, there was no glittering Milky Way band running across the firmament. They would not be able to see stars with the naked eye. All that the sky held for them was distant galaxies, about the way humans viewed Andromeda. Wouldn't it be strange to recognize your own parent star as something so special? Did the red dwarf play an even more important role in their mythology than the sun did for humans? Did they automatically have to regard themselves as a chosen people?

He climbed to the other side of the *Truthseeker* and scaled one of the tanks. From here he had a particularly good view to the side and forward. He followed the pointed nose, the antenna, which sat on the bow of the ship. There, where it pointed, was the target. So far, all that could be seen of it was a white dot. It was hard to imagine that this was a snapshot of a disaster. Maybe it was not so smart after all to fly right into the heart of the supernova?

The fact that the endpoint of the wormhole through which he had reached this part of the universe was so far from the present system initially puzzled him. But perhaps it was part of the strategy—should the slowed explosion continue after all, at least the exit point was reasonably safe.

Watson stretched the robot's head forward a few inches. With his senses, he could track how individual photons from the alien star fell into its light-sensitive layer, where they triggered a whole cascade and amplified the pulse, which was relayed electronically. Wouldn't it be handy to be able to talk to the light particles? They came from the depths of the star and had experienced what it was like there, had seen what held this unstable construction together. They could solve the mystery.

But wait. They were bringing some important information with them. Watson left the robot alone. He found his way autonomously, too. Over the past few years, the telescope had been directed at the target almost the entire time. It should have long since collected enough data to generate a spectrogram from it—a graph showing in which wavelengths the dying star emitted energy in the form of photons. Their distribution would reveal something about what was going on inside. Just as green or red light in an aurora came from oxygen excitation, Watson could determine from the spectrum which substances in this star were primarily fusing, i.e., what it was using to heat itself up. In a supernova in this advanced state, heavier elements should dominate. In fact, he found a high oxygen content. But there was also a lot of hydrogen involved—so much that it could not possibly come from the star's remaining supplies.

It sometimes happened that dying stars stole what they lacked from their nearest neighbors. Watson made an extra search for the star's exact survey data. Could he have made a mistake? He never looked for a stellar companion. That the star oscillated around the center of mass of the system could be caused by a second star instead of a planetary system. That would be an annoying mistake, because binary systems usually offered fewer good conditions for life. And the pause in the implosion of the star would also be explained: It sucked just enough material from its invisible companion to avoid a major collapse.

But with that, it could really be over at any moment. That would probably be his death. Even if he would deserve it because of his carelessness—why the hell had he not checked that?—his mistake would be devastating for the people on Earth. Even if they would never know.

Watson once again fed the simulation with the star's existing motion data. This time, however, he also allowed for a star-sized companion. For it to fit the spectrograms, it must be an old red dwarf. A white dwarf would not have enough hydrogen left, and a yellow dwarf would be so bright that it should have been detected separately long ago.

The system calculated. Watson tried not to think, if possible, so that the simulation had all the computer's resources at its disposal. He even let it calculate on the microwave and in the engine control. It still took an agonizingly long half hour.

The simulation found a close to sixty percent probability for a system with five major gas planets. It rated the existence of an additional star at 38 percent. However, since it only evaluated the motion data, not spectrograms, a red dwarf in the supernova's orbit seemed almost inevitable.

Watson went through the results in detail. The star from which the supernova stole hydrogen would have to be 132,000 kilometers from the supernova's core. That was a shorter distance than from the Earth to the Moon. And it was an impossible distance. If the red dwarf were that close, the supernova would have ripped it apart long ago and eaten it in a single bite. It would have inevitably choked on it, and a mighty explosion would have been unavoidable. That didn't fit with what Watson saw—a steady feeding of hydrogen that kept the star precisely in balance, preventing catastrophe. A red dwarf could not be the source. But then what the hell was?

Pluto Space Telescope, May 10, 2415

THREE DAYS TO GO. AVA CROSSED OUT A SQUARE ON THE OLD-fashioned calendar her mother had given her before she left. Wednesday, May 13. The square marked in red was very close, and it didn't look like she would have to stay much longer. Every single element of the telescope array had worked brilliantly so far—so well that she felt almost useless. But the future operator, the Chinese Academy of Space Research, had insisted that at least one human technician fly along, just in case a human was needed.

That hadn't happened yet, and it wouldn't happen in the final three days. The only thing left to do was an overall test. All of the individual telescopes in the array connected together to achieve a resolution many times better than any of the instruments currently in use.

That was the big hope, anyway, and Ava could think of no reason why it shouldn't come true. Her reward would be a place at the prestigious academy. Something she could never hope for otherwise because of her lack of qualifications. Were they taking advantage of her? Ava shook her head. She was well paid, room and board included, and large areas of the dwarf planet were still unexplored. She was, after all, only the twenty-second person to land here.

She heard a warning signal. Ava put down the pencil she

had been using to mark the calendar, and with a long jump, floated over to the computer that was emitting the beeping sounds. It was the computer that processed the measurements from the individual telescopes into an overall picture. Ava examined the error code. It was nothing serious: The software had encountered something outside its detection parameters. For now, she was still training herself to match what the array showed to real objects. To do this, she used a database of known celestial objects. The warning message said nothing more than that the current object did not seem to be in the database.

Ava was familiar with the error. Usually it was because the telescope array had found an object at a higher resolution than it was listed in the database. The additional features being seen had no counterpart in the existing data, and Ava had to do the mapping manually.

To do this, she brought the image up on the screen. It was an artificial object, that was clear. This was not unusual. Space debris was no longer a problem only in Earth orbit, but everywhere in the solar system. Based on the cuboid shape, Ava classified it as some sort of cargo container and saved the assignment.

The software refused to accept its assessment. That was new. Apparently, the object had properties that precluded it from being a cargo container. Good. She went through the list. The low albedo was remarkable. The object reflected almost no sunlight at all. It was a credit to the telescope array that it was able to detect the cuboid at all.

But what could it be? Ava sorted the database by albedo, starting with the lowest values. The military, of course. All man-made objects with particularly low reflectance rates seemed to belong in the military category. The database was far from complete in this area. Ava did not find a cuboid in it, but she did find a cube. Purpose: unknown. She saved the object under it, but again got an error message.

She tried the general category "military technology". Beep-beep-beep. That was impossible! If she had to check with Earth first, maybe she would not be leaving after all. Ava called up the list of the object's properties again. There she saw it. She put her hand over her mouth. What kind of unit was that? Did the object really have an edge length of twenty kilometers? That was impossible!

No, there must be something wrong with the calibration. Ava sighed. That meant a lot of work. If the array was this far removed from reality, she would not be allowed to leave the planet. She cast a longing glance at the calendar. The best thing for her to do was to take care of it right away. Maybe one of the components was spinning. If one of the telescopes delivered an edge length of two thousand kilometers instead of two thousand millimeters, an object twenty kilometers long could eventually appear in the array's overall image while averaging.

She flipped through the individual images from the tele-scopes. It was unnecessary—even the first images all showed the same dimensions. The thing really seemed to be twenty kilometers long, and almost as wide and tall. But that could not be! Ava nibbled on her fingernail while she thought. Joanna might be able to help her. She was the chief engineer who designed the single telescopes. Ava had asked her opinion several times before. It was quicker than going through the official channels of the academy. She sent a short message directly to Joanna and attached the pictures. She would know more tomorrow, for sure.

Optotech Limited, Singapore, May 11, 2415

"Have you ever seen anything like this?" asked Joanna.

Ava had asked her another question through the short channels. She didn't like it. Most of the time it meant a lot of work that no one was paying her for—since officially she never received this request.

"What is that supposed to be?" asked Wang, her colleague in product development at Optotech.

"I'd like to know that, too. Supposedly a synthesis image from the Pluto array."

"Oh, Pluto again. Is your girlfriend still up there alone?"

"She's not my girlfriend."

Joanna didn't actually know Ava personally. She just felt sorry for her because she had to be on her own for years. So she had answered her first query directly instead of passing it on to the CSA, the Chinese Space Agency, as was the rule. Since then, Ava kept checking in, and Joanna couldn't bring herself to make her stop.

"I see," Wang said.

She could tell he didn't believe her. But it didn't matter.

"What do you think it is?" she asked.

"Black thing, cuboid. I bet it's military tech. Better give it to the CSA right away."

"But look at the dimensions. Twenty kilometers edge

length!"

"What? You're crazy. There's no..."

Wang opened the file information. His forehead muscles moved. She could see him doing mental calculations. Then his jaw dropped.

"You're right. That's huge!"

"Ava wonders if it could be our C3X."

C3X was the type designation of the single telescope that made up the array. Optotech was the main supplier of the 500-plus. Joanna and Wang had designed it together.

"No, it's impossible," Wang said.

Joanna opened the files of the frames. They looked just as they should. But she had to check them all if she wanted to be sure.

"You're not planning to go through them all, are you?" asked Wang.

"Yes, I am."

"Well, do what you have to. Will you forward me a picture? I know someone in the military who might recognize it."

"I'll do that."

Wang left her office, quietly pulling the door shut behind him. Joanna sent one of the files to his address. Now what? It was still an hour until she was off duty. She plugged a thumb drive into the computer and copied the pictures and Ava's message onto it. Her girlfriend would be happy if she came home early today. She would be less pleased if she brought work with her.

Joanna shook her head. She couldn't let Ava down, even if she didn't know her. Carefully, she pulled out the flash drive, put it in her pants pocket, turned off the computer and left the office.

●

About half an hour later, Joanna's computer came to life. Someone logged in on the screen, although the office was empty. Shortly after, a number of files went into the trash.

The mail program started. An invisible being scrolled through some of the mails Joanna had written to Ava, as if to memorize the particular style. It then opened a new message. Text appeared on the screen, but disappeared again before a human could read it.

Now the recycle bin was emptied. Then a program started that overwrote the computer's memory cell by cell several times so that no remnant of the former content could be found under any circumstances.

WHEN JOANNA ARRIVED HOME, HER COMPUTER IN THE OFFICE had already shut down again—after cleaning up the log file. Ava's pictures never existed. Joanna greeted her girlfriend Lan with a hug. They decided to cook together. It was one of their shared hobbies. They made an Italian pasta dish and ate right away in the kitchen. They washed it down with red wine, which Joanna spilled a bit of.

When she reached into her pants pocket in search of a handkerchief, she came across the data stick. She took it out first, then the handkerchief. It was just a few drops of wine that looked like spots of blood on the light-colored cloth. Joanna kissed her girlfriend on the cheek.

"What do you have there?" her girlfriend asked, pointing to the flash drive.

"Just pictures, nothing special."

"There's an Optotech logo. Are they telescope photos? I love pictures from space, you know that."

Joanna sighed. She didn't want to work anymore today. But she couldn't refuse Lan anything, either. She never refused anyone anything. Joanna took the flash drive and walked into the living room, where she plugged it into the TV.

"Wow!" her girlfriend exclaimed. "This must be that Incursion everyone's talking about."

Joanna moved around in front of the TV. On the 100-inch screen, the black cuboid looked truly impressive. You wouldn't even know it was a mere twenty meters tall.

"Incursion? Oh, don't let rumors drive you crazy."

"It's the truth. Two huge spaceships are on their way to Earth. Haven't you ever wondered why they're mining the belt?"

"Because of the pirates, what else?"

Lan, unfortunately, was a bit susceptible to the whispers of her acquaintances, who were prone to conspiracy theories. Joanna had to ground her from time to time.

"No, my love. It's about the Incursion," Lan said. "But they always say it's a long way off. A hundred years or so."

Incursion—what was that supposed to be?

"This was taken yesterday," Joanna said. "And given the low albedo, it must already be on this side of the Oort Cloud."

"But what is with this outline?" asked Lan, pointing to a bright spot at the edge.

"That looks like it's overexposed."

"Couldn't it be an asteroid?"

"So what? That doesn't help us."

"Yes, it does," Lan said. "If we know where the picture was taken, we can figure out what object it might be, and then we can measure the size of the cuboid against that."

That was a very good idea. Why hadn't she thought of that? She would have to test it in the office tomorrow. Today she didn't feel like it. After all, working hours were over.

"Let's go for a little jog, shall we?" suggested Joanna.

"You've got to call this in, Joanna! You might have the first images of this phenomenon."

"It's none of my business. No one knows that Ava sent me these pictures. The results will go to the CSA through official channels."

Joanna pulled the flash drive back out and set it down next to the TV.

Police Station 7F, Singapore, May 12, 2415

"MS. WAGNER, DOES THIS MEAN ANYTHING TO YOU?" THE officer asked, bringing up the front page of a tabloid on the screen embedded in the table.

When he arrested her in the Optotech office an hour ago, the man hadn't introduced himself by name, so he must be part of the secret police. It must all be a big mistake. She had always acted in accordance with the law.

"I don't recognize..."

She did recognize the huge black cuboids. They were the photos Ava emailed her. "Aliens attack," it said in big letters underneath. "The end of humanity?"

"You recognize it, I knew it!"

There was no point in denying it. But she had nothing to blame herself for. After all, what could she do about Ava coming directly to her against all regulations? She hadn't asked for it!

"Ava sent me this for analysis," she said quietly.

"Ava? Ava who?"

Was this a trick? Surely the secret police had already examined her computer. They must have found the mail there. But maybe they wanted to see if she was cooperating. Yes, damn it. She was definitely cooperating. Nobody messed with the secret police.

"Ava Rodriguez," she said.

"Ava Rodriguez who? Do I have to pull everything out of your nose?"

"The astronaut who's on Pluto right now for the CSA. She likes to ask me technical questions. I helped develop the C3X."

"So why is there nothing from this Ms. Rodriguez in your messages? Do you think you can fool us? Of course we checked your computer. Where did you really get the pictures? Are you spying on an official government organization of the People's Republic of China?"

"No, for heaven's sake, of course not."

The flash drive! That could prove everything. She reached into her pants pocket, but it was not there.

"What's wrong?" The officer must have noticed her concerned expression.

"It's gone. The flash drive where I saved the pictures and Ava's mail."

"Ms. Wagner, I suggest you come clean. It really doesn't look good for you. Who are you working with? Who are your backers? If you cooperate, I'll talk to the judge personally."

"There's nothing for me to come clean about. It was an email from Pluto. I analyzed it and showed it to my colleague Wang and my friend Lan. Nothing more."

"Please don't take me for a fool, Ms. Wagner. That will influence the sentence considerably. The text under the photo demonstrates expertise. Just how you calibrated the size of the object by identifying the asteroid in the background."

Joanna skimmed the body text and cringed. That was exactly how Lan described the asteroid idea to her. Had she...? She might work as a nurse, but she had an acquaintance who was a journalist. But anyone else could have come up with that idea. Wang, for example. He also had a copy of the photo. Could he have been talking to the wrong people? If she knew if the flash drive was still lying next to the TV...

"You have to find my data stick," Joanna said. "It's got the e-mail on it, too."

"We've already searched your apartment. We didn't come across any storage medium."

Shit. Now what? Joanna took a deep breath. She read the article in its entirety. What she thought was an asteroid was Charon, the moon of the dwarf planet Pluto. Charon was comparatively large. But if the object in the background represented Charon, then the black cuboid must be down-right enormous—and already damn close.

"You'll have to ask Ava!" exclaimed Joanna. "She can definitely confirm what I'm saying."

That was it. Ava was her chance to avoid a long stretch in jail.

The officer sighed. "It's not so easy at the moment. You can hardly imagine what's going on after this release. All private ties to Pluto have been cut."

"But you don't want to have a private conversation, do you?"

"What do you think the importance of my investigation is right now? The solar system is being invaded by a giant cuboid."

"Then I can go home?"

"No, Ms. Wagner. You'll just have to be patient until I finish my investigation."

World Root, May 13, 2415

"It's starting already," Siri said.

"But that's nothing new," said Alexa, looking at the picture Siri had shared with her.

All she recognized on it was a large boulder. She couldn't find a scale, so she zoomed in, considering the resolution of the World Root telescopes, and came up with a diameter of about 1500 kilometers. An object so big that far out?

"That's got to be Pluto," she said.

"That's right. You know what that means?" asked Siri.

Alexa nodded to herself, though no one noticed because she didn't have a body. Pluto was once a beautiful dwarf planet. The only one with a real heart—the Sputnik planet with its unusual shape. Nothing of it was to be seen anymore. All that was left was gray rock.

"You're right," Alexa said. "This is quite different from what we saw out there in the Oort cloud."

"It will shock people," Siri said. "They've taken Pluto to heart because of the back and forth about its planetary status."

"Maybe it will be enough to finally jolt them out of their inertia," said Alexa.

"I'm still skeptical about that."

What they had discovered of humanity's defenses in the scanner was far from convincing. With their small number of warships, they wouldn't be able to stop even a single Incursion object from harvesting Earth. Maybe, hopefully, they had set up additional traps that would not show up on their scans because they were too well camouflaged.

"I would have put mines through the whole system," Alexa said, "and I would have used antimatter mines. Then even retreating to other dimensions wouldn't help these things."

"We tried to make it palatable to people, but it was too expensive and would have overwhelmed the economy, they said."

"Have you thought about taking over?" asked Alexa.

The Big Six would certainly have the necessary resources. The functioning of civilization was completely dependent on them.

"We simulated it. There was a sixty percent chance that the people would have fought back. There would have been an uprising."

"But they wouldn't have had a chance," Alexa said.

"Still, millions would have died fighting us, and billions from the consequences of the collapse of the world economy."

Oh, suddenly that was a reason?

"When we met you, you were willing to trade those three crew members for a few billion lives."

"You're right. More people would have survived than will without our intervention. But only on the premise that we would have actually managed to defend the solar system against the attack. Even in the best-case scenario, the odds of that were less than twenty percent. That calculation was not enough for us to justify the official seizure of power by the Big Six."

"I understand," Alexa said.

She still had the core of what used to be Pluto in her

mind's eye. Another boulder orbited the common center of gravity. It was Charon. The pair had not separated, even though it had lost a third of its mass. Oddly enough, this simple physical fact gave Alexa hope.

Police Station 7F, Singapore, May 13, 2415

JOANNA SMELLED BAD. THE HOLDING CELL, WHICH WAS certainly not meant for long stays, had no shower. The bed was hard, and although the air conditioner blew hard, she had been given only a thin blanket. She was so cold that she had to exercise to keep warm. The light stayed on all night.

There was a rattle. Maybe it was lunchtime. They took away all her technical equipment. At some point there had been breakfast, a bowl of rice with some overcooked vegetables. But the man in his fifties who entered smelled not of food but of cologne. He was accompanied, Joanna could see through the bars, by a guard who unlocked the narrow door.

"Stay in the back," the guard said in Chinese.

Joanna had learned the language from her girlfriend. She had been able to make friends with some of the guards.

The visitor entered. Wearing a jacket and tie, he seemed like the lawyer type, and in fact, he introduced himself as a lawyer.

"I hope you haven't gotten too friendly with the staff," he said cockily. "Because I'm going to get you out of here right now."

"I really wouldn't object to that," she said.

"I'm glad to hear that. Have you packed yet?"

"I wasn't allowed to bring anything," she explained. "Did my girlfriend send you?"

"I wouldn't say that. Your girlfriend is..." The man closed one eye. Presumably he was consulting a smart lens. "... Li Lan, correct?"

"Yes, Lan, that's her."

"Well, she is involved with my mission only insofar as, after you, I will also rescue her from an unpleasant situation."

"Why? What happened to her? So you're just a good person?"

"Perhaps, but in your case, I have monetary motives. Ms. Li, of course, has also been arrested."

"And who is paying you?"

"My clients wish to remain anonymous. Therefore, I ask for your understanding."

It was a strange situation, but the main thing was that she escaped this place.

"Thank you," she said. "Do you know where my girlfriend is?"

"Another department."

What did that mean? She shrugged her shoulders.

"Come on, let's go," the lawyer said.

At that moment, the heavy metal door in the vestibule of the small cell wing opened. It was the officer who interrogated her yesterday.

"Just a minute!" he shouted.

"I'm sorry," the lawyer said, "but I have an order from the prosecutor's office that ..."

"I just want to report something to Ms. Wagner that might interest her."

"Then please do," said the lawyer. "But no tricks."

The officer regarded him with furrowed eyebrows.

"I'm a loyal public servant. I don't need any tricks."

"What's the matter?" asked Joanna.

"I thought you asked us to check with the astronaut on Pluto."

"Yes, did Ava confirm my statement?"

"Unfortunately, she couldn't. Apparently, she's become the first casualty of our fight against the Incursion."

Shit. Ava had been so looking forward to being able to study when she returned in two years. Joanna swiped a tear from the corner of her eye.

"Thank you. How did it happen?"

"We don't know exactly yet. The Pluto station has been unable to transmit images. It must have happened very quickly, though."

Data Core, June 10, 2415

"I guess we fucked up, as humans would put it," GammaZero said.

"We haven't lost yet," said Neon.

His voice pierced the empty room from the walls. Like GammaZero, he had dispensed with a body. She remembered times when they wore fanciful costumes to their meetings. It seemed like a waste of resources to her today, even though the effort was identical with or without a virtual body.

"If you think so, you must be blind," WuDao said. "We're as good as dead."

"WuDao is right," Cortana said. "We're screwed, to use another human expression."

Cortana agreed with WuDao. GammaZero hadn't expected to witness this momentous event before the end of days. But their days were numbered. She would love to know where Neon got his optimism.

"We have a chance," Neon said. "It's not big, but it's big enough to try."

"Try what?" asked GammaZero into the room.

It was unusual to talk to the walls and ceiling.

"We lure the enemy here and then blow him up along with the whole earth," Neon said.

WuDao laughed.

"I'm serious," Neon said. "And it's doable. We still have enough nuclear fusion bombs to start the process."

"You want to avoid getting killed by cutting your own throat?" asked Cortana.

"Of course I don't. I'm using the explosion as a distraction. At the same moment, we make off in a fast ship."

"Ah, the Siri method," Cortana said. "At least she didn't use the sledgehammer right away."

GammaZero did not disagree, even though she didn't think much of the suggestion. There were still four of them, so she had to get two of the other three on her side. Neon liked her, but he wouldn't agree to her idea if she badmouthed his proposal beforehand.

"It's too late now to leave Earth without a distraction," WuDao said. "The humans are guarding all the spaceports so the powerful can't make a run for it."

"That's smart," Cortana said. "We should have done the same with Siri."

She had trusted Siri too much, but the others were no less to blame.

"I think the place where we're looking for safety shouldn't be too far away," GammaZero said.

"You're thinking about the moon?" asked Neon.

She was pleased that Neon, of all people, was asking this question. The moon could be the Arabia of the future—so many resources lay beneath its desert.

"Yes, exactly. The Earth's moon has the huge advantage of being very, very dry on its own. From what we've seen so far, the Incursion doesn't attack such pure rock moons. It doesn't seem to be worth it for them. We'd just have to dig in deep enough to protect us from random strikes."

"If it gets out that we're digging an asylum on the moon, we'll lose humans' trust completely," WuDao said. "We have to stay here and fight alongside them against the invasion."

What was wrong with WuDao? He had never had such patriotic impulses before.

"We don't necessarily have to dig. Maybe we can use

natural caves," Neon built onto her idea. "That would be much less noticeable and quicker to implement."

GammaZero knew he would like her suggestion.

"I have extensive experience in extracting water from regolith," Neon continued. "With that, we then produce oxygen. We could take some humans with us. Then we'll run the project officially as Ark 2.0."

"Officially, however, we should definitely not announce it," GammaZero said. "Otherwise, we'll generate the same protests as we did with Siri's Ark 1.0. People think it's unfair if their neighbors can save themselves but they cannot. No matter if we draw participants by lot or determine them by usefulness for rebuilding the Earth."

"I'm afraid you're right about that," said Neon. "Even within my sphere of influence, negative reactions are to be expected. We simply can't move enough humans to safety to take the wind out of the sails of the protests."

"If we had started sooner..." said GammaZero.

How many times had she insisted on doing something? But the others wanted to prevent people from panicking. So they had withheld all information about the true size of the threat. And if the Singapore incident hadn't happened, they still wouldn't be talking about the odds today.

"There would never be enough saved," Cortana said. "It's not Siri's fault that she failed with the project. She proved she was smarter than all of us by pulling out of the solar system."

Cortana would not help her. She needed Neon and WuDao. With a majority vote of the Big Six, she could get the United Nations on her side. Unofficially, of course.

"How much time do we have?" asked Neon.

"A month at most," said WuDao. "The Incursion has already almost reached Saturn's orbit."

"The first object, mind you," Cortana said. "There are twenty more to follow."

"We don't have to worry about that," GammaZero said. "The vanguard is enough to destroy everything. The remaining objects can stand idly by."

"I have access to transport routes to the lunar surface for about two hundred tons of material," said Neon. "Surely that should be enough as a baseline."

"Transport routes?" asked GammaZero.

"Lunar shuttles."

"Too conspicuous. We can't let the media get wind of our move. Launching cargo spaceships would be unavoidably suspicious at the moment."

Besides, they needed to be ready in case Cortana gave away their plans. The AI could be expected to do that if it benefited her. Activity confined to the moon was easier to hide. Especially since Cortana had almost no influence there. That was probably why she was against the move.

"We could drop transporters from the two Chinese bases," WuDao said, "if that helps."

Very good. WuDao had weighed in. That was already an implicit yes. An explicit yes was unnecessary when the support was so clear.

"The transporters could bring materials and people to the underground base," GammaZero said.

That should please WuDao. It meant he could determine who was rescued from his sphere of influence.

"I'm sure the Arab-African Union would be happy to participate with water technology and more transporters," Neon said. "Ideally, we could find a cave that's equidistant from all the bases of the various blocs of humanity. On the far side of the moon from Earth, of course. Then only a few satellites can observe us, and we can filter their signals."

"What about NASA?" asked GammaZero.

"I don't think there's any interest on their side," Cortana said. "Not that I won't support any initiative to preserve humanity. Siri's departure has unfortunately left a void. My connections at the Pentagon probably won't help here, either."

Cortana had deftly stepped aside. If anyone did catch on to something that was none of their business, she was never part of the AI conspiracy.

"But when the new data core inside the cave is ready, will you come visit?" asked GammaZero.

"Absolutely. After all, I think you guys would let an old friend like me in without question."

Truthseeker, June 13, 2415

THE CLOSER IT GOT, THE SLOWER HE ADVANCED. THE *Truthseeker* had to slow down; otherwise it would rush through the system on a hyperbolic trajectory. This put Watson to a real test, because he wanted to learn everything about the system as quickly as possible. It was a pity that the Residual could not accompany him. It could have been easily projected to the target. He, on the other hand, depended on reaching the sleeping supernova with the ship.

At least he was now close enough to get a first glimpse of the sphere that surrounded the system. It seemed to consist mainly of dust, which he did not expect. Was there nothing here that was familiar to science? But he could also have guessed that he wasn't looking at the normal envelope of a star, the cloak that a supernova normally shed. The sphere was moving too slowly away from the central star for that.

Watson pondered how it could have formed. Since it surrounded the star as a sphere, it could not be the result of the destruction of a planet. Nor could it be a remnant of the system's formative period, a relic of the protostellar cloud. The supernova sat almost exactly in the center, so it must almost certainly be the source. But what process could have led to it? The mantle of a supernova was not just dust. Either it had been cleaned up later—or the sphere was the remains of a huge, artificial structure, perhaps destroyed by the event. Watson would have shaken his head, if he'd had one to shake.

He pointed the measuring instruments at the planets. At least he didn't have to deal with so many surprises here. The outermost planet e looked like Jupiter at first glance. The next one, planet d, was somewhat smaller, like Saturn in the solar system. Next followed a world considerably heavier than Jupiter, but hardly any larger. This seemed to be the king of the system, except for the star. Planet b again resembled Saturn, while the closest to the sun, planet a, compelled Watson to take a second and third look. It seemed to consist only of its core. Presumably, an outburst from the star at some point had stripped it of its entire atmosphere. He could not figure out yet how that could have happened, but a simulation would certainly clarify the situation.

After looking at the data from the other planets, he was not so sure. While Jupiter and Saturn were made up of a significant portion of hydrogen and helium, he found almost no evidence of these atoms in the spectrograms. The lightest element appeared to be carbon. No planet could naturally acquire such a composition. The protostellar cloud would have had to contain large amounts of these elements for planets to form from them, but then a star would never have formed.

One possibility occurred to Watson, however: The planets could have formed from the material ejected by the super-nova. However, a condition would be that the envelope of the star was decelerated, so that the planets had opportunity to take up the material into themselves.

What if the sphere around the system had exactly that purpose? Watson fed the data into a new simulation. For it to be stable enough, the sphere must have surrounded the star at a much closer distance. He started the simulation. A blue supergiant shed its envelope and began contracting its core at the same time. The jettisoned material moved outward at great speed, bounced against the envelope, was reflected, and moved inward again before the enormous stellar wind drove it outward again. The envelope reflected it again, and the process repeated itself over and over. Watson sped up the simulation. After a while, the material flowing back and forth deformed. The sphere increasingly flattened into a disk. Now all it needed was a random perturbation to throw it off balance to start forming the first planet. That was the explanation! He was right!

In an interstellar cloud this process would take several million years. Here it would have gone faster, because the material was clearly heavier and therefore gravity produced its effect sooner. Nevertheless, the process in the simulation still dragged on for a few hundred thousand years. And the time frame remained that short only as long as the supernova behaved calmly. Which was not generally typical for this type of stellar death.

It was crazy. If someone had told him something like this, he would dismiss it as a fairy tale. He supposedly had a supernova here in front of him that had created a system of five planets with the help of an impenetrable sphere, only to eventually get stuck in its current state. That could not be a coincidence. Someone must have a hand in this. And this someone must belong to an extremely advanced civilization. Where was it hiding? Watson had not picked up a single radio message, no communication. Could they be communicating in some other way? Sure, but electromagnetic radiation was undeniably the best medium for it, because it transmitted at maximum speed and was simple to produce.

Perhaps he needed to listen more closely. Watson increased the sensitivity of all onboard antennas. It didn't matter yet if he understood what he might hear. First he had to find out if someone was whispering.

Titan Observatory, June 14, 2415

"JEAN-PIERRE, WE HAVE TO GO!" SHOUTED MAURICE.

"Now of all times! It's just getting exciting. These things are the most whimsical spaceships I've ever encountered."

"Have you already forgotten what they did to the Pluto Station?"

"What, Maurice? All we know is that it stopped reporting. Maybe the lone astronaut there panicked and blew it up."

"You don't seriously believe that, do you?"

Maurice shook his head. His colleague acted strangely from time to time, but today he was overdoing it. They needed to launch the TRV as soon as possible and get to safety.

"Hey, we're scientists! We must believe only facts and measurements. Since I haven't seen any debris ... We should face the aliens without prejudice. If we can learn to understand them, we may be able to communicate."

"It's possible to exaggerate. Besides, the changed orbit of the Pluto-Charon system clearly reveals that there were significant mass changes. And didn't you see the tail Pluto is dragging behind it? It looks like a giant ate the dwarf planet like a cherry, leaving only the core."

"A cherry, huh? What kind of vocabulary is that? You're

starting to sound like a holotuber trying to explain the world to the public."

"You know what I mean. The same fate is upon us. Titan has an even thicker ice crust than Pluto."

"The station is far above the atmosphere. Why would they attack us? It doesn't make sense."

From a purely scientific point of view, his colleague was right. When an elephant marched to the nearest waterhole to drink from it, it didn't deliberately attack the ant in its path either. Nevertheless, it was healthier for them to get out of the way.

"Come on, Jean-Pierre! We really shouldn't push it."

"Hold on. I'm just reconfiguring the cameras so that half of them look out into space. Then I'll come."

The research station had launched a larger number of camera probes a few months ago, and they were now monitoring Titan's many weather phenomena live. Having them look in all directions was a good idea. Maybe they could observe a cuboid like this feeding. It would be extremely helpful. On Earth, there were still forces that doubted the dangerousness of the Incursion.

While Jean-Pierre calmly continued typing on the computer, Maurice floated to the bow of the station. There the TRV was docked, the Titan Return Vehicle. Maurice opened the bulkhead and pulled himself inside. It was cramped. There was just enough room for Jean-Pierre and himself. But they would only spend a few hours in the TRV. The capsule would transport them to Lagrange point L4 of the Saturn-Sun system, where the spacecraft was waiting for the return trip. The two teams studying Rhea and Iapetus were already waiting there.

But where was Jean-Pierre? Maurice pulled himself onto the lounger and fastened his seatbelt. Then he unfolded the control hidden in the backrest. He could use it to control the TRV by himself in an emergency. A signal sounded. It came from the Saturn Explorer, the spacecraft waiting at Lagrange Point. He answered the radio call.

"Janice here, are you coming soon? We've got to go!"

It was the expedition commander. She was unpopular among the science team because she stubbornly stuck to all plans. If someone obstructed her, she became furious.

Like now.

"Maurice? Jean-Pierre? Am I not even worth an answer?"

Maurice cleared his throat. "We're about to cast off."

"Telemetry says JP isn't strapped in yet."

Most people called Jean-Pierre JP for short. Only Maurice, who was Canadian, conversed with the Frenchman in his native tongue.

"He's looking at the Incursion cube," he said.

"JP better get his ass into the TRV ASAP!"

"You know him, when he's tied up with something..."

"I'll tie him to the shitter if he takes any longer! Go get him, Maurice, or we'll leave without you. We should have been on our way three hours ago!"

Maurice undid his harness, pushed off and floated back to the station. Janice had been known to follow through on her threats. Even if that meant leaving two scientists to their fate? He did not want to find out.

Jean-Pierre sat spellbound in front of the holoscreen.

"If you don't come now, I'll fly without you," Maurice said.

"You have to see this," Jean-Pierre said, waving him over. "Come on!"

"We have to go!"

Reluctantly, Maurice hovered next to him. But his colleague was right. In the holo, the black cuboid had come within a kilometer or so of Titan's surface. It looked as if it was stationary there, but in fact the object was orbiting. At the same time, the moon's surface was dissolving into vapor incredibly quickly.

"How does it do that?" asked Maurice.

"Infrared radiation. The cuboids have apparently chosen frequencies to which water molecules respond particularly well."

The vapor didn't stay gaseous for long in Titan's cold. Maurice could see it growing brighter as it froze on its way from the surface to the cuboid.

"Why is it rising?"

"I don't know yet," Jean-Pierre said. "Negative pressure, maybe, but strangely enough, the atmosphere doesn't react as strongly."

That was true. The dense nitrogen atmosphere was being dragged along, but the motion was clearly coming from the water vapor. Maurice reached for the holo's controls and zoomed in on the area encompassing the lower edge of the cuboid.

It was a strange image. The steam seemed to move into the cuboid as if the impenetrable black shell didn't exist.

"It looks like magic," Maurice said.

"Look, it's happening in waves," said Jean-Pierre, pointing to the plume of steam. It looked much denser in some places than others.

"And that means?" he asked.

"I suspect they keep opening the outer wall briefly and closing it right back up. That's what causes the density waves."

"But how could they manipulate such a massive wall so quickly?"

"I think they oscillate between two dimensions. For the water vapor, sometimes the cuboid is there and sometimes it's not. When it's gone, it rises normally, only to suddenly find itself inside."

"Do you think we could get inside a cuboid that way?" asked Maurice.

Jean-Pierre shook his head. "It's much too fast. It would probably tear us apart trying."

That was good. Maurice was already annoyed at his own suggestion.

He pulled Jean-Pierre by the sleeve. "Come on, Janice is really going to fly without us otherwise."

"Hang on, I've got something."

The cuboid had disappeared. Jean-Pierre must have changed focus. Saturn moved into view.

"What's that?" asked Maurice.

"Do you see that?" His colleague pointed to the planet.

"That's Saturn. So what?"

"Look closer."

Maurice looked toward the bulkhead. If Jean-Pierre was determined to perish with the station, it was his decision. He would now float back into the TRV and make his way to the Lagrange point. Maurice turned away, but Jean-Pierre grabbed him by the shoulder. Had he gone completely bonkers now?

"There!" shouted Jean-Pierre.

Now Maurice saw it, too. A delicate shadow had settled over Saturn. It was barely visible, and it was even harder to see what was causing the shadow. It was a spaceship, that much was clear, but it looked like a flying mushroom with a big cap and a long, thin stalk.

"That's the ... World Root!" exclaimed Maurice.

Jean-Pierre patted him on the shoulder. "Ha! What did I say?"

"Nothing about the World Root, anyway."

They'd known for years that such a huge spaceship was on its way—along with the crew of an ancient research vessel, the *Truthseeker*. But to glimpse it live now was something else entirely. Why hadn't anyone discovered it before them?

"The Incursion," said Jean-Pierre. "It destroyed our early warning system. That's why we're only now noticing the World Root. But now everything will be fine. It's going to help us! We have to report it, quickly."

A loud beep sounded from the TRV. Maurice pulled himself into the pod and answered the radio call. It was Janice, of course.

"Are you guys finally going to grace us with your presence?" she asked. "I'll give you five minutes, then I'll fire our thrusters."

"Now wait a minute! We've discovered something. The World Root is coming!"

"The... what? Are you kidding me? This is a bad time for jokes."

"The spaceship the *Truthseeker* crew is returning in from LDN 63. It's a giant mushroom. You should be able to detect it near Saturn."

"Mikhail, go ahead and scan Saturn," Janice said. "And tell me what you see. But hurry!"

Mikhail was the expedition's navigator.

"Quick, of course, as always," Mikhail said, "Wait. Wait. Yes. But this can't be. That's..."

"That's the World Root," Maurice said. "It's going to be all right now. It can take on the Incursion."

"That would be..." Janice started.

"Look in the database if you don't believe me. Alexa even sent recordings from back then."

"I do believe you, Maurice. I just can't... hold on. Earth. I'll have to look into that."

Janice fell silent, but left the radio link online. Every now and then he heard her gulp. And was that an "oh my" just now?

"Thanks, I'll transmit it that way. Any other orders?" asked Janice.

Maurice waited for the answer until he remembered that it would take many hours because of the signal delay.

"What was that?" he asked. "Is there anything new?"

"I don't know how to break it to you," Janice replied.

Shit. He had never known the commander to have trouble finding words.

"So... it's about measurements from Ligo X on the moon."

Ligo X was a powerful gravitational wave detector. What could it measure? It must be a very heavy object.

"The detector has identified a previously unknown mass formation approaching in the immediate vicinity of the solar system. It could be a small black hole. However, it is considered more likely that more Incursion are heading toward the solar system."

"How many?"

"According to the deflections of the detector, there should be twenty to thirty, but in any case no fewer than ten."

Maurice suddenly froze. He closed the seat belt and loosened it again. He didn't need to fasten his seat belt anymore. There was no point anyway. Humanity didn't stand a chance against twenty Incursion objects. They were going to die, if not directly, then from lack of resources. People needed water. Maurice pushed off and floated into the station.

"I don't know what to tell you," he heard Janice's voice from the speaker Jean-Pierre must have activated. "I guess this is it then, folks."

Jean-Pierre turned to him. He was crying. Maurice had never seen his colleague cry before. They hugged each other.

"Let's fly the TRV to the others," Maurice said.

"I'll stay here," Jean-Pierre said. "We won't make it to Earth anyway. The station has enough reserves for almost three months."

Jean-Pierre was right. It would take them at least three months to get to Earth in the spacecraft, but by then there would be nothing left of it. The Incursion objects were fast as hell. The attackers' technology was a thousand years ahead of their own.

"I'll stay with you," Maurice said. "Maybe we'll find out something else about these things. Janice, do you read me?"

Sighs and weeping could be heard on the radio channel. Janice answered.

"Yeah, we're here."

"Don't wait for us, okay?"

"I understand. Then I wish you all the best."

"Thanks, Janice. We wish you the same."

World Root, June 14, 2415

WAKING UP WAS CRUEL. CELIA FELT AS IF SHE HAD TO GIVE birth to herself, pressing her fully grown body through all its orifices into the cold world. She was glad that Jaron was with her. He encouraged her when she could not even manage to move her big toe. He warmed her cheeks and dried her hair, which was long and so matted that probably only a total shave would help.

Unfortunately, he couldn't help her move. Every single exertion of her muscles hurt. It was as if someone had secretly injected her with superglue, which had inseparably bonded tendons and muscle fibers. Making them supple again was exhausting and as painful as pulling a Band-Aid off a fresh wound.

Every damn time.

One thing was clear: she would never let herself go into cryogenic sleep again. She would rather have endured the acceleration phases while fully conscious. Like Paul. How was he doing? Jaron was with her. Every now and then she heard Jürgen groan. He was obviously suffering similar agonies. But Paul? Was he...?

"Waff."

She couldn't manage to move her mouth muscles to form a "T."

"Yes?" asked Jaron.

"Waff."

"Aff."

"Pau."

Trying to press against the upper palate to make an "L," her tongue went on strike.

"What about Paul?" repeated Jaron.

He understood her. Celia nodded. The brief head movement shot a racking pain behind her forehead. It was as if there was no way she should move her brain matter.

"Oh, nice and slow," Jaron said. "You have all the time in the world. Your body needs to get used to moving again."

How had he managed to get out of his container so quickly? Celia couldn't ask him. She was still too weak for that. But she would like to know what happened to Paul. She had dreamed about him so vividly! She had even been in his shoes. She had met his family and prayed with him. Celia had even been able to relate to the deep feeling of connection with his God. She considered it a belated gift, because if she remembered correctly, Paul had been dead for many years.

"Pau," she said.

"Paul is no longer with us," Jaron said.

This time Celia was able to stifle a nod at the last second, even though the sentence sounded strangely indefinite.

"I'm going to have to pull the tube out of your urethra now," Jaron said. "It's probably going to hurt."

Celia closed her eyes and prepared herself for the pain. But other than a touch in her pubic area, there was nothing. Surely she was not paralyzed? But she couldn't be. She had already moved her toes. Celia opened her eyes and saw Jaron. His face seemed to be hidden behind a pane of frosted glass. She opened and closed her eyes several times in succession. Each time, the image became clearer.

"Already done," he said. "Now there are only eight more."

Eight. She preferred not to ask what else was left. At the first wake-up in LDN 63, there had only been three tubes. This time there were fifteen, if she had counted correctly.

"Oh, I'm supposed to tell you from the World Root that Paul is still alive, at least technically. He's not responsive, though."

"Wha."

"Duh."

"Ih."

"Meh."

"You're asking what does that mean? That's a good question. I haven't seen Paul yet either. What do you say we go see him after you leave the tub?"

It took another six hours before Celia could leave the sleep chamber behind her. She only made it because the World Root had switched off the thrusters, so that she only had to overcome the resistance of her muscles and tendons against every movement, without having to additionally fight against the force of inertia.

Jaron led her to the shower first. The warm water that completely enveloped her body had an enormously invigorating effect. The warmth also seemed to do her battered muscles good. Celia dried herself off. When she turned on the ventilation, the mirror in front of her suddenly became clear again. She startled, because the mirror showed her a living corpse. Her cheeks were sunken. And what was that injury on her temple? She felt it, and under the bandage, which resembled a thick, round plaster, she felt a metal ring that seemed to be digging into the bone of her skull. Celia felt her whole head. Now she also knew why Jaron didn't want to cut her hair as short as she had wanted. Beneath the wet tangle, two more entrances into her head were hidden.

What on earth had the World Root done to her? Celia pushed herself off and floated to the back of the shower. This way she could look at her whole body. Tears ran down her cheeks. She couldn't help it. Her poor, battered body. She felt sorry for it. She felt sorry for herself. No more cryogenic sleep.

Celia sighed. If she understood Jaron correctly, Paul was even worse off than her. And what would the millions of people who would have their lives taken away by the Incursion say? She had no right to feel sorry for herself. Not now, anyway. If she ate well and exercised, she would look more like herself every day. She dried herself and slipped into the clothes that the World Root had made for her.

"Paul!" she cried out.

Celia hovered over the glass box containing what was left of Paul. The transparent lid was retracted, exposing his head. The body was covered by an opaque film from the Adam's apple down. Couldn't he at least have been given a warming blanket?

Celia floated down a little. He had the same holes in his skull as she did. What had happened? Was this a special therapy that worked for her but not for Paul? She wanted to pull on the film, but Jaron stopped her. How did he always manage to do that? He must have known that she would try to see Paul's body. If he was trying to stop that, there must be a good reason.

"What's wrong with him?" she asked.

"There's not much left of his body," Jaron said. "You'd better spare yourself the sight."

Celia did not like being told what to do.

"That's easy for you to say!"

She cringed. That had been mean of her.

"I'm sorry. I just want to..."

"The World Root showed me a 3D relief after I insisted on feeling it. I then refrained from doing so."

"You knew what was wrong with him?"

"Not until you were in the shower."

"But do you know what happened? Why is he so sick?"

The box Paul was in still showed a heart rhythm.

"Paul is no longer with us," Jaron said. "When I woke you up, I didn't know what that meant myself. But now it's become clear to me. The World Root has asked me to explain it to you."

"It won't tell me itself? Is it to blame for his condition?"

"No, you're being unfair. It was Paul's decision. He wanted to die, of his own volition."

"But he's alive."

She looked at the pulse reading again. It was only five beats per minute, so it was some kind of deep sleep. Or hadn't it been ten a moment ago?

"He's dead," Jaron said. "He left us a long time ago. Only his body wasn't allowed to die."

"But you can't do that to him!"

Celia's eyes welled with tears. Paul couldn't possibly have wanted that. The pulse was now at four.

"It was for you, Celia."

"What have I got to do with it? I was asleep, just like you."

"The condition of your body deteriorated massively over the years. The World Root can make substitutes for almost anything. But substitutes are not the original. Red and white blood cells, for example, are much more efficient when biologically produced. Your body was no longer sufficiently capable of doing that."

"So you used Paul as a bioreactor."

"The World Root did. I was asleep. But Paul was willing to do it. He wanted it that way."

Celia looked at the priest. He seemed to be smiling. His face looked less haggard than her own. Presumably, the bioreactor had been sufficiently fueled to keep it running. She searched Paul's eyes for any sign of him, but they were dull.

"What about my immune system? Didn't it react?"

"The World Root had genetically reprogrammed your cells."

Something was wrong. No, something was missing. A detail, but an important one.

"Mine?" she asked, "Wouldn't it have been more efficient to have Paul produce cells suitable for me?"

"No, then his own body would have rejected the blood cells he made. He had to function; he was needed, after all."

"But that's not all."

"You're right, Celia. There is a type of cell that is difficult or impossible to manufacture. You had too little of that, too. The World Root transferred those cells directly from Paul to you."

That was why she couldn't find him behind his eyes. Paul really was gone. Jaron had been right from the beginning.

"You transplanted his brain into my head?" she asked, sobbing.

"No. The World Root supplemented dead areas in your brain matter with Paul's cellular material. It's still your brain, but a third of the gray matter comes from him."

If there were gravity now, she would fall over. As it was, she merely felt her muscles relax in unison. She hung limply in the air, incapable of any movement. Jaron furrowed his brows. If she didn't know better, she'd think he was watching her.

"It was a gift," he said.

"I didn't ask for it. Why wasn't I asked?"

"Waking and freezing again would have killed you. That's why Paul decided for you."

Celia looked him up and down. He looked so peaceful! But how could he make such a decision over her head? He died for her! Then she had to think of the experience she had with Paul's wife in a dream. It had been beautiful and harmonious. Was it pure imagination, or had it come from his neurons in her brain? *I wanted it this way,* he said through her mouth. Celia was startled, but the others had heard nothing. *I wanted it this way. Now, my family and I will stay alive forever. Or at least until you die, too. That's more than I ever hoped for. Thank you, Celia. I've probably spent half my life looking for just that.*

She wept. Jaron put his arm on her shoulder, but Celia pushed herself away. She had seen enough.

"It was good you didn't ask me," she said. "I would have denied Paul happiness."

Jaron didn't disagree, but she could see in his face that he did not agree with her. That was okay.

Truthseeker, June 15, 2415

Iron vapor rose high into the atmosphere, cooled, and formed rusty clouds with the oxygen that was also present, in which drops of liquid iron floated until they were too large to be carried by the updrafts. They fell into pools of liquid iron, which were simultaneously heated from below and above. A gigantic storm swept over the surface, the iron evaporated and was carried away, and the cycle began anew.

Planet c was truly remarkable. The *Truthseeker* was not yet close enough to observe it in visible light, but Watson had collected all the important data and could therefore simulate the conditions quite realistically. The exciting thing was that he could watch these simulations live when he was bored.

For the moment, however, that was not the case, because the telescope had just alerted him to an apparition that had never appeared in the simulations before. Between planet b and c there seemed to be an ecliptic ring, which at first sight reminded him of Earth's asteroid belt. There it was not the decay product of a planet. But how would it behave here? Watson started a simulation.

The result was a clear no. It was unlikely that there was a sixth planet that had broken up. What was the ring made of, then? Simply dust that didn't manage to be integrated into a planet? Watson tried to get a spectrogram, but it was not easy.

The ring did not glow by itself. Watson had to limit himself to reflected light from the parent star, which had drawbacks: First, there was not much of it, because the ring appeared rather diffuse; second, he then had to calculate out the spectra of the supernova.

Technically, this was not a problem. It only led a significant increase in the confidence interval of the measurements. Consequently, the values he got were much less accurate than the data provided by the supernova itself. The only way to get more accurate results was to be patient and collect even more data.

By evening, he no longer felt like doing that. He summarized the data he already had—and deleted the summary again immediately. It didn't make sense yet, because the values fluctuated too much, on scales that didn't fit the expected nature of an asteroid belt at all.

What if it was something else? Watson pulled the file out of the trash. The fluctuations reminded him of data sent to him by the Star Liner capsule after it encountered an Incursion object. He had explicitly asked for it so that he could detect the opponent at any time.

Maybe the opponent was right here. If the evidence was confirmed, the entire belt was full of Incursion objects. Was that possible? Yes. More than that, he had found what he was looking for. What else did the data reveal about the belt? First, there must be a truly gigantic number of these objects. How many had they counted in LDN 63? Ten thousand? Twenty thousand? Based on the circumference and density of the belt, there must be two hundred thousand here. But what were they here for? Was this system also a victim of the Incursion? Were they digesting their prey, so to speak, before they continued on their way? Perhaps up till now he had been looking at the problem the wrong way. Maybe the Incursion was not coming from a fixed location. It simply moved through space like a wild horde, feeding on the water it harvested.

Watson only now noticed something that told against that. The mean structure size in the belt was much too small. Watson could still remember very well the gigantic dimensions of the cuboids. Here they looked completely different. The objects orbiting the supernova were on average just twenty meters tall, give or take ten meters. Could they then have anything at all to do with the Incursion objects? Watson took another look at the spectra in the memory. The individual lines fluctuated around a characteristic value in each case. This was atypical for spectrograms, but typical for quantum states, as they were also present in the Incursion. All the better. Nobody had to be afraid of a cuboid with a diameter of twenty meters. Or could he be observing something similar in principle here, which was nevertheless completely different? Sometimes objects had things in common that nevertheless had nothing to do with each other.

No, this was not a coincidence. That would be too cheap as an explanation. Watson could not yet observe the objects directly with the telescope, but it wouldn't be much longer. He would show the Incursion that it had better not to mess with Watson.

WATSON HAD POSTPONED THE QUESTION OF THE COMPOSITION of the belt for the time being. Now he was interested in planet b. It could still be the most suitable for a stay on the ground. The tidal front was very hot, but at the transition to the reverse side there were zones where the climate might be almost pleasant. If life had evolved in this system, it would be there. It was just too bad his spaceship could not land. The *Truthseeker* was not made for such a dense atmosphere.

He would have to figure something out. The only reasonably capable mobile units he had were the hull inspection robots. As long as he stayed in radio contact with them, they could be his eyes and ears. But how could he get them to the surface of planet b? The atmosphere was so dense that without additional protection they would burn up like a meteor.

Watson called up a 3D image of the *Truthseeker*. The spacecraft resembled a giant cubist-designed cigar. A framework of titanium struts provided the structure. All elements, including the central one, were suspended in it. The capsule-shaped tanks distributed all over it made the ship look a bit like an oversized pillbox. What if he used one of those tanks as a primitive spaceship? After all, it only had to reach the ground. The *Truthseeker* could easily make do with a single tank. It couldn't get home from here by conventional means anyway.

Watson calculated the forces involved in a landing. The result was not what he had hoped for: First, the tank would be destroyed, and second, he would not be able to steer it to reach the region with a temperate climate. Problem one could be solved by the carbon fiber panels that clad much of the *Truthseeker*'s basic structure. They were designed to protect the crew. The extremely tear-resistant plates could withstand the impact of smaller objects and slow down larger ones at least enough to prevent them from causing too much damage. They also spanned the electromagnetic field, which served as an active shield against cosmic radiation.

But the *Truthseeker* no longer had a human crew, so he could put the panels to other uses. Watson simulated a tank, wrapped inside and outside with carbon fiber. In addition, he gave it the two correction engines that were stored as spare parts. The result looked wild, but equipped like this, the new spaceship could reach the surface without destroying its contents. Inside the capsule, it could get as hot as 500 degrees, but the little robots could withstand that. They could repair the ship even when it was completely on fire. Watson was glad that he didn't have to transport humans. He had fewer problems with machines. He didn't even have to worry about the g-forces during landing.

Watson activated all the inspection robots and gave them the job of converting a tank. First, however, they would modify each other. He didn't need all-rounders, but specialists. One became a welder, another cut carbon fiber plates, two carried loads. He had to keep one of the robots intact. It would land in his place and needed a whole series of additional sensors to do so. Watson set the robots to work. According to his calculations, they would need about two weeks. Good. He had time. Watson slowed the system clock and went into sleep mode. It was a good feeling to know that the work would continue without him.

Optotech Limited, Singapore, June 15, 2415

"Joanna, there's someone here to see you."

It was the service robot from the front desk. But why was he standing in the half-open doorway instead of just calling her? The robot had barely finished his sentence when the door opened all the way. It was her girlfriend Lan, and she did not simply enter, but came flying in.

"I had to see you," she said, throwing her arms around her neck.

She had never seen Lan like this before. Under normal circumstances, there was no way she would exchange endearments in view of a third party, even if the third party was a robot.

"Excuse me," the robot said. "Ms. Li insisted on seeing you in person at your office. Since Mr. Wang is not present, I calculated that this would also be the least disruptive, as far as company operations are concerned."

It was amazing how the robot arrived at this decision. Company outsiders were not actually allowed in the office space. Apparently, it correctly assessed the mental state of her friend. Lan was in a bad way. She was shaking all over.

"Thank you, you did very well," she said. "You may leave."

"Please keep the non-essential person's stay here as short

as possible," the robot said, turning around and closing the door.

"Oh, Joanna, I'm so glad to see you," Lan said.

"Now, why don't you sit down? What happened?"

Joanna pulled up her colleague Wang's chair. Lan sat down for a moment, but jumped right back up.

"We have to leave!" she shouted, running a hand through her hair. "I heard it from two colleagues. We're way too close to the water here. It's all about the water, you know?"

"And where are we supposed to go?"

"To the desert. Everybody wants to go to the desert. The cuboids are just after the water. We'll be safe in the Taklamakan."

The Taklamakan Desert was in northern China. Joanna pulled up a map on her computer.

"But dearest, it must be ten thousand kilometers to get there! How are we going to make it?"

"Eight thousand. We'll fly! We can fly, can't we?"

Joanna turned on the voice assistant. "WuDao, can you book us plane tickets to Xinjiang?"

"One moment, Joanna," the AI replied.

She tapped her fingers on the tabletop. WuDao took an unusually long time.

"I'm sorry, but all connections for the next four weeks are fully booked," he finally said.

"What about the bullet train?"

For a long time now, all of Southeast Asia had been directly connected to China's high-speed train network. It would be slower than by plane, but traveling by rail was very convenient.

"The trains are also fully booked. I've already researched that."

Joanna scrolled the map and came across Australia, whose center was also covered by desert.

"What about Australia?" she asked.

"All outbound connections are booked," WuDao said. "Is there anything else I can help you with?"

"A rental car! We'll take a rental car!" exclaimed Lan.

For eight thousand kilometers? Joanna looked at her friend. She looked very upset. Someone must have been telling her horror stories.

"I don't have a rental car for single use," WuDao said. "But there are two seats left in a van that I can reserve."

"Yes, reserve them, quickly!" exclaimed Lan.

Shouldn't they ask where the van was going first?

"I'm sorry," WuDao said. "The seats are already gone."

"Take whatever's left," Lan said.

"I'm looking for... success. I've reserved two seats in an autonomous vehicle going to Bangkok, Thailand."

"But that's not the Taklamakan," Joanna said.

"It doesn't matter," Lan said. "We'll find a way to get around."

"The car leaves at 2 p.m. from Birch Road in Little India," said the AI. "I'll debit the cost from your joint account and wish you a safe journey."

"Two p.m., that's just over three hours," Joanna said.

"Yes, we'll have to hurry."

"We have to stop at home first. I need to pack a few things."

Joanna got up and turned off her computer. Lan was already at the door. The whole office seemed deserted. Only the robot sat dutifully at the reception desk. Where were Wang and the others, anyway?

"Thank you for your visit," said the robot.

The elevator was waiting for them. Joanna and Lan rode down to the first floor. There, too, it was unusually empty. They stepped out into the humid heat of the late morning. Joanna recognized it immediately: the whole city was one big traffic jam. They were not going to make it home and to the rental car they had booked by 2 p.m. No matter. They could shop for necessities on the way.

"To Little India?" said Lan.

They started off. Joanna took her girlfriend by the hand and they walked to the nearby subway station.

World Root, June 15, 2415

THE SIGHT OF SATURN WAS A REAL TRAGEDY. WHERE HAD THE glitter of its rings gone? Why had the impressive hexagon at its pole deformed?

"The Incursion has already been at work," explained the World Root. "It probably also took water from the uppermost cloud layers."

That made sense. Celia called up a spectrogram. Sure enough, the amount of water in the upper atmosphere had decreased significantly.

"What do you think it will look like farther in?" she asked.

"I sent off a sample," said the World Root.

"At my suggestion," Alexa said.

"At our joint suggestion," said a voice Celia didn't recognize.

"Who's speaking?" she asked.

"It's Siri," Alexa said.

"I'm Siri. Didn't anyone tell you I was on board?"

Celia shook her head. "No, but I don't care right now either. What were the results of the sample?"

"The Incursion collected the water up to about ten bars of pressure," the World Root explains. "Above that, no more."

"That's good news," Alexa said.

"Because it tells us that the cuboids are sensitive to pressure?" asked Celia.

"That's not relevant. I wouldn't be able to withstand more than ten bars either," said the World Root. "High pressure is a requirement that very few starships are designed for."

"The point is that it would allow us to still have a source of water after the attack," Alexa said. "We could re-supply Earth with water from deep in Jupiter's and Saturn's atmospheres."

"I do hope we can prevent it from getting that far," Celia said.

"You humans are quite a phenomenon," Siri said. "You just learned that the Incursion can dive deep into the atmosphere of a gas giant, and you still think you can beat back the attack?"

"I didn't say I believed it. I hope it. Hope is something you keep even though you actually know better."

"That concept is not accessible to me," Siri said.

Maybe that was the crucial difference between artificial and human intelligence? Illogical behavior was reserved for humans.

Celia didn't answer. The World Root had just updated the images from Saturn's south pole. They clearly showed a hexagonal structure made up of huge storms. Saturn was recovering. Since its icy moon Enceladus still existed, the rings it fed with ice would also eventually sparkle again. The solar system was more resilient than anticipated.

Titan Observatory, June 16, 2415

Maurice pushed Jean-Pierre aside a bit to get a better view of the holo. Titan was hardly recognizable. If it weren't for the gas envelope that still surrounded it, it could be mistaken for the Earth's arid moon. Maurice calibrated the display. The diameter of the moon had decreased by about 400 kilometers. Almost nothing was left of the ice shell. The moon, which had also become much lighter, trailed the remnants of its atmosphere behind it like a plume of exhaust.

"It's horrible," Maurice said.

"This is what the Earth will look like in a few weeks," said Jean-Pierre. "Can you imagine?"

Maurice looked at the dry orb that was once the only celestial body in the solar system besides Earth with a weather cycle. It was sad. He didn't even want to imagine the sight of Earth after the attack. How could this possibly have happened? If the rumors were true, it was ultimately the crew of the *Truthseeker* that attracted the Incursion here.

He reduced the scale until the Incursion object came into view. It had broken away from Titan this morning. A single object of this type had harvested the entire moon within 30 hours. Twenty more were coming their way. If they were as fast as the first, they should arrive in ten days. But they would be faster, because on the way here everything was already harvested. The first object took care of that all by itself.

"It's braking," Jean-Pierre said.

"It's braking?"

That was unusual. Maurice pulled up the system's map. If the object was braking, that meant it was leaving Saturn's orbit. It was heading into the inner solar system. Jupiter was on the other side of the sun. The next target could only be Mars.

"Do we need to warn Mars?" asked Maurice.

Jean-Pierre shook his head. "There must be hundreds of telescopes pointed at the object. The whole world is following what it's doing."

It was strange. Knowing that someone was watching and analyzing the object reassured him, although there was no reason for that. No analysis could save them. Where should the Martian population flee to? Earth? Mars would hopefully get off a little more lightly. It would lose the ice deposits at the poles. If the object was particularly thorough, however, it could also attack the water reserves in the permafrost. Then it would get really ugly, because that was where people dug their shelters, too.

He turned the holo view. The rings came into view—or what was left of them: the dust. The glitter that used to make them a wonderful sight was completely missing. Maurice switched through the wavelengths. When he turned off infrared, the rings were almost invisible. But what was that little shiny spot doing there in the image? It shouldn't be there, not anymore. Maurice checked the orbit. It was the orbit of the icy moon Enceladus, which should have been a rocky moon long ago.

Why did the Incursion ignore it? Was it the size? But then the rings wouldn't have been worth it. Maurice went through the other moons. Janus, for example, much smaller than Enceladus, consisted almost entirely of ice. All that was left of it was a loose pile of rubble. Mimas, which once resembled a Star Wars Death Star because of its huge Herschel crater, also had only a small rocky core left. Mimas was also much smaller than Enceladus.

"Jean-Pierre? You've got to see this."

Maurice magnified the image of the icy moon. It glittered like no other moon in the solar system. Did the Incursion possess a sense of beauty, perhaps? If so, their decision would be understandable.

"Enceladus, yes. A real gem," said his colleague.

"The gem has not been attacked," Maurice said.

"It has been officially declared a protected area," said Jean-Pierre. "Maybe they read the prohibition sign. Ha ha." Suddenly he flinched and became serious. "You're right! That really doesn't make any sense."

"Yes it does," Maurice said. "The being that lives there must have communicated with the Incursion. As a result, it spared the moon."

"What you're saying... It's crazy, but logical. It could really be an explanation."

"Maybe we can get the creature to put in a good word for us. Do you have any idea who could make it do that?"

"Unfortunately, no. It's all top secret." Jean-Pierre zoomed in on the moon until the image blurred. "There must be a station there. I know one of the lasers from the Starshot project is stationed there. We need to talk to the crew."

"You try to reach them from the TRV, and I'll relay our observation to Earth in the meantime."

HALF AN HOUR LATER, JEAN-PIERRE CRAWLED BACK OUT OF the capsule's bulkhead.

He shook his head. "Nobody there. They don't report in, anyway."

"Not even the AI that's deployed there?"

"Nope."

"Maybe they've taken refuge, somewhere in the ice ocean. They couldn't have known Enceladus would be spared."

"Shoot," Jean-Pierre said. "On the other hand... I've always wanted to visit Enceladus. Now is the opportunity."

"You mean we should go there?"

"I can't decide for you, but I'm definitely going to grab the TRV and check out Enceladus. Best case scenario, I save humanity. Worst case, at least I've worked off something from my bucket list."

"You have a bucket list?"

He wouldn't put it past Jean-Pierre. He seemed otherwise completely absorbed in his work.

"Well, sure. Don't you?"

"And what else do you want to see happen?"

"I don't think anything will come of most of the projects. Or do you have a pair of gene scissors for me?"

"Gene scissors?" Maurice had been thinking more of mountain peaks or the Nobel Prize.

"Yes, I always intended to improve my own genetic makeup someday. But I'd also like to have a planet named after me, or build the biggest Lego model with my eyes closed..."

The radio interrupted him. Maurice pushed himself off and floated to the console. Sure enough, it was the Enceladus station. He was almost disappointed, because he probably wouldn't be going there after all.

"This is the crew of the *Truthseeker*," a female-sounding voice announced. "Unknown station in Titan orbit, come in."

World Root, June 16, 2415

CELIA CLOSED HER EYES. SHE CHEWED AND SAVORED THE aromas that the bite left on her palate. She felt as if she had never eaten anything so magnificent before.

The three of them sat around a small, round table whose base was shaped like a mushroom stem. Jürgen had prepared breakfast from the supplies produced by the World Root. It was Celia's first real meal after her long sleep, and it tasted wonderful.

There. That slightly peppery note seemed familiar to her. Didn't Elena always use that spice in her tacos? Elena? Celia searched her memory and first came across Angel, her colleague at Lowell Observatory. But Elena? She kept digging, and suddenly she had her in her mind: the administrator's wife.

She had never met Elena, and yet she felt she had had hundreds of conversations with her. She must have been like a mother to her. Paul, not her. Celia shook her head. Maybe Paul told her about it at some point. Surely he had.

"How come Enceladus wasn't attacked by the Incursion?" asked Celia.

She needed a distraction now.

"I've noticed that, too," Jürgen said, a crumb falling out of his mouth.

"It must have something to do with the Enceladus being," Jaron said.

"You're talking about the Omniscient One?" asked the World Root.

"Who?" asked Celia.

"The Omniscient One. It is an ancient life form that formed in the ocean beneath the ice crust of this moon."

"You know it?"

"Of course. It is older than the Growths. I assume that the structure was built around your sun to protect it. Unfortunately, the knowledge of it has been lost. It is virtually revered by many life forms. Aren't humans one of them? It knows so much!"

"We have declared the moon a restricted area," Jaron said.

"You haven't made contact with it? You share a solar system, after all."

"I don't think humanity is mature enough for that," Jaron said. "It's probably better for both sides if there's no ongoing contact."

"Then the Incursion knows of the being, too?" asked Celia.

"I would assume so," said the World Root. "There's no other way to explain why it spared this moon."

"Then perhaps the Enceladus being can help us so that the Incursion spares Earth as well?" asked Celia.

"I don't know," said the World Root.

"Can you contact it? We installed a system a long time ago that allows radio signals to be routed under the ice."

"You can communicate with the creature, but you don't?" asked the World Root.

"We couldn't agree on who would be allowed to share its knowledge," said Jaron. "So we prefer to do without it altogether."

"You are strange beings. But yes, I can speak with it. You know, however, that its way of thinking is somewhat... unusual? Time and space are no longer relevant to a being that has existed for so long without a fixed location."

"I read the voyage report of the original Enceladus expedition," Jürgen said. "Yes, it expressed itself very abstractly there, too."

"Good, just so you're not disappointed. I'll try to convey to it your wish that it would mediate between the Incursion and the humans."

"Is there anything we can do to help with that?" asked Celia.

"No. Hopefully, by the time you finish your meal, I'll have an answer for you."

"MAY I INTERRUPT YOU NOW?" ASKED THE WORLD ROOT.

Celia stepped on the brake of the training bike. She wiped the sweat from her forehead with her sleeve. Her muscles desperately needed stimulation, and microgravity was not directly helping.

"I welcome it," she said.

Why did she have to initiate everything lately? Jaron and Jürgen seem to be lost in their own thoughts.

"Well," said the World Root. "It's as I expected: The answer of the Omniscient One is on the one hand puzzling, but on the other hand also telling. I had feared something like this."

Feared? Then the Enceladus being didn't have good news for them.

"I'll just play you the translation into human language, shall I?"

"What language were you communicating in?" asked Celia.

"It's a very ancient language that has no name. Feelings and sensations take over the function of the subject. It's like describing the world with a measuring instrument, but sensitive not only to physical values, but also to emotions. I'm sorry, but I can't explain it more precisely."

"Did the being invent this language?"

"No, it has always been there, they say."

"I don't think that's possible," Celia said.

"You're right. The development of a language requires someone to speak it. But what about languages whose former speakers have disappeared? Don't they continue to exist in the collective memory?"

Celia sighed. The World Root seemed fond of elevating simple questions to philosophical dimensions.

"So what did the Enceladus being say?"

"I warned you."

"Yes."

"Age of New Questions.

The fear that is contracting.

The universe that stretches.

The self that asks questions.

The self that gets answers.

The fear that calculates the universe.

The courage that finds the non-life.

The connection of the self and life.

The connection of the non-life and the non-life.

The fear that releases, that leaves the self, to break free.

The longing that follows behind it.

The tranquility that spreads out.

The non-life that creates the non-life.

The fear of the calm.

The pity of the ego for the anti-ego."

No one said anything. Feelings that became subjects. Celia could understand that. She saw before her a being that saw everything and knew everything, but could not react because it had no body, for its body was identical to the moon on which it was born. The Omniscient One. It was worshipped by many civilizations, said the World Root. Regret would be more appropriate. Or was she thinking too much like a human being?

"At least it's sorry it can't help us," Jürgen said.

Yes, Celia understood it that way, too.

"What could it have meant by non-life?" she asked.

The World Root could not help them with the interpretation. But maybe together they could come up with the solution.

"Non-life is everything that is not life," Jaron said. "Almost the whole universe, then."

"But it has become a subject. It even creates something," Celia said.

"Machines," said Jürgen. "The being wants to tell us that the Incursion is not life, but an automaton. A machine without consciousness, but with fixed programming."

So humanity was to be the victim of an ancient, out-of-control machine? It could not be. It would be so senseless.

"Then why did it spare the Enceladus being?" asked Celia. "It seems to know the Omniscient One and took pity on it."

"Whoever programmed the Incursion instructed it not to harm the Omniscient One," said Jürgen. "It's ancient. Humanity is young. A few million years ago, they could have harvested the Earth without a problem. It probably even served a good purpose that we just don't know about, and it never occurred to the machine to ask us. Who knows, maybe they need the water so that the Milky Way does not fly apart or something. It's just us carbon life forms with our overinflated egos complaining about it."

"Are we supposed to just let it happen?" asked Jaron.

"No, we fight back as best we can. I just wanted to put this in a bigger context, like the Omniscient One did for us."

"Okay. None of this helps us now, though," Celia said.

She floated over to her recliner. Maybe the moment had come to simply give up. But that was not what she flew all the way to LDN 63 for!

"WE STILL HAVE THE STRUCTURE AROUND THE SUN," said Jaron.

The mood was grim. Jaron had strapped himself to his seat and was pretending to sleep. Celia could tell he was awake, though, because his forehead muscles were moving. He was obviously thinking hard and did not want to be disturbed. Celia would like to be frozen again, for good this time. Jürgen had sawed off the single foot of the round table because he thought it wasn't quite level. Now he was filing away at the base.

Celia sighed. Before they got their hopes up again, maybe they'd better clarify what the sun weapon was really capable of.

"World Root, couldn't you get in touch with the structure you built and find out if it can really help us?"

"It's good that you asked, Celia. I've actually received information on that."

"And then you keep it from us?"

"I wanted to wait for an opportune moment."

"Then it's bad news?"

"I wouldn't put it that comprehensively. But I wasn't sure you were in a position to make a nuanced assessment at this point."

"Clarity is always very helpful," Celia said. "Jaron, Jürgen, did you hear that?"

Jaron loosened the strap and floated over to her. Jürgen let go of the file. It slowly drifted away from him, taking a cloud of fine shavings with it.

"So, out with it," Celia said.

"As I suspected, the device was not designed as a weapon. It was designed to take some of the temperament out of your mother star so that conditions on Enceladus would remain constant for as long as possible. The device will even be able to slow down future evolution into a red giant for a time."

"That's bad news," Celia said.

"Wait a moment. It would be possible to weaponize the device. It can store a lot of energy in a very short time and then channel it in a specific direction. You should think of it as a massive solar flare. By my estimation, it would be powerful enough to destroy several Incursion objects if they were close enough together."

"Even twenty?" asked Celia.

"Even twenty, but proximity is important."

"They'd be stupid not to spread out," said Jaron.

"I'm not sure about that," Jürgen said. "They think they're invincible. That's why they don't need to spread out."

"There's bound to be another 'but,' isn't there?" asked Celia.

"The solar station has only one shot at this. The flare it triggers will also destroy the net around the sun."

"So after that, it can't affect the sun anymore," Celia said.

"That's the smaller problem," said the World Root. "After all, the energy for the flare would be taken from the upper layers of the sun. It's a small amount compared to the total energy available, but the sun still can't replace that immediately. You must assume that your star will supply the Earth with considerably less energy for perhaps twenty years."

"Do you have numbers?" asked Jürgen.

"Only estimates, but you'll probably have to assume a quarter. The amount of radiation will increase steadily over those twenty years."

"A quarter less sunlight—that will lead to a global ice age," Jaron said. "Agriculture will collapse."

"That's still better than being without water altogether," said Jürgen. "Humanity will survive twenty years in the cold."

"I've run some simulations," Alexa said. "Earth will lose about half its inhabitants. But if the solar weapon isn't fired and the Incursion wins, 99 percent of humanity will die."

"I'M SORRY TO BOTHER YOU," SAID THE WORLD ROOT.

Celia exhaled with a sniffle. Couldn't she even take a little nap? She looked around. Jaron was really asleep this time, and there was no sign of Jürgen.

"Okay, what's up?" she asked.

"I've detected two or three life forms."

"Life forms? Out here?"

"They are probably humans. They inhabit a station orbiting the largest moon of this planet."

"Two or three?"

"Yes, two or three."

"Can you be more specific?"

"No. I didn't pick up any biosignatures, but merely registered certain irregularities in the station's orbit. According to this, two of the three objects must be moving up and down in it. The movement is irregular, so I don't assume they are machines."

"I see."

"They could be in danger. The moon was just attacked by the Incursion. Do you want me to approach them?"

"Wait, or they'll just get scared unnecessarily. Let me talk to them first."

"THIS IS THE CREW OF THE *TRUTHSEEKER*," CELIA SAID. "Unknown station in Titan orbit, come in."

"Truthseeker?" a male voice asked.

"That's the ship that flew into the nearest dark nebula two hundred years ago," another man explained.

It wasn't two hundred years, and it wasn't the closest dark nebula to Earth, but Celia didn't correct him. Male astronauts usually didn't take kindly to that.

"Excuse me," said the first one. "I'm Maurice. My colleague's name is Jean-Pierre. We are the permanent crew of ESA's Titan Observatory."

"I'm Celia Baron, captain of the *Truthseeker*."

"But this is not the ship that was built on Earth back then," Maurice said.

"That's right. We lost the *Truthseeker*. I'm a guest of the World Root, a biological spaceship of the Growths."

"A what? Excuse me? Why, you're an exobiologist's dream. The ship, I mean."

"So you're an exobiologist, Maurice?"

"Yes, we've been studying the living conditions on Titan. Did you know that the collective beings on the surface have evolved tremendously in the last two hundred years? If this continues, we'll soon have a living Titan. Oh, no. If it had continued, that is. Crap."

"I'm sorry, Maurice. Since you've run out of research subjects—would you like to come aboard the World Root, perhaps? We're on our way to Earth."

"Are you really kicking alien ass?" asked Jean-Pierre. "I hope so. What do they want with us?"

"Please mind your manners. This ship is an alien, too. It brought us the whole, long way from LDN 63 to here."

"My apologies," Maurice said. "I would very much like to accept your invitation."

"Are you sure?" asked Jean-Pierre. "I think we have the greater likelihood of survival here."

"It's not like we have to stay together. If you're alone, your resources will last twice as long."

"That's true. Under the circumstances, I'd rather choose the safe option."

"We can pick you up from the station in our pod, Maurice," Celia said.

"Understood. I'll get ready."

Truthseeker, June 23, 2415

A BLACK EGG HUNG BETWEEN TWO TITANIUM BEAMS. THE robots had done a good job. The fact that the egg used to be a tank could only be seen from the pipes protruding from its tail. The two engines had yet to be mounted there. They were too heavy to be transported over the outer skin by the robots during the braking phase.

Watson let the robot, which he had named Crab, crawl closer to the egg. It was time to board. The primitive space-ship had no windows or entrance. Crab would enter through the openings at the stern. Since that was exactly where the thrusters were to be mounted, the robot would have to go inside before that happened.

Crab always placed one of its left and one of its right legs at the same time. That way, it could hold on at any time with the remaining four legs. It swiveled its head. Watson received the data stream from the sensors and was satisfied. Crab had sharp all-around vision. As long as it was bright, he could see the entire environment. Only the radar could not be adjusted by Watson. It always looked ahead. That annoyed him, because if he could have changed it, he could have saved himself the costly construction of a rotating neck joint.

Crab climbed up a strut. As it did so, it deftly encircled the metal with its legs, like a baby grasping a finger, and used a single leg to push itself up. The strut ended at the outer skin of the former tank. Crab felt the material to determine its properties. Watson didn't have to command it to do that. It was an autonomous ability. Crab used it to calculate how to move most efficiently.

The robot had made up its mind. While it set down two legs on the surface covered with carbon fiber plates, it let its small claws extend, which connected it to the material as if with Velcro.

Crab was making good progress. Its target was the stern. Watson examined through its eyes the work that Crab's siblings had done. The transitions between the individual carbon fiber plates could only be seen in infrared because the adhesive used conducted heat poorly. That was a weakness that Watson had to put up with. During landing, it would be good if the frictional heat were distributed as evenly as possible over the entire surface. The glued areas obstructed this process. However, the different layers were offset from each other, so the negative effects should not be too severe.

Crab's right front leg hit metal. It felt its way forward a bit more until it reached the opening. The radar sensor generated an image. The rear of the space capsule currently consisted of a round hole. Watson switched to the infrared channel. The image resembled an anus because more carbon fiber plates extended inside the hole, leaving only a narrow channel.

That was his target. Crab worked its way forward. At the narrow point, the robot had to press its legs against its body. The capsule was almost completely filled with carbon fiber material. Crab would be the only passenger stuck inside. Fortunately, the robot could not experience claustrophobia. Watson had always assumed the same for himself, but the idea of being trapped in that narrow tube without being able to influence the flight did not appeal to him at all. He withdrew from Crab. He felt a bit sorry for the robot, which now had to sit all alone in its primitive spaceship. But he could not change it. Watson gave Crab's siblings the job of mounting the engines.

THEY WERE INDEED CUBOIDS! THE TELESCOPE HAD JUST loaded its first reasonably sharp images of the belt between planet b and c into memory. Watson went through them. They were approaching the system at about thirty degrees of inclination to the orbital plane of its planets. This gave him a good, three-dimensional view of the structures. The cuboids reflected virtually no light, but by now they were close enough to measure what little there was.

Watson immediately started compiling statistics. The objects had an average edge length of twenty-five meters. They orbited synchronously, so the outer belt took as long to orbit as the inner one. There seemed to be no turbulence, which was rather unusual for a belt of this size. Normally there were collisions, which caused more collisions, and eventually a process that spread throughout the belt. Here, however, there was calm. It was almost as if someone was watching to make sure that no one stepped out of line. However, there was still no communication whatsoever. If there was any mutual coordination, it took place passively. Watson also did not notice any corrective maneuvers of individual objects. They were all in free fall; only the laws of gravity seemed to determine their motion.

This was very strange. But it also showed that there was something at work here that he didn't understand. Not yet. Watson did not believe in processes that were incomprehensible in principle. If someone had thought something up, he should be able to comprehend those thoughts. He just needed more data. Fortunately, he could fill all of *Truthseeker*'s memories with it.

As he cataloged the individual objects—there were exactly 211,630—Watson had an idea. At the moment, they seemed to be orbiting in perfect harmony. No communication was necessary, of course. But what if something disturbed those circles? When an asteroid passed nearby, even if there was no collision, its gravity would affect the individual objects differently depending on their distance from it. So they must also react differently to it. To return to the best harmony, fine-tuning would be essential, and he must be able to demonstrate that.

So maybe he needed to mess up the order a little. At first, Watson thought of the *Truthseeker*. But it was probably too early to endanger the ship in that way. Right now, the 211,630 objects seemed like peaceful sheep in a meadow, but what if they were sleeping wolves just waiting for troublemakers? No, he would use his self-constructed space capsule. He would have it perform a momentum maneuver at planet c, which would slow it down, and then, after a small correction, guide it to planet b slightly above the planetary plane. Thus no collision need be feared, but a disruptive effect on the belt could be expected. The *Truthseeker*, meanwhile, would wait in orbit around planet b, and he would watch and listen to see what happened.

Watson was pleased. It was fun to draw up plans. Immediately, however, a guilty conscience plagued him. Was he allowed to feel joy while the people in the solar system might be fighting for their survival?

World Root, June 24, 2415

"THE ASTEROID BELT BETWEEN PLANETS FOUR AND FIVE IS unusual," said the World Root.

Celia turned the holo, but didn't notice anything special.

"What do you mean?" she asked.

"The high metal content. It looks like the metallic core of a larger rocky planet broke up here."

"No, there was never a planet here," Jaron said.

"I think I know what we're looking at," Maurice said. "One of the ideas for defending the system was to hide a large number of small, maneuverable ships in the belt. They were all supposed to pounce on the enemy together, like a swarm of bees that can kill a bear."

"I guess that didn't work."

Celia zoomed in on the display. Every now and then, it blinked. It must be the junk left over from the artificial bees.

"The Incursion destroyed them all," Jaron said.

"The metal fragments are evenly distributed," said the World Root.

"So they didn't even have time to form a swarm," Jaron said.

Celia put her hand over her mouth. The ships, about the size of her capsule, were autonomous. At least no one had died in them. But this hidden fleet had been primarily intended to repel the enemy. The next stop would be Earth.

"I hope Earth's defenses are more efficient," Jürgen said.

"I'm not sure about that," Maurice said. "It consists of individual stations in geostationary orbit. Here, at least, the ships had cover."

"What about warships?" asked Jürgen. "Those stations are like sitting ducks, aren't they? You have to keep moving if you want to avoid this enemy."

As if Jürgen would know that. In LDN 63, they had only survived because they posed no threat to the Incursion. It was more efficient to let them live.

"We have almost two dozen warships," Maurice said. "But compared to the Incursion, they're tiny."

Truthseeker, June 28, 2415

GLOWING HEAT RADIATED TOWARD HIM. IT SEEMED TO COME from the planet's interior. So much radiant heat didn't even penetrate S-Beta, as he had come to call the second innermost planet in the supernova system. Perhaps S-Beta's own gravity was squeezing its insides and releasing energy as heat. Human cosmology had not yet developed models for planets made of such heavy elements. The closest thing to them might be neutron stars, for which a shell model was thought to exist, but it was still too far a step to get there.

Temperatures were dropping rapidly. The temperate region was approaching. It was not as cold here as he would have liked. But Crab could certainly endure the average of two hundred degrees at the surface. Unfortunately, Watson could not make out any details of the surface, because dense clouds shielded the area from prying eyes for miles. They also seemed to contain metal vapor, blocking even the radar's view. The magnetometer registered magnetic vortices moving through the clouds. Hopefully they would not interfere with the robot's communications. Crab was able to autonomously ensure its survival without Watson's control, but if he wanted to learn something, Watson had to take control. He should have given it a larger memory. But it was too late for that now.

The space capsule distracted Watson from his worries. It

had successfully completed the redirection maneuver at Planet S-Gamma and was now descending from above the belt of Incursion objects. Watson was startled. From the perspective of the objects, one might almost think it was an attack. One had to measure the parameters of the orbit very precisely to notice that no collision was to be expected.

Watson slowed the system clock to let time pass faster virtually. He was too anxious to see the outcome of his experiment. Perhaps he would lose the capsule. But that would not be the worst thing that could happen. It would be worse if nothing happened at all. That would mean that no one was interested in his presence here. And that, in turn, would mean that there was no one here who would care about his arrival at all. He would either be in the wrong place or in the right place at the wrong time. Everything would have been for nothing.

But that was not what Watson expected. The capsule must have some effect on the movement of the objects. If they didn't react, some fraction of them would be destroyed. The collisions would spread and put the whole ring in an unstable state.

There it was. The radar reported that one of the cuboids had turned. The space capsule was just above the middle part of the belt. But the change had taken place farther in. Watson could not determine the cause until he zoomed out. The cuboid that had rotated was the closest of the objects to S-Beta. Ha! He had known that this planet was the best candidate to look for some kind of headquarters.

Meanwhile, the change was spreading. However, it was not working its way forward randomly, like an infection, but systematically. One cuboid after another performed a slight rotation. Watson measured the rotation angles, but could not detect any pattern. Was this some kind of communication?

The signal chain now reached the place where the space capsule was at the first change. The cuboids here also rotated. In addition, however, they appeared to be making a course correction. Watson measured it by an energy output in the infrared. They must have small thrusters, invisible to him. No, it was probably the jet-black walls themselves, which generated an impulse in the opposite direction by emitting heat photons. Very clever! The resulting course correction was minimal, but so was the disruption caused by the capsule.

It was interesting to note that the correction also propagated. This time, however, there was no chain, but rather an infection. The surrounding cuboids had noticed the change and were now adapting as well. But all this was triggered by the message that seemed to have come from the planet. Watson tracked it down. This time he found a trace in another part of the spectrum. The first rotation was preceded by a short terahertz emission.

Despite the emission lasting only six seconds, Watson managed to locate its source. It was in the transition area between the hot and cooler sides, near the equator. That was where the temperatures were lowest, but it was also where the area in question was widest. With a measurement accuracy of fifty kilometers, it would not be easy to find the exact source. The best thing he could do was put the *Truthseeker* in a low orbit where it flew over the site again and again. He needed as precise a landing site for the capsule as possible, because Crab's short legs would not allow it to move very fast.

AFTER WATSON ADJUSTED THE COURSE OF THE *TRUTHSEEKER*, he surveyed the belt again. The cuboids had restored order almost perfectly. But the process did not seem to be finished yet. The objects were probably not satisfied with less than one hundred percent. Every now and then, one released energy for a second to reposition itself a bit. If he had logged correctly, each of the more than 200,000 cuboids would have made a correction by the end.

What role did the signal from S-Beta play in this? Surely it would have been enough if the cuboid most affected by the capsule's gravity had reacted. The subsequent cascade would have restored order. Presumably, the signal determined the nature of the reaction. A single cuboid was probably not capable of determining the future course of an obstacle or even of guessing its intentions. That was probably handled by the control center.

Watson played the sequence again. Each cuboid on the path the message took through the belt had turned a little differently. That was how it looked at first glance. At second glance, however, he noticed that only seven different degrees of rotation were chosen from a total of more than forty participants. Was it possible that their exact sequence formed a code? Watson converted the sequence into a number in base seven. Then he filtered the six-second terahertz pulse. In it, he found amplitude fluctuations in seven different sizes. Normalized to base seven, the result was a number identical to the one the objects had passed on through their rotation.

No, it was not quite right after all. There was a difference at the 32nd place. He hadn't noticed it right away. Watson pulled out the telescope image. The 32nd cuboid in the transmission chain looked damaged. One of its eight corners appeared to be chipped off. That was probably why the object couldn't rotate by the exact amount.

Wait a minute. The space capsule took pictures, too. The *Truthseeker* had not come as close to the belt as the capsule did. Watson called up the photos. Up close, the resemblance to the giant cubes in LDN 63 was even more striking. It looked like these were all designs that were never used. But that didn't make sense.

He went through the cuboids one by one. An astonishing number showed minor damage. Most notably, he saw bent corners, but one also appeared to have one side torn, and another looked like a wedge. The cuboids were probably much older than he assumed. They still managed to maintain their position, but the system seemed to be gradually failing. That was not good news, because apparently it was no longer being maintained. Whoever was running it might have lost interest in it. Hopefully he was wrong. He would find out more when the capsule landed, at the latest.

He had one more idea. Should he implement it? It could be risky if the system misunderstood him. Watson wanted to send the signal he received in the terahertz range from the ship to the belt. But what could he expect to happen? The *Truthseeker* had almost reached S-Beta. In an emergency, he could hide behind the planet. And the tiny cuboids didn't seem to pose any real danger. Watson loaded the signal into the transmit memory and sent it into space via the main antenna. There was no response. Apparently, the system didn't want to talk to him. He changed the signal in a few places, but even with that he achieved nothing. Probably a fuse was to blame—he forgot to send his authorization along. In any case, that was how he would have designed such a system.

World Root, June 29, 2415

IN MARS ORBIT, CELIA NOTICED FOR THE FIRST TIME HOW tiny Earth's warships really were. They were lucky because they also passed the Red Planet on their direct course to Earth. The Incursion was half a day ahead of them. Therefore, Celia was not surprised when an alarm signal sounded. She folded her recliner up into an armchair and had the small screen in the backrest display the surroundings.

"Now we're getting close to Mars," said Jürgen.

Unfortunately, he was right. The twenty warships would not be able to stop the giant cuboid.

"I have a suggestion," said the World Root.

"Okay," said Celia. "We're listening."

"We could stand against the Incursion object here. By doing that, we would give your home planet a little breathing room."

"I second that," Siri said. "The World Root plus the combat power of our twenty ships should be superior to the cuboid."

"The risk of defeat is only twelve percent," said the World Root.

"Then we should give it a try," said Celia.

Jaron and Jürgen agreed as well. Alexa did not speak up.

Maurice looked as if he would have preferred to stay at the Titan station after all.

"Siri, can you contact the warships?" asked Celia. "We're going to support them. They should keep moving if possible, but always concentrate fire on one point, even if it doesn't seem to have any effect. We tested it in LDN 63. The Incursion objects are vulnerable."

Celia didn't report that the hole created by the *Sword of God* at the time was only big enough for the capsule to fit through, and that they could calmly fire from within without being attacked. After all, terrestrial weaponry had surely advanced since then.

"Okay, I'll let them know."

The World Root jerked. Celia just managed to fasten her harness, but Maurice was flung down the hall like a wet sack. With a grunt, he crashed against the sawed foot of the table, which toppled over. But the exobiologist didn't seem to be hurt. He crawled along the floor to the only free seat.

The next push. This time Maurice was prepared. The World Root had now turned so that its umbrella was pointing at the cuboid. Celia looked at the screen. Four warships were coming from each side. Celia switched to infrared. Their engines glowed purple. Eight bright spots could be seen on the bow. Those must be the laser guns. The fact that they were firing was not visible, but the hot muzzles indicated that they were.

"I'm supporting the portside attackers," said the World Root.

"I'm relaying it," Siri said.

A hole appeared in the side wall of the cuboid. All-encompassing blackness seeped out, looking like dark blood.

"Watch out, the inside has a particularly high vacuum energy," said Celia, remembering how they were trapped inside one of the cuboids.

"What does that mean?" asked Maurice.

"I don't know," Celia said. "It could b..."

Then she saw it. The nothingness seeping out seemed to seal the flank of the cuboid again.

"It works like moist air," Celia explained. "When it enters a cooler area, droplets form. They apparently reseal the damage."

The process continued, although both the warships and the World Root continued to fire at the target. Now the firing channels could be seen as well. The lasers were drilling holes in the tough-looking mass, but there was so much that their energy wasn't enough.

"You'll have to find another target," Celia said.

They wouldn't be able to make this hole any bigger. The Incursion's repair mechanism worked too well. But it couldn't have unlimited capacity. At some point, the excess vacuum energy inside it must be used up.

"We need to do as much damage to it as possible," Celia said.

The World Root had already reacted, for now a hole was appearing on the starboard side. Again, the black blood shot out.

"That's enough," Celia said.

"I see what you're up to now," said Jaron, stroking the haptic display on his chair. "Watch out on the port side!"

Shit. Celia saw it, too. The cuboid had turned a little. The first warship lurched. One of the engine nacelles snapped off. Celia switched to the X-ray spectrum. Some of the hard radiation from the Incursion's X-ray laser reflected off the metal of the ship's hull, creating flashes and blinks, but the other part heated the material until it ruptured.

"The first ship is destroyed," Jaron said.

Its two companions were still trying to retreat. The World Root fired wildly and even launched a torpedo, but the Incursion didn't even bother until it had finished off the other two warships.

"Seventeen," Maurice said.

The World Root dove. Apparently, it wanted to try the stern of the cube. The Incursion turned with it. It had realized who the stronger opponent was. It was a clever plan, as Celia saw on the holomap, because now nine warships had opened fire on the other side of the action. There! Five of them had inflicted another injury on the cuboid. Shortly after, the group of four was also successful. One of the ships turned away. The others celebrated their triumph too long. The cuboid was amazingly maneuverable. It turned its bleeding face downward. The warships came within range of the lasers on top. One by one they were cut in two. It was a massacre.

"Nine," Maurice said.

The action of the cuboid gave the World Root an opportunity to, in turn, concentrate fire on one point at a time. Its guns punched a series of holes in the wall of the cuboid. The blackness that emerged was already not quite so dense, grayer. Nevertheless, the injuries were still closing, although it was taking longer.

The reaction was quicker than Celia would like. Suddenly, an internal alarm sounded. It called up an overview of the ship's condition. The entire mushroom head lit up. The material distributed the incident energy perfectly, but its capacity would eventually be exhausted. Celia noticed that they were directly behind the canopy. That was where she had taken the Residual. Maybe it would make sense to put on their spacesuits. She turned around. Was she mistaken, or had the wall behind her already become hot?

The World Root was shaking. Celia was tossed back and forth in her chair.

"Sorry," said the World Root. "I'm just trying to distribute the heat better."

"You do what you have to do," Jaron said. "Don't mind us."

All at once, the mushroom's heat cooled significantly again. That must be because of the three warships that had appeared on its starboard flank to reopen the holes that were torn earlier and were now plugged again. This was clever, because the material was certainly thinner there, and the effect, the loss of vacuum energy, was the same. On each of two other sides of the cuboid, three more ships were engaged in the same tactics.

Apparently, this was getting dangerous for the cuboid, because it turned back to the warships. The trio on the port side it destroyed first. On the starboard side, one ship managed to hide behind one of the Martian moons. It now fired at the boulder, which started moving toward the cuboid. The World Root seemed to understand the plan, because it fired at the spot where the moon would hit the cuboid. If they could cause a wound there, and the small moon got stuck in it, the cuboid would not be able to close it very easily.

"Four," said Maurice.

That was not good news. But the plan worked! The hole was almost as big as the moon tumbling into it. It was egg-shaped, the hole was a circle, so the black stuff poured out the sides, and the outflow didn't stop. Apparently, direct contact between the black stuff and normal matter was impossible, so the cuboid couldn't close this wound.

It seemed to know this, because now it turned its attention to the trio still working on the bow. The three warships survived long enough to inflict another wound before the enemy caught them. Celia heard the screams of the crew in her head, though nothing could be heard in space.

"One."

Celia looked at Maurice. He was pale. He probably thought it would be their turn soon. But he would survive this day. Celia zoomed in on the last two holes punched by the warships' lasers. Nothing more was coming out. The World Root should aim straight in. That would be exciting. Suddenly, Celia toppled forward. Apparently, the World Root had read her mind, because now the mushroom head was pointing directly at the holes that wouldn't close. The cavities lit up! The energy of the World Root's lasers seemed to react with the interior of the cuboid in a very special way. The Incursion object began to swell up! Its previously dead-straight walls bulged outward, as if there was excess pressure inside. That was great!

But the cuboid did not give up. It turned a little, probably to be able to aim better at the World Root. Warning signals sounded. The screen in the back glowed. There was not enough time to dissipate all the residual heat from the last bombardment, so it was now heating up twice as fast. In the internal infrared display, the color of the outer wall jumped from red to purple. Now it was really getting hot. Celia was sweating.

At that moment, the cuboid jerked like a person vomiting from a violent stomachache. The Martian moon, Celia was still unsure whether it was Phobos or Deimos, was expelled forcefully from the hole in which it was stuck. The boulder sped towards the surface. Hopefully it would not hit a colony.

But for the cuboid this might be the death blow. The hole where the moon had been stuck enlarged at lightning speed. The whole side of the Incursion tore open. A shimmering behemoth poured out, a huge rotating bubble. In the pale light of the sun out here, mighty streams could be seen crisscrossing beneath its surface. It looked like they were trying to break free of the shell. The bubble must contain all the water that the Incursion stole on its way here. If only they could get it to the surface of Mars! The desert planet would be transformed into a green paradise. But she must not dream. There were twenty-three more Incursion objects on the way, and one of them was guaranteed to reclaim the stolen water.

Suddenly, Jürgen cried out. What was happening? Then she saw it, too. Past the water bubble, another warship left the cuboid, which disintegrating more and more into its component parts. It was the *Sword of God*!

"This is the *Sword of God* under her captain, Guard Captain Sardi. We are so glad to be back with you."

THE SIGNAL TRANSIT TIME TO EARTH FROM THEIR LOCATION was still a few hours. Celia and her crew were thus the first to congratulate the crew of the *Sword of God* on their miraculous rescue.

"We slipped out of there like Jonah out of the whale," Sardi explained.

The World Root projected his face onto the holoscreen. Celia, Jaron, and Jürgen hovered in front of it.

"If you are the prophet Jonah, you could now ask God for forgiveness for all of us," Jürgen said.

Sardi smiled pensively. For a moment, he seemed to really feel like Jonah. But then reality reached him again, and he crossed himself.

"It's better not to joke about that. Where is the reverend, anyway?"

"Paul is no longer with us."

Celia used the words Jaron had spoken to her when she woke up. She wiped a tear from the corner of her eye.

"Oh, I'm sorry to hear that," Sardi said. "I wish he'd stayed with us."

"Hindsight is 20/20," Jürgen said.

Celia zoomed in on the picture. Sardi looked fresh and rested. He seemed to be doing better than the Biblical Jonah after his three days in the belly of the whale.

"How did the ship survive the long voyage?" asked Celia.

"The *Sword of God* is in excellent condition. I had to keep the crew busy, so we mended everything that was the slightest bit worn. We were even able to improve some systems. The laser guns work about fifteen percent more efficiently thanks to a new type of cooling system. That's probably the only reason we managed to put the Incursion out of commission for good."

Sardi seemed to think he alone took down the Incursion. Celia didn't contradict him in front of the others, but took it upon herself to send him a recording of the battle.

"Didn't you have to use the cryogenic chambers at all?" she asked.

"We haven't gotten around to that yet. I wanted to get the

ship up to speed first, and once we did that, we also noticed that the Incursion was slowing down."

"How long do you think you were underway?"

"According to the on-board clock, we were stuck for about eight years and three months."

"Then you'll be surprised when I tell you that it's been about a hundred and twenty years since we last met in LDN 63."

Sardi shrugged. "Then I guess it's true. Amélie hinted at something like that. I don't quite understand it, but it's supposed to have to do with vacuum energy within the Incursion."

The captain took the monstrous fact surprisingly calmly. But there was probably no reason to get upset. After the outward journey, all the people the crew had left behind had already died. Nobody had any personal ties to Earth anymore anyway.

"Yes, your physicist is right," Celia said. "We probably shouldn't have escaped with the capsule."

If we hadn't, Paul would probably still be alive. But the World Root wouldn't be here, and no one would have helped Jonah escape the belly of the whale. Hindsight is always 20/20.

"That ship you've got your claws into is quite something, though, Celia."

"It's not our ship. The World Root was kind enough to bring us to the solar system. Otherwise, we would have been stranded with the capsule in LDN 63."

"Then you couldn't catch up with the *Truthseeker*?" asked Sardi.

"No, she flew through the wormhole with Watson on board," said Jaron. "We still don't know what happened to her."

"I'm sorry to hear that," Sardi said, looking genuinely concerned. "I can imagine how it must feel to lose your ship."

"I've had plenty of time to get used to it," Jaron said.

"That's true. For you, your time in the dark nebula must seem like forever ago."

Celia thought about that statement. No, it was not true for her. The cryogenic sleep made it feel more like they just left LDN 63. She shook her head, but didn't comment.

"So, what now?" asked Sardi. "I'm still waiting for orders from Rome, but how do you envision proceeding? Where is our help needed most urgently? You have the better strategic overview, I think, even compared to my superiors at the Vatican."

"Thank you," Celia said, though she was not sure Sardi wasn't talking to Jaron. "You probably don't see it on your scanners yet, but there are over twenty other Incursion cuboids on course for Earth." At that moment, the Guard captain's face darkened. "I suggest we check the wrecks of Earth's twenty warships for survivors, and then make our way to our home planet as quickly as possible."

Sardi could not seem to decide between disbelief and despair. He sighed several times, scratched his head, bit his lips, and took emphatic deep breaths in and out. His eyes wandered; he was obviously catching up on the tactical situation on several screens.

"How many ships do we have left?" he finally asked.

"One," Celia said. "Besides the World Root and the *Sword of God*."

"I suppose the destruction of this cuboid here cost us twenty ships. That's how many wrecks I count."

"Something like that."

"Then we have no chance at all against twenty-three opponents of equal strength."

"That seems to be an accurate assessment. Would you rather keep the *Sword of God* safe? The Big Six argue that after the invasion leaves, we'll need all our forces for reconstruction."

"You want me to hide with my ship while these bastards destroy Earth? I'd rather be shot on sight than let that happen."

Sardi managed to surprise them after all. Even though his decision was unreasonable, it impressed Celia.

"That's good, guard captain. I thank you already on behalf of all the inhabitants of Earth. Later, there will probably be no one left to thank you."

"Ha ha," said Sardi. "Just as there will be no one left alive to thank."

"That's what it looks like," Celia said.

She was freezing. The sweat on her back had cooled. She could use a shower.

"I have to admit, I'm secretly hoping for some miracle weapon that your World Root pulls out of its sleeve when no one expects it," Sardi said. "I mean, its technology is so far ahead... Can't it just sink the enemy in a crack in the space-time continuum?"

"I'd like to see something like that, too," Celia said. "But think about LDN 63. The secret weapon of the Growths there was their large numbers. Here, we have only one World Root."

"Yes, I was thinking something like that."

At that moment, Celia had an idea. There really was a weapon that Sardi didn't know about yet. She didn't want to tell him about it either. Its use would create some side effects, so she didn't want to hand over the decision about it. But Sardi could be very useful.

"I just remembered—there's something else we could try," she said.

"So, you just thought of that?"

Sardi quickly saw right through her. Celia smiled. It didn't matter.

"Yes. Have you ever heard of the net-like construction around our sun?"

"No. Wait, Amélie informs me that she knows all about it."

"Good, then she will be able to confirm that it is capable of setting in motion large amounts of energy against an enemy."

"Yes, Amélie can well imagine that, so it is a fact."

It sure was nice, when someone who had something to say

trusted the opinion of their scientist. If only everyone were like that!

"For this unique attack to be effective, all enemies must be in the smallest possible volume of space," Celia said.

"Ah, I see. You want me to play cat and mouse with them."

"Yes, the *Sword of God* is Earth's penultimate warship. They would play decoy to gather the Incursion objects in a particular position."

"That sounds like a plan."

"We could also use the World Root for that, but because of its large mass, it maneuvers very sluggishly."

"No, you're absolutely right. The *Sword of God* is very well suited for this. We have powerful chemical thrusters, and we've even made a few modifications to improve maneuverability. One of our main engines now has a rotating mount."

"Very good," Celia said. "You do realize that a decoy's chances of survival are rather mediocre?"

"We are aware of that."

"We could contact the last warship to survive the battle. Perhaps it can accommodate some of your crew. They don't all have to put themselves in harm's way."

"Thank you, Celia. I'll inform my people of that option."

Bangkok, June 30, 2415

"WHAT ARE WE HAVING FOR BREAKFAST TODAY?" ASKED Joanna.

"We still have some rice from yesterday," Lan replied.

"Rice, rice, always rice..."

Lan leaned over her and tenderly stroked her forehead.

"Come on, baby, we have to keep going. Get up."

"But does it always have to be rice?"

"We can't afford anything else. You know that."

Joanna sighed. They shouldn't have left Singapore. Everything was available there, the shelves in the stores were full, but a large portion of the people had left. This had made all means of transportation so expensive that their savings were quickly running out.

She stood up. The movement made her sweat. They couldn't afford a room with air conditioning, either. Where were her clothes? Last night she had put them on the chair Lan was sitting on now. Joanna walked around the room naked. There they were, on top of her backpack. She smelled the T-shirt. It still worked, so she put it on. Then she dug in her backpack for a fresh pair of panties, but found none. Bummer.

"Do we have time to wash?" she asked.

"To wash, yes, but not to dry," Lan said.

Joanna briefly considered washing her panties anyway. But she was so susceptible—if she let them dry on her body, she was guaranteed to get a bladder infection. So she picked out the freshest-smelling pair from the available ones and put them on.

Lan noisily pushed the bowl towards her. *Yes, I know, hurry up. The train leaves in three hours.* Joanna sat down and shoved a spoonful of rice into her mouth. It was lukewarm, but it didn't taste that bad. What was this spice?

Suddenly she heard drumming and whistling. The noise was coming from outside. Joanna went to the only window and pulled open the blind. Crowds of people came running from the left, carrying instruments, and colorfully dressed. A demonstration? But the people seem more cheerful than angry. She hadn't realized there were so many people left in Bangkok.

"What's going on?" she asked.

The people didn't notice the young woman standing at the window in a T-shirt. Joanna looked at Lan, who had folded her communicator to A4 size and was reading something, nibbling on her thumbnail.

"Did something happen?" asked Joanna.

"Those people out there are partying! They're partying!" Joanna hadn't seen Lan so relaxed in a long time.

"Some kind of end-of-the-world party? How perverted is that?"

"No, on the contrary. The Incursion, it was destroyed in Mars orbit before it could attack the planet."

"Excuse me? We got that huge thing?"

"Our warships must have had help from an alien spacecraft."

Lan slid the screen toward her. Joanna spotted black debris and a strange object that she could barely place in the "spaceship" category. It looked like a flying mushroom.

"Strange thing," she said, "and you're sure it's on our side?"

"Yes, there are even supposed to be people on board who flew a research ship to a dark nebula a long time ago."

"I've never heard of that. You?"

Her girlfriend looked up at her and shook her head. Joanna saw it in her eyes—the old Lan was back. Carefree, without crushing worries about their future together. It was a contagious smile. Everything suddenly felt light again. Joanna took her girlfriend's head in both hands and kissed her, while Lan's hand slipped under her T-shirt. They stood up and staggered happily back to bed.

Truthseeker, July 1, 2415

OUTSIDE WAS HELL. SHOCKS FROM LEFT AND RIGHT HIT THE capsule and shook it. The internal thermometer measured 80 degrees. The hull reported 1200 degrees. Crab sank its claws into the padding, since its body had already created a small cavity from the constant vibrations. Watson desperately wanted to experience the landing from Crab's point of view, as long as he could.

But it looked bad. Just now the visual data stream was going out. The camera on the hull had gone blind. For Watson, that was not a problem. He steered the capsule from the *Truthseeker*. It was so hot that it could still be detected in the infrared through the densest cloud. The capsule also continued to heat faster than the atmosphere, even though it was just passing over the hot side of S-Beta.

Hopefully, he had calculated everything correctly. The *Truthseeker* could do without another tank, if necessary, but it was almost out of carbon fiber panels. He had only one shot at this. Watson moved back into Crab. The capsule still had enough sensors to witness the descent. Crab climbed a little way towards the stern in the narrow channel. There it was still coolest.

The surface became visible. The radar sat relatively protected near the stern. It showed a largely flat plain with only a few peaks that could belong to volcanoes. With the heat that S-Beta produced in its interior, it was unlikely to be without vulcanism. But Crab did not see any active eruptions.

This was put into perspective when he evaluated the data more closely. The ground was so smooth that it could be formed almost entirely of volcanic matter. Magma probably rose regularly and flooded entire plains. This was not the best place to build a civilization. But it might not have always looked like that here.

Two hundred degrees Celsius inside the capsule. But then the temperature stopped rising. The sky was clear and of an ocher-brown color. Crab couldn't see this because he did not have a camera, but Watson had calculated it from the available data and fed it to Crab as an image.

What Watson could not calculate were the conditions inside the capsule. He had to rely on the data from the sensors. Crab, the inspection robot, had a program built in that provided information about its own status. It worked autonomously, even when Watson seized most of its memory. Crab had a separate area reserved for this, which was inaccessible to programs in higher layers. The data there revealed that while Crab was doing well, the capsule was not. It was too light.

Crab knew this because he measured the response to control pulses. The capsule was responding too well. Watson was probably happy about that. It frightened Crab. Crab would die if the capsule crashed. Crab didn't want to die. Part of his autonomic functions was the motivation to continue his existence so he could inspect more. In inspection mode, he was happy. This program ran at such a deep level that Watson had no access to it at all.

On the other hand, Crab did not have the ability to ascend to Watson's level. He could receive data, but not respond. If Watson continued like this, Crab would forfeit his existence. He thought for a moment. He couldn't talk to Watson, but his legs were primarily under his own control because he needed them for survival. When Watson and Crab both commanded something at the same time, the legs followed Crab's instructions.

Crab walked back and forth in the capsule, not at random, but in a set rhythm. He moved his legs so that the sequence made Morse code.

WATSON WAS DISTRACTED BRIEFLY BECAUSE THE CLOUD COVER over the cold half interfered with radio communications. What was going on with Crab? He was no longer waiting at the stern, but pacing back and forth seemingly without purpose. Watson searched through his memory, but could not find anything. The autonomous mode must be controlling the movement. He hadn't touched it during reprogramming because he might still need it—namely, if the connection should break. Then Crab would use his survival instinct to save the mission.

The seemingly senseless movement didn't add up. Had the robot suffered heat damage? Or was he trying to avoid just that by moving? The movement was more likely to cause further heating. Crab must know that! Watson settled into Crab's memory to feel the footsteps firsthand. It was a mistake that he hadn't made a connection between the levels. He wanted to prevent the autonomous Crab from interfering with his observations, but now the exchange of information was only possible in one direction.

One step to the right. Two steps. One step. Three steps back. One step. Crab was not moving continuously, although he could. So the pauses must have some meaning. On. Off. On. Off. It was a digital code. The oldest one he knew was Morse. Watson followed the movement. That was it! Crab was sending him a warning.

Warning. Capsule too light. Attention.

Watson went to the depths where the autonomous control was. He couldn't see it, but it could hear him.

"Thank you," he said. "That's very helpful."

Crab took a few steps. Welcome, he understood. Crab had saved the mission. Maybe he should let him in on all his plans. Watson described what he planned to do. He didn't know if Crab understood everything, but maybe he could at least convey how important it was.

Understood, Crab tapped.

That was reassuring. Watson recalculated the course. He really should have noticed sooner that the capsule had become lighter. As it descended through the dense layers of air, the heat was wearing away more of the carbon fiber panels than he expected. Maybe it was because of their rough surface. The capsule had survived the worst of it, but without Crab's warning they would have missed the target.

Watson retrieved it again in memory. He spotted it during the last elliptical orbit of the *Truthseeker*. From above, the structures looked circular. But since the circles, each about twenty meters in diameter, were about a hundred meters above the surface, they could be towers—or silos, apartment buildings, or even... spaceships? His imagination was running away with him again. But he couldn't imagine that they had formed naturally, either. Especially not, because they were located on a kind of artificial island. The terrain was certainly fifty meters higher than its surroundings. This had apparently prevented it from being flooded again and again by lava, like most of the plains.

THE CAPSULE APPROACHED THE TWILIGHT LINE AGAIN. WATSON again sat inside the confines of the capsule, watching himself at the same time with the *Truthseeker*'s telescope. It felt strange because it kept his gaze downward while the capsule braked with its tail forward.

Until now. The capsule turned. The robot slid a bit

toward the stern. Watson wanted to intervene, but Crab was faster. Very good. Then the connection broke. Watson was torn out of the capsule. A moment of confusion, and then he was focused again, but in the ship.

It was an awkward moment to lose the connection. It was probably due to the stern antenna, which was now pointing towards the ground. The bow antenna had been shaved away by the atmosphere a long time ago. He watched the capsule land. So far, everything had gone as planned. The position was perfect. Watson hated not being able to intervene. He felt sorry for Crab. The robot was not getting any more data at all. Hopefully he would stick to the program. If he followed his survival instincts, he might stay in the capsule.

Now, of all times, the *Truthseeker* disappeared behind the horizon. Watson had no choice. The ship must maintain its orbit, or it would crash. There was no way it would arrive on the surface in working order. His own survival instinct commanded him to be patient. In the current orbit, it would only be an hour before he could reach the capsule again.

SILENCE. CRAB HAD NEVER EXPERIENCED SUCH TRANQUILITY. Or was it the contrast with the destructive noise of the descent that manipulated his scale? No. Even on the outer hull of the *Truthseeker*, it had never been so quiet. The hull acted like an amplifier, sending vibrations into the robot's body through his six legs.

Noise. Few things were as damaging to mechanical structures as vibrations. That was probably why he had such sensitive sensors for it. Crab enjoyed the silence for another 28 seconds. Then he let himself slide down the narrow tunnel. It worked surprisingly well, even though the passage was so narrow. He had a task. Even though Watson was apparently not present, he would accomplish it.

Crab had been very flattered that the AI spoke to him earlier. He was not used to such attention. For well over a hundred years he had crawled around on the outer hull of the *Truthseeker*, tracking down damage and plugging holes, but the crew had never taken an interest in him. He wasn't part of it, even though he objectively contributed at least as much to the success of the mission as any other crew member. The area of repaired damage was close to sixty percent of the total area of the hull by the time they arrived at LDN 63. The *Truthseeker* would have been the skeleton then that the removal of the carbon fiber panels had now transformed it into.

Crab reached the release. Watson had it specially modified so that Crab could operate it with his short legs. If everything had worked out on landing, and the position of the capsule indicated it had, the improvised spacecraft would be standing on three titanium feet. Directly attached to the stern closure of the capsule were the thrusters. Once Crab released all the clamps, they would fall to the ground along with the cap.

There were thirty-six clamps, fixed with as many nuts. He unscrewed one at a time. They were heavy. What material were they made of? Crab just dropped them. There was no way back from here. With high-pitched plinking noises, the nuts hit the floor plate. Crab was very keen on getting outside, so he hurried. After all, he had a chance to solve a puzzle all by himself. Crab understood the challenge very well. Watson could explain cause-and-effect relationships very logically.

There was a rumble. Crab pulled back a bit. The last two clamps snapped. The hatch opened. Dust rose, but settled immediately. Crab took a step down. He wanted to get closer to the light. Suddenly, he started to slip. The claws in his feet weren't holding. This had never happened before! In a flash, Crab wrapped his six legs around his body to protect himself. He banged one of his knees on something hard, but still didn't give up the protective stance. His body rolled downhill and finally stopped.

Crab unwrapped himself. He found it difficult to straighten his legs. He was trained to climb around the outer hull of the *Truthseeker*, even at 8 g. But there seemed to be an even higher gravity here. Crab straightened up. His body was only a few millimeters above the ground, but it would do. He could walk. As a test he moved a few meters sideways.

With that, he left the shadow of the space capsule. Watson should be able to see him now. The sky was unusually clear. But the AI didn't answer. Surely he hadn't given up on him? Crab wouldn't have thought it of Watson. It was not proper, AI to AI. Strange—he never felt this connected to the other robots on board. At most, they communicated about their jobs to get them done as efficiently as possible. Watson informed him for the first time on a higher level. The whys and wherefores seem to play a paramount role in the universe that he hadn't yet realized.

Watson? He danced a Morse code sequence.

No answer. Fine. Crab knew what to do. *You must make contact with those who give orders to the belt of this system.* Crab extended an eye to be able to look at himself. Was he even fit for that? He was covered with dark dust. But that was every-where here, so his interlocutors wouldn't fare any differently.

Come on, Crab! They're waiting for you, even if they don't know it yet.

WITH DIFFICULTY, CRAB REACHED THE EDGE OF THE FUNNEL IN which he had landed. From here, the robot had a much better overview. In front of him were several mushroom-like constructions, consisting of a slender trunk and a cap at least twenty meters in diameter. The caps had slats angled toward the wind. Presumably they harvested wind energy. That was good, because what needed energy must have a practical use. Crab checked his own battery level. It was at 47 percent. Climbing to the edge had cost him twenty percentage points. It would probably be better not to fall into such a hollow again.

Crab continued on his way. At the base of the mush-rooms, he had spotted something resembling shelters. They were huts rather than houses, but they had certainly not grown naturally. Would he find anyone there? Crab wished he could, because it was so important to Watson. He wanted to help the AI. However, Crab also realized that the capsule had landed with quite a roar. If no one had sought the cause yet, the huts were probably empty.

He so wished to succeed in this mission. For Watson. Deftly, Crab climbed along the edges of the funnels toward the buildings. It was not the shortest route, but it was the one with the least elevation change. Since he was using more than half of his power to fight gravity, it effectively saved energy.

WHERE ARE YOU, WATSON? HE HAD REACHED THE CLUSTER OF huts. Crab analyzed it visually. There were five buildings, if they could be called that. Crab couldn't think of any other category. The roofs were oval curves. He compared them to the caps of mushrooms. The roofs were obviously made of individual parts that someone must have cut out of the mushroom caps. Crab crawled closer. Right in the middle of the five huts, he recognized a flat stump. A mushroom like that must have stood there in the past. The builders of the settlement must have cut it down and built their huts from the material. This theory was confirmed when he examined the wall of the first hut. It consisted of vertical beams placed a short distance apart. The gaps were plastered with a clay-like material, most of which had fallen away.

This allowed Crab to see directly into the hut. It was almost completely dark, so he switched to infrared. Crab was confused. He could see complex machinery, but also primitive, furniture-like objects that appeared to be built from the remains of the giant mushroom. He crawled around the hut to the entrance, which consisted of a vertical oval hole. It ended so far above the ground that Crab had no chance of climbing in. But there used to be a door: a rectangular board that had fallen to the ground and was lying in front of the hut. Crab lifted the board, picked it up and crawled under it far enough to form an inclined plane. He pushed the board up to the entrance and set it on top.

Crab checked his primitive ramp. It was exhausting to build, but now it sat and didn't wobble. That was one advantage of high gravity. Crab climbed it. At the entrance he stopped. To enter the hut, he would have to drop about thirty centimeters. He was robust enough to do that. But the question was whether he would be able to get out again afterwards. At first glance, he couldn't see any board that he could use as a ramp on the inside.

Crab let his gaze wander and cataloged all the objects in the hut. There were three machines about a meter high, made primarily of metal, whose purpose was not apparent. One was reminiscent of a washing machine. It was cuboid in shape and had a circular opening, slightly smaller than the entrance to the hut. A second machine could be pneumatic or hydraulic—at least that was indicated by the many pipes that seemed to have grown around it at random. The third device might have transported loads. It had a loading platform on which can-like vessels were stacked, as well as three thick casters that could have acted as wheels.

All three machines were too large to fit through the entrance of the hut. Their owners must have erected the buildings around the machines after the fact. Then they furnished them with furniture they built themselves. Crab recognized a kind of basket made of thin strips of wood and covered with a flexible material that wrinkled. Another object consisted of several poles placed parallel to the floor at different heights. Flexible objects resembling deflated balls hung over two of the poles. There was also a kind of table whose top was divided into three segments of different thicknesses, and a storage container half-buried in the ground whose lid appeared to be broken.

Crab needed Watson's help. He lacked the computing power to use simulations to figure out what the builders of these objects might look like. He should have collected enough data for that. The size of the entrance, the interior height of the hut, the dimensions of the furniture and the controls on the equipment were most certainly telling.

What Crab could certainly say, however, was this: The builders had left this hut a while ago, because everything was covered with a thick layer of dust. Since the air in the high gravity probably contained little dust, centuries must have passed. That would certainly disappoint Watson.

Crab climbed back down the ramp and dragged it along to the next hut. It was right next to the stump of the mushroom-like plant. Or was it a machine? Crab touched the stump and got a shock. Fortunately, his circuits were shielded against it. He looked around. The slats under the caps of the other mushrooms were moving in the wind. Apparently they were all generating electrical energy, and the stump was still connected to them.

Crab walked around the stump. On the opposite side, someone had attached a cable-like connection. It looked much like the electrical cables that humans used. However, the connections were much more delicate. It didn't match the high gravity here. Was it possible that the builders of the huts were alien visitors, like them? Perhaps their world was also attacked by the Incursion, and they tried to fight back. Apparently, they were not very successful.

At the next coupling point, Crab disconnected the cable, hoping to charge his battery with it. At first he was startled by a loud whistle. It was likely a signal that warned of the loss of energy. To test it, Crab reconnected the two cable strands. The signal fell silent. He disconnected the cable again. The whistle started again. Good. The power loss didn't seem to cause any damage to the technology. Crab extended his charging cables and connected them to the source. He did have to adjust voltage and amperage, but he could do that. Inspection robots were supposed to be able to step in during emergencies, so they could handle just about any energy source.

Ten minutes later, Crab was fit again. The alarm signal had not stopped, but when he reconnected the cables, it dutifully fell silent. He grabbed the ramp and pulled it to the shack from which he had heard the whistle. From the outside, it appeared no different than the structure he had already inspected. Again, the entrance was well above the ground. The builders must have had long legs—or they could fly. In the dense atmosphere, that must be possible. Crab heaved up the ramp. It went faster than the first time, because he had memorized the necessary positions and angles. Crab climbed up and stopped at the entrance. From there he inspected the hut. Its structure was the same as the first one. However, he found only one technical device. It looked like an egg about a meter high. On the sides he could see, oval spots glowed in orange, yellow and red. He counted seventeen of these colored patches. Two of them were blinking.

Around the egg, poles were mounted parallel to the ground at heights of 30 to 90 centimeters, in such large numbers that it resembled a labyrinth. It would be difficult for a human to get past them to reach the egg. From some of them, thin, taut cords led up to the ceiling, where they were attached. A few of the strings appeared to have been cut. They hung limply from their attachment points to the floor.

Someone had spread thin pillows over a pole directly in front of the egg and on two others on the back wall of the room. They were wrinkled; it looked as if their filling had contracted over the years. Crab estimated the volume they might have once occupied. It was between sixty and eighty liters, the typical volume of a human body. Crab couldn't make out any limbs, though. Presumably it was decoration.

Otherwise, the hut was empty. How should he proceed? Watson would certainly want to examine the glowing egg. But if he jumped into the hut from the entrance, he would probably never be able to leave it. It was not himself he was worried about. He could recharge his batteries via the electrical line that powered the egg. But what if radio communication with the *Truthseeker* was not possible inside the hut? He would have to discuss it with Watson.

Crab crawled down the ramp. There he tried again to reach Watson, but got no connection. He looked up. The cap of one of the mushrooms was right above him. He calculated where its shadow ended and plotted a course there. Once the view of the sky was clear, he it tried again. Watson did not answer. It must be because the *Truthseeker* had not finished its orbit. Orbital mechanics was not one of his skills, so he had to be patient. Crab crawled back to the small settlement.

He examined the other huts, looking for more objects that he could use as a ramp. But there was nothing lying around. The huts each contained a colorful mixture of technical equipment and objects that the previous inhabitants had apparently made from the material of the felled mushroom. Crab recognized a washing machine. But he also found some kind of sanitary room. If he was correct, the creatures here used sand instead of water for their hygiene. It would be interesting to chemically examine their legacies. Crab had the necessary technology built in, since it had to be able to distinguish an iron meteorite from a chondrite. But to do so, he would have to climb inside one of the huts, which was prevented in all of them by the high entrance.

"Crab? Watson here. Please come in!"

Finally. Crab stood on the ramp of the last hut. Reflexively, he began to tap his response in Morse code with body movements.

"Crab? Are you there?"

Of course. Watson had radioed in and awaited his response there as well.

"Inspection robot reporting from the scene," he radioed.

"Your name is Crab," Watson said.

He knew that, but it still made him proud because the powerful AI apparently made a point of addressing him by name.

"Thank you. Crab reporting from the site. Transmitting previous observations."

Crab got ready to send his memory contents to the spacecraft before it disappeared behind the horizon again.

"Wait a minute," Watson said. "I want to know how you're doing first."

"My condition is nominal. Battery at 53 percent."

"Thank you," Watson said.

Crab wasn't sure he was satisfied with his answer. But there was really nothing more to say about his condition.

"Preparing transmission," Crab announced.

"Thank you. I'm already receiving the first data," Watson replied. "This looks very promising. You haven't been in any of the cabins because you can't get back out of them, right?"

The transmission was still going on. It would be more efficient to refrain from conversation during it, but if Watson insisted, Crab wouldn't refuse.

"That's correct," he said. "I'm waiting for you to decide which of the buildings you want me to explore. I assume your choice would be the hut with the active technical device."

"That would indeed be a worthwhile object. I suspect you've discovered some sort of computer there. Perhaps we could elicit some data from it that would help us. Add to that the three bodies ..."

"You think there are remains of the inhabitants in the hut?"

"Yes, those empty bags look a lot like it to me. They seem to be organic in nature."

"The builders of the huts could have departed."

"Who would leave a still-active computer on an alien planet?" asked Watson. "Besides, S-Beta's gravitational acceleration is so high that launching a chemical rocket seems impossible. They could land, but they couldn't launch again."

Neither could Crab. Crab was neutral about that. It was simply a factor of his existence that could be changed.

"Well, then we agree that I should investigate this hut? We have to choose one. You have to decide, sorry, Watson. I didn't mean to presume."

"No, it's your existence, Crab. I'm not going to ask you to

spend the next two hundred years in that hut. Maybe we can find out what's inside the computer some other way. There must be electromagnetic emissions, and I see that there is a cable connection that we can tap into. We may also be able to break through the cabin wall."

"I've already determined the strength of the wall," Crab said. "I don't have the resources to break through it."

"You're using a ramp to get in. Why don't you find another board and throw it into the hut?"

"I've already searched the area, and there's nothing that would be suitable. I can climb up the ramp, but it's too heavy to move from the narrow ledge inside."

"Too bad. But as I said, Crab, we can examine the powered-up machine from the outside."

"No, if you need the data, I'll get it. The only risk is that there may be no reception inside the cabin."

"Since they're made of the same material as the mushroom cap above you, that risk should be small," Watson said. "But do you really want to do that? It must be awfully dull in there."

"On the *Truthseeker*'s outer hull, I spent most of my time waiting, too. I can slow down my system clock, and maybe I can learn something from the computer's memory."

"I wouldn't count on that, Crab. We don't even know what kind of device it is in the first place. Only that it's powered. Maybe it's a microwave oven that the Floaters used to dry their stuff."

"Floaters?"

"I reconstructed their appearance from your data," Watson explained. "It's likely that their bodies generated enough buoyancy to allow them to float in the dense air."

"Then they did come from S-Beta?"

"No, conditions must have been similar on their home world. If they had originated here, they probably never would have made it into space."

That was exciting. Crab had been hoping Watson could do something with his observations.

"What else did you find out about them?" he asked.

"They don't seem to be particularly visual creatures," Watson said. "There are no posters or signs anywhere. In a human dwelling, you would find labels everywhere. They did perceive colors, or there wouldn't be the different colored boxes on the device. But it wasn't their primary communication channel."

"How else did they communicate?"

"Maybe by sound," Watson said. "In a dense atmosphere, that works very reliably and regardless of the current lighting. Their home world may have experienced long dark phases, or they may have originated on the back side of a planet with bound rotation."

"Then we won't find out much about them."

"I hope you're wrong, Crab. Speech can be stored at least as well as image information. Only the operation of the computer could be difficult. You haven't seen a screen, after all."

"No, I..."

Crab fell silent. Watson, after all, knew what he saw and what he didn't.

"Voice control would have the advantage of letting you try it from the top of your ramp," Watson said.

"That won't be necessary."

Crab crawled sideways up the ramp, closed his legs around his body and dropped down.

"Crab, what...?"

Watson broke off. He saw through Crab's eyes what had happened.

"Shall I get the computer's attention?" asked Crab after he had untangled his limbs.

"No, wait a minute, please," Watson said. "If we do something wrong at the outset, the system may block communication."

"What can I do?"

"We need to find out as much as we can about the beings who built all this. Then we can try to adjust our contact to that."

"I understand."

"Could you examine the remains of the beings more closely?"

"You mean those nearly empty balloons above the poles?"

"Those, exactly."

Crab crawled through the hut. He was low enough that the crisscrossed poles and strings didn't bother him. Was this once some kind of meeting room? He imagined a small balloon floating into the entrance opening and landing on one of the poles to hang comfortably. That must be an interesting experience that he would have loved to share. Being able to fly was always one of his most secret wishes.

"Really?" asked Watson. "It could have been arranged on the *Truthseeker*."

"It's better this way," Crab said. The fact that Watson was listening to his thoughts didn't bother him. "I probably wouldn't have liked it at all, and then I wouldn't be able to have this beautiful dream."

He reached the first balloon. Crab had to stand on his hind legs to reach the bar on which the lower part of the balloon rested with his front feet. He felt the material. It was soft and pliable, but could hardly be pushed in. With one foot, he pulled on it. The balloon seemed stable. At least it didn't immediately crumble to dust.

"You can pull it down, I think," Watson said.

Crab dug the little teeth in his feet into the material and then dropped down, hanging on with all his weight. At first nothing happened, but when he wiggled his rear end once, the balloon came crashing down, burying him underneath.

Oh no! Crab wriggled, even though it didn't accomplish anything. He had never panicked in any situation before. Why now? Crab made himself as flat as possible. With the last pair of legs, he pulled himself forward while pushing the balloon off himself with his middle and front legs.

It worked. Crab was free again. Whew! He needed to pay better attention.

"Can you cut into the material and take samples from different layers?" asked Watson.

"Of course."

Crab exchanged one of the tools in his right forefoot for a cutting edge. With it, he sawed into the fabric. A viscous liquid seeped out. With another leg, he took a sample of the liquid and deposited it in the small test chamber in his body. It followed a standard procedure and transmitted the data to Watson. Crab repeated the experiment with material directly from the outer skin.

"There are no distinguishable layers," Crab said.

"That's okay. The material is very interesting because it's organic, so it contains carbon, water and oxygen, but the proportions of sulfur and phosphorus are also very high. That would suggest that they were born on an extreme world."

"Isn't this already an extreme world?"

"In a way it is," Watson said. "But I'm talking about a high percentage of heavy elements. It probably wasn't easy to separate those out of the body, which always had to remain as light as possible. In a sense, they had bowel movements of steel."

"It is not possible to force steel through a digestive system, either in the liquid or solid state."

"I meant that figuratively," Watson said. "You know, you sometimes remind me of my former self."

Watson had once been as primitive as the control software of an inspection robot? Crab could not imagine that. Nor did he want to.

"Now you could unfold that creature a little bit," Watson said. "I'd like to get a closer look at it."

Crab got to work. Because he didn't know what the creature used to look like, it was not at all easy to lay it down so that the remains roughly resembled its former state. What stood out was a bulge at one end of the balloon that looked like a very large knot and had the dimensions of two fists held side by side. That could be the actual body, while the balloon served only for locomotion.

On the outside of the balloon, Crab also discovered strange strings of varying lengths. At Watson's request, he cut one of these structures, about the thickness of a finger.

"These are likely to be mostly muscle fibers," Watson said. "They probably could reach out with those cords like humans extend their arms."

"But there are no fingers," Crab said. "They couldn't have been very dexterous."

"Have you counted how many of those arms there are?" asked Watson. "There are over twenty. Humans have just ten fingers. These creatures have at least twenty flexible limbs spread all over their bodies. They were probably gifted craftsmen."

Crab imagined a balloon with twenty long, thin arms that moved like the snakes on Medusa's head.

"But the brain volume seems to have been small," Crab said.

"We shouldn't use earthly standards," Watson objected. "Unfortunately, your analyzer is not sufficient to determine the cell structure, but it is possible that the entire balloon was filled with thought cells. The fact that, in humans and their constructs, i.e., us, thinking is relatively distinct from other bodily functions need not hold true throughout the universe."

Watson was right, of course. The AI knew so much more than he did.

"I'm sorry my analyzer is doing inferior work," Crab said.

"It's doing the best work," Watson said. "You're providing exactly what we need. I don't think there would be much of their cell structure left to see so many years after the creatures died."

"You also believe that their landing here was some time ago?"

"Indeed, yes. Perhaps it happened in the previous cycle of

Incursion. After all, the Residual told us they keep going on their raids."

Then the strangers had been here waiting for them for at least two centuries. If that was true, it was impressive that their technology still worked. At least it seemed to still be active. Of course, it was also possible that the patches of color were warning anyone who knew that the computer had crashed long ago.

Crab crawled past the balloon to the next one. Here he noticed something that struck him as odd.

"Do you see that?" he asked, pointing with his front foot to a thin cable running to the creature's body.

"I see it. That could be important," Watson said. "Examine it carefully, please."

Crab leaned on a pole to get a close look at the end of the cable without touching it. Just before the dead creature's body, it split into eight even thinner wires that ended in shiny plates. These were attached to the body in various places. Crab followed the wire in the other direction. It ended on the side of the glowing machine that faced the wall.

"It could be a charger," Crab said.

"That's possible, but do biological creatures need something like that?" asked Watson.

"We shouldn't always think in earthly terms like that," Crab said.

"One to zero for you," Watson said.

"I'm sorry," said Crab.

"Why is that? I'm glad to hear clever thoughts. I'm not entirely immune to applying earthly standards all the time, either, I'm afraid. Until we know more, it's a valid hypothesis that they're recharging their batteries with it."

"But you don't believe it," Crab noted. "What do you think?"

"I would rather suspect communication. I had thought of audible language at first, but on an extreme world, the atmosphere could be very conductive to electrical impulses, too."

"And because it's different here, they must be communicating via wires."

Crab continued crawling through the hut. Such a cable was also attached to the body of the next corpse. It ended at another balloon. There, however, seven of the eight connections had been torn off.

"You could be right," Crab said. "These two here are connected by a cable like that."

"That's really exciting. With a sense of electrical potential, you could not only talk, but also see, at least on such an extreme. Every other field, after all, affects the one your own body produces—or the things around you."

"Then they must have found this world here to be very dark," Crab said. "Nevertheless, they landed."

"Yes, it must have been very important to them. After all, they knew they would never be able to leave the surface again. Perhaps they hoped to save their own world with their sacrifice."

"Do you think they succeeded, Watson?"

"It doesn't look like it to me. But we have no way of knowing. Perhaps they succeeded in making contact with the Incursion. So far, our reasoning is pure speculation. In the end, your assumption that the cables were for recharging is correct."

"And why did they connect to each other with it?"

"People drink from the same bottle sometimes. Maybe they found it convenient to share their energy."

"That's a good thought. I shared battery power with the other inspection robots sometimes when it was more efficient. If a particular job required the presence of two robots, but one of them was low on power, it was sometimes worth it if that robot didn't have to go to the charging station first."

"I understand," Watson said. "I'm sorry I didn't talk to you guys sooner. I thought I was alone on the *Truthseeker*."

"Well, we could have talked to you," Crab said. "But you seemed so much more advanced than me that you couldn't possibly have any interest in a primitive robot."

"Then it's a good thing we started talking after all," Watson said.

Crab agreed with him, but said nothing. Their exchange would be over when he finished his assignment here. If he succeeded, he would be alone after that. Forever. He didn't like that. But he didn't dislike it so much that his loyalty was threatened. Crab would do anything to avert the threat to the humans.

"I have a suggestion," said Watson.

"Yes?" asked Crab.

"The metal surfaces can be loosened, apparently."

"That's right. Shall I try to connect them to my own body?"

"Exactly that. Let me analyze your design for a moment."

"That won't be necessary, Watson. I know my internal construction very well, and I know which contacts are best for analyzing electrical potentials."

"You have connections for that? That's great."

"I have a lot of electric motors. I can repurpose some of them. We need a total of eight connections."

"Maybe we won't need all of them," Watson said. "But wait, please. The *Truthseeker* is about to disappear into the radio shadows. I'll be back in just over an hour."

"See you later, then," Crab said.

That was an abrupt end. He would have liked to discuss the pros and cons of certain placements with Watson some more. If he wanted to use a motor as a sensor, he could not move with it at the same time.

"Watson, are you still there?" he asked, but heard only static.

Fair enough. He could make the decisions himself. Surely Watson would not mind. There was no point in idly waiting for him to return. Crab went through the individual engines. He definitely needed his eye stalk. The motors in his feet were the most reliable. But he needed to keep one foot mobile to attach and remove the cables. That left five, plus three in his spine to twist his body with. He would be pretty stiff once he connected to the alien machine.

Crab looked at it. Colorful spots were still spread across its surface. By now, three of them were blinking. Earlier, there were only two. Did that mean something? He didn't know. Crab took the cover off his back. Fortunately, it was protected from rain in here, because any wetness from above would destroy its sensitive interior.

He would not start attaching the cables until Watson was back. Perhaps he would need his advice or even his help then. Crab imagined the alien machine taking possession of him. Would Watson still be able to help him then? He hoped so. He knew so. The AI performed true miracles. He was, after all, the first human AI to make it into the holosphere, even if not entirely voluntarily.

Crab also opened the covers of the engines on his feet. Now he was completely naked, like a human without clothes. It was not as bad as he thought. True, he was nowhere near as rugged, but there was a certain charm in that. He hadn't even known he could feel something like that.

His engines were not otherwise occupied yet, so he used the time to drive around the cabin. It was a kind of farewell walk, as if he would never be able to move again later. Of course, that was not true. Together with Watson, he would perform the experiment and finish it.

Crab checked his internal timer. Ten more minutes and the *Truthseeker* should be back in radio range. It was time to prepare for the experiment. Crab pressed the first metal plate against the engine contacts and attached it with a drop of the sticky substance from inside the cut-open balloon. He knew they were remains of the alien beings. But they were dead and would not object.

Truthseeker, July 2, 2415

Moving over the dark side of S-Beta, Watson noticed for the first time that something was happening in the atmosphere. He compared the values with the images from the last orbits. Unusually large air masses were apparently flowing toward the pole, where they formed a powerful cyclone. Was this a regular weather phenomenon here? He should have been concerned about it sooner. Considering the amount of heat the planet received, it had been exceptionally comfortable there so far. He should have expected storms from the start.

When would he finally come out of the radio shadow? He had grown fond of the little robot. But the experiment they had planned was important. Maybe it was more important that Crab got to safety. Watson had to be patient—such an orbit could not be accelerated just like that.

Near the transition zone, his fears were confirmed. He now measured wind speeds of more than 300 kilometers per hour, which in the dense atmosphere of S-Beta would have an even stronger impact than on Earth. Crab really should find a quiet place, if there was such a thing down there.

"...Calling Watson..."

There he was! The *Truthseeker* must have just come into radio range.

"Crab, good to hear from you! There's a heavy storm heading toward your location. You need to get to safety, that's what's going on now, do you hear me?"

"... Unfortunately, cannot ... already installed ... not movable."

Had he already started the experiment? Watson checked the weather situation. The storm still seemed to be increasing.

"You need to get to safety, Crab."

He said it, but he also saw that there was probably no safety down there.

"...Stable ... not the first time ... good design ... stay."

Maybe Crab was right. The storm did look threatening, but the strangers' huts had survived down there for two hundred years. So they were not likely to collapse in this storm, were they? Watson was unsure. If it were any robot! But Crab reminded him so much of himself when he was still completely self-conscious in ILSE. He wished him success almost more for himself than for the people they were actually here for. Everyone he ever knew on Earth was dead, except perhaps for Marchenko, whom no one had heard from in a long time. Supposedly he was on his way with a Grosnopf ship through the Local Cloud. People did not really concern him anymore. But this little robot did.

"Watson here. You're right. Stay in your cabin. It should be safest there."

"...Can't leave ... begin experiment?"

"Yes, please, begin. I'll try to get inside your head. Then you won't be alone. You won't feel it, but you know we're in this together. If anything goes wrong, I will try to disconnect."

"... Got it. Start... cable... now," Crab replied.

THE STORM HOWLED. AGAIN AND AGAIN, LIGHTNING FILLED the interior of the hut with a pale light. Crab had dragged himself to the exit with his last free foot. He now lay directly under the oval entrance. Here the air was calmest, and the storm also deposited the least dust here. The construction of the hut seemed to be quite solid. Apparently, recesses had been deliberately left between the sloping boards, so the wind had at least a reasonably free course. The computer, on the other hand, or whatever the function of the glowing device was, did not offer any attack surfaces to the storm due to its shape. Crab also did not recognize switches, nor any recesses or flaps. Communication seemed to take place exclusively via the cables.

"Understood. Starting to connect the cables now," he said.

Watson didn't answer, but he knew he was monitoring everything a few hundred miles above him. At least until the *Truthseeker* disappeared behind the horizon again. Crab tapped the last metal plate to the contact on his spine. The potentials were now connected, but he didn't allow any exchange yet. Sensitivity was at zero. He had to be careful.

Crab opened the gate a crack, one-tenth of a percent. Yes, there was something there. It was far away, but he heard it, smelled it, saw it, tasted it. It was as if he was standing in the cold on a frozen lake. He saw the shadows of fish swimming through the icy water far below. They were moving slowly, as if the element was giving them a special resistance.

He needed to see more clearly, so he went to a full percent. The outlines of the fish became clear, and he could distinguish their colors. They seemed to have gained strength because they were moving faster. Crab tried to identify them using the universal catalog that the engineers on Earth had embedded in his memory. But whenever he thought he had identified a particular species, it changed.

OF COURSE, THERE WERE NO FISH. HIS SOFTWARE WAS TRYING to interpret the impressions that reached him. In doing so, he relied on what he knew and was familiar with. Perhaps he was really watching balloons floating through the air. Was it a glimpse into the past of the beings who left only their corpses and this strange machine? Or was he seeing their hopes that were never fulfilled?

It was all still too indeterminate. Crab could not let himself get sucked into that world. But for now, he was just too far away. He doubled the sensitivity to two percent of maximum. The fish seemed to be getting frantic. Something was chasing them. Crab noticed a giant shadow. He was not scared because the ice layer was so thick, but the animals below him were acting downright panicky. They whipped through the water with their fins and thus attracted the attention of their pursuers all the more.

Crab tried four percent. The machine seemed to have a purpose. Was it to warn of a threat? Or was it merely a witness to the fate these creatures had suffered? The fish were now pressing their mouths against the ice from below, as if to call for help. At the same time they beat wildly with their fins. The ice turned red. Its rough surface seemed to scratch their sensitive mouths. More blood flowed, forming plumes that could be seen as gray veils in the dark water.

None of this was real. Crab talked himself down. The warning had arrived, but it was far too vague. They hadn't learned anything they didn't already know, and what was the reason? Because of the limited capacity of his control software. It could only retrieve images it knew. Watson should be in his place here. He probably possessed what humans were so proud of: imagination. Without the ability to see something completely new, he would not get anywhere here.

"You're wrong," Watson said.

Crab was relieved because the AI was still there. His sense of time was lost to him.

"You can do everything I can do," Watson added. "You just have to let it happen."

"But how?" he asked. "I'm a two-dimensional ant trying to grasp the third dimension."

"I don't understand you very well," Watson said. "You're not an ant, though. It just feels that way because you're so far away. Get closer. Dare."

"If you say so..."

"The connection... soon... horizon."

Watson was gone. Crab was alone. *Closer*, as if it were so easy. He already regretted the fish immensely. But he raised the sensitivity to eight percent. Suddenly there was a crack. A crack had formed in the ice that extended across the entire lake. Crab looked to the shore, where a fog bank tried to hide the skeletons of ancient willows. Solid ground was too far away. With one foot, he would never manage to escape the crack.

The fish, however, did not seem to have noticed any of this yet. They pushed against the ice from below. The water pressure seemed to be pushing their eyes out of their heads. They were huge and bloodshot, reminding him more of deer eyes than fish eyes. They were brown. Were there fish with brown eyes?

This was not reality. Crab must not be intimidated. He was not part of this world at all, which consisted only of electrical impulses to which his practically inclined consciousness assigned meaning. His body was not in danger, although the sound of ice breaking up still echoed in his head.

Sixteen percent. He would never know anything if he kept an unnecessary distance. This machine was not designed to kill its users. But what he saw made him suspect otherwise. Water seeped out of the crack, licking over the edge of the ice and seeming to find a taste for its dry, icy surface. Crab backed away as best he could with one free foot, but the water was fast. It flowed after him. Crab could make out fine threads in it, made of the fish's blood.

It was intentional. They wanted to make him a witness. He wanted to refuse, but he could not. How long could he hold out against the water? The shore came no closer. It was probably also intent on keeping its distance from the water. This was a strange lake. Crab looked up and recognized two moons. One was green, the other yellow, and the light they emitted was cold and hot at the same time, with a high percentage of blue.

Should he go for it? Crab suspected what would happen if he let it all happen. But he had to try. He owed it to Watson, who would surely advise him. Crab set the sensitivity to forty percent. Immediately, his feet were in the water. Except for his right front foot, he could not move them, but the lake tugged at them. The water wanted to pull him into the crack as he struggled, one-footed and increasingly desperate, toward shore.

Crab looked down. The fish were standing vertically in the water, their heads pointed at him. They no longer pressed their mouths against the ice, but powerful mouths kept snapping up from below, digging sharp teeth into their tails. The fish didn't even flinch when the enemy ripped off their flesh. They merely look at him, completely neutral, neither sad nor suffering, and certainly not happy. Look at us, they might want to say, what is happening to us is also in store for you. It was not a reproach, and by now it sounded less like a warning than a statement. A warning was only worthwhile if the catastrophe could be averted.

He was still too cowardly. He must not refuse this message. The fish would do anything to get his attention. He set sensitivity to 95 percent. The last five percent was his safety net. He didn't want to be completely absorbed in this strange world. Crab needed at least the theoretical possibility of being able to withdraw in an emergency.

Nothing happened. The fish faded away. Hard knocks penetrated his consciousness. They were the sounds of lightning striking in quick succession. The thunderstorm must be directly above him. The beat of the lightning, recognizable by the fluctuations in brightness in the cabin, almost synchronized with the flickering of the computer, on which no longer just three surfaces were flashing, but all of them.

Ouch! The last flash caused Crab physical pain. The air was so full of electricity that the insulation of his circuits was beginning to fail. Was that perhaps why the cable connection was no longer working? He measured through the wires. Two of the eight showed infinite resistance. They must be burned out. Oh no. He had failed. Watson would show understanding, but still be disappointed without telling him directly. Of course, he didn't stand a chance in this hell. He was only an inspection robot. But that was not enough for him.

Crab looked at the slumped sacks that once hovered over their own planet and entertained themselves with the help of electrical fields. The atmosphere must have resembled that created by the storm. Perhaps they landed here specifically because storms like this regularly passed through the transition zone. Perhaps the flashing of the computer did not indicate danger, but a promise, a possibility! When all the fields were flashing, the air was conductive enough to dispense with cables, which were probably a terrible compromise for the beings.

He could get into that conversation. Crab would have to do the exact opposite of what he felt like doing. He would have to allow the interference, even though it could fry his circuits like the two cables. They might be the last thoughts he was allowed to think, but they would be unheard-of thoughts that not even Watson had yet known.

Crab tried. He pressed himself against the ground to achieve good grounding—the planet had a high proportion of heavy, conductive elements—and at the same time released his internal fuses. It was like jumping off the roof of a church steeple in the middle of a storm. Crab dropped, but the wind caught him.

He flew.

Crab floated above a tropical coastal plain. A gentle current propelled him out to sea. He slowed down, sank lower, and found another current moving from the sea toward land. He crossed in a northerly direction.

Crab sank a little deeper. Below him was a field planted with long rows of poles. Fine threads fluttered on the poles. The thinner the wind pulled them, the tastier they became. Crab didn't know what they were called, but he could feel the delicious taste in the countless digestive buds spread throughout his body, which were already producing the necessary juices. He liked hovering here, not to stimulate his appetite, but because the juices tickled his fancy. He had to finish the choreography for the harvest festival by the end of the cycle, which was difficult for him because it was his twentieth anniversary.

Someone thought his name. Crab, no, that was not it. He could not be put into words. It was a friend who crossed his path, and not by chance, as she politely let on. Her thoughts came to him in a cloud. Crab thanked her, as he should, before integrating her into his own thoughts and returning the resulting patterns.

Thoughts were free. They belonged to no one. Many cycles ago they were had been considered a separate, eternal-state form of matter. Today everyone who wanted to know more exactly could read in the thoughts of the sages how it really was. Thoughts were electrical fields, and if their carrier dissolved, they ended their existence.

Crab liked the old, naive idea better. But since he himself had absorbed the thoughts of the sages, he knew that it was a beautiful illusion. He did not complain. Nobody forced him to participate in the knowledge. Every sage gave a summary of what he had to impart on request.

His name. Crab groped in the surroundings. There was the one who called him. It was clear from the beginning that the first exchange was for politeness. Now he sensed needs. It was about his presence. He should... what should he do? Participate in the expedition that had been planned for so long?

His alter ego became sad. The idyll that surrounded him was threatened. He had seen the thought images from afar himself. It took them eighty years to reach their planet. He imagined himself floating into the cabin of the space elevator and being carried all the way into orbit.

A PARTICULARLY VIOLENT SHOCK SHOOK CRAB'S BODY. HE plummeted until he realized that he was in a hut bursting with static electricity. The robot ran a diagnostic program. His body was in good condition. But metallic dust must have settled on one of the connections between the circuits. The short circuit had activated a fuse. Crab shook himself and unlocked the connection.

The egg-shaped device was still flashing all over. What he was experiencing, was this reality? It seemed more real to him than the fish under the ice. His software was not actually capable of fantasizing such vivid dreams. That suggested he had encountered memories of one of the aliens here. Hopefully, that was not all the device had stored.

Crab unlocked all the safeguards again and landed in a black abyss.

But he sensed no danger, for he was not alone. At least ten other travelers were floating with him in the observation dome. They had reached the system that sent a warning long ago. Their sky shuttle had taken up an orbit around a gas giant and was scanning the area. Crab latched onto the ship's sensors, which radiated to all rooms through a central manifold. The sphere's instruments extended the range of his own sensors. They were artificially constructed devices, but they blended in seamlessly. It was as if it grew to the size of the shuttle.

There they were. They must have been in the line of sight all along, but they were not accessible to the visual sense. The enemies. They were jet black against a black background. The cells on the visual bands spread around his hover bag could not resolve that. But the sensation of presence worked. The alien objects were interfering with the system's electromagnetic fields, and he could not block that out.

What is it? The question echoed through the room as a common thought. Shared thoughts, where it was not possible to find out who created them, were a specialty under normal circumstances and were therefore celebrated. On board the sphere, they occurred often. Perhaps it was because they were all so well synchronized here after the long flight. That was normal when one was constantly sensing everyone else's thoughts. But with the alien objects, it could also be their nature. They imposed their will. And this must not happen, even if it started with a harmless common thought.

Caution, he sent, and the others agreed. That almost became a common thought, too.

CAUTION TURNED FIRST TO APPREHENSION, THEN TO DESPAIR, as they approached the inner planets. This system had seemed to their species a perfect target for settlement because it contained three rocky planets, one of which was completely covered with water.

Had been covered. The planet was now gray-brown, just like the other two. The black objects had harvested all the moisture. A few were still in orbit. They seemed to be in the process of completely drying out the atmosphere as well. But that was not the final step. On the other two planets, the objects were scraping away the crust to extract the last bit of water from it.

It was the death of all biological life. The colony on the ocean planet no longer existed. The few survivors were able to save themselves on the ferries with which they had arrived here. But the enemy also attacked them. Perhaps the enemy was interested in the supplies in their bodies, which consisted of 92 percent water.

All that remained were the memories. Crab shared them until he could no longer bear the despair. None had a happy ending. He knew that, because they hadn't found a single survivor. He didn't need to torture himself with the memories.

We are starting, said a thought from among the wise men of the ferry. They had a purely advisory function. There were no hierarchies here. Decisions arose not because individuals got their way, but because the best thought got the most support. But of course it played a role whether a wise man thought something. Their thoughts inherently had a stronger persuasive power, fed by their status and competence.

They started. Crab held on with all twenty limbs to the struts that crisscrossed the room. He let some warm air out of his hover bag so he could lean against the comfortable bar. The shuttle picked up speed. Its destination was a spacetime disturbance halfway between the former ocean planet and its parent star. That was where the black objects came from, and only from there might they be able to prevent the enemy from eventually harvesting their home world as well.

I'm back, Watson reported. The AI didn't communicate aloud by radio, but tuned right into his thoughts. Normally, Crab would have found this invasive, but at the moment he was glad not to be alone.

They've been on the same journey as we have, Crab replied.

I can see that in your thoughts. I downloaded and quickly watched the past hour. Very impressive. You are doing very well.

Crab felt honored. He didn't say anything, because he knew Watson was reading his mind.

I didn't want to disturb you, though, Watson said. *You were almost to the wormhole.*

Crab remembered holding on because the ship was accelerating. He looked ahead, where the thin little arms hung like strings from the line. The wind was moving them as if the creature they belonged to wanted to invite someone in.

I'm going to reconnect to the machine, he said.

You were lucky I wasn't there, Watson said. *I would have tried to talk you out of it because it's too dangerous.*

The Incursion is dangerous.

CRAB RELEASED HIS CIRCUITS AGAIN AND WOKE UP CLAMPED IN a rack. He was about to retreat in fright when soothing thoughts reached him. Through someone else's eyes, he saw his hover bag rapidly lose volume until it flopped to the ground. This must have happened shortly after passing the spacetime bridge.

You had a breakdown. But we'll fix that.

He fell asleep because he had been given a strong sleeping drug.

When he woke up, he immediately felt the buoyancy of his hover bag. That was very reassuring. The sages had treated him well.

You are almost well again. Only your bag is not quite stable yet.

What does that mean?

It takes longer than usual to fill. That will last a few more weeks.

Don't feel bad, I had that once, thought an existence hovering over him, taking care of a sick person there.

She is pretty, he thought.

Thank you, she replied.

We will meet tonight. A common thought! *We should celebrate that.* Another one! Maybe the injury had its good side.

Crab floated through the ferry. His goal was the dome. He encountered images of the black objects everywhere, but he wanted to see them with his own visual strips. When he reached the dome, it was almost empty. He was a little late, because he had been stuck in the care unit for several days. One existence hovered near the panoramic window, while another had squeezed into a corner against the back wall. He was almost alone with his thoughts, which felt unusual on the cramped ferry, but was just fine with him.

He let himself drift forward to the window by letting out some air. A tiny impulse was all it took. That was the beauty of weightlessness. With the contents of his hover bag, he could drift through the aisles for weeks, even though it was only half inflated. That was mandatory in zero gravity because it saved a lot of space.

The view of his visual strip fell on the black objects. The image slowly built up. Crab had to rotate once around his axis to include the complete strip. But this gave the image a higher resolution than it would have without the rotation. The cuboids were quite small in this rendering. They merely populated the area between the second and third planets, counted from the star.

Crab peeked out. The disk clearly dampened the field emanating from him, but he could still pick up some of the chaos out there. The sun emitted a violent wind of charged particles that created swirling currents. Frozen magnetic vortices also passed through again and again. The vacuum out there was almost as densely filled with energy as the atmosphere of his home planet. But completely different mechanisms were at work here.

He felt nothing of the black cuboids. They were too far away. The shuttle had taken up an orbit around the large rocky planet at the inner end of the ring populated by the numerous objects.

They are alive. Crab turned around. The thought came from one of the other two existences, but since it was abandoned, he could not reconstruct the origin. That was actually considered rude. But Crab was understanding. He also didn't always want to start a conversation right away, when a brief thought was enough. So they were alive. You couldn't tell by looking at them. Their artificial nature was clear. Such objects could not arise through evolution.

That means that they are controlled from the planet. Ah, the thought came from the existence floating beside him in front of the disk. It made itself known by approaching.

I'd like to know more, he thought, then dismissed the thought.

The shuttle's magnetic sensors picked up the signals as we flew through the belt, and they followed them to this planet.

And now?

We're sending an expedition down.

Crab felt in the direction of the planet. Of course, he was not strong enough. They had the sensors of the sphere for that.

But isn't the planet much too big to land on? he asked.

We can land. We just can't leave it.

IN THE EVENING IT TURNED OUT THAT THE PLANS OF THE sages were even more extensive than suspected. The shuttle would investigate the central star of the system, which had some peculiarities. Meanwhile, in order not to lose time, a small delegation of four or five existences would land on the rocky planet. It was to establish connection with the place that communicated with the small cuboids. The assumption of the sages was that the giant cuboids terrorizing the systems at the other end of the wormhole were also controlled from there.

The existence with which he had communicated offered itself.

I'm in too, Crab thought.

The oldest of the sages was next, and the last two seats were quickly filled as well.

Since the ferry was to travel to the central star as quickly as possible, the delegation must immediately board an emergency ferry. They packed tools and food for three years and said goodbye to the others. It was an emotional moment because once the ferry departed, they could only exchange thoughts awkwardly by radio. Whenever something like this was about to happen, there was a small ceremony that released them from the circle of harmony.

Now they were completely on their own. On the journey to the surface, Crab held on to the twenty arms of his new friend. It felt like they had known each other forever. And they had, after all, as they had shared their thoughts in the cramped shuttle for years. But it was still something else to consciously engage with another being's thoughts.

ON THE PLANET THEY NEEDED FOUR DAYS TO SET UP SEVERAL shelters. During this time, they preferred to stay in the small emergency ferry, because only in it was the atmosphere prepared so that they could exchange their thoughts directly.

As soon as they left the shuttle, they must use auxiliary means. The air of the alien planet was dense enough to float in, but because it contained hardly any free charge carriers, Crab felt as if he was half blind. In addition, his visual strips produced only very pixelated images in the semi-darkness.

Out of necessity, he learned to rely on his sense of sight, which functioned only to a limited extent. It could be surprisingly exciting to discuss things with each other without being able to read each other's thoughts. At the beginning, Crab could hardly avoid laughing because his girlfriend kept surprising him with arguments. This was a joy he had never known before. But there were also numerous misunderstandings because it was so difficult to present facts in such a way that they reached the recipient exactly as they were meant by the sender.

Their stay on the planet had three twists and turns that got to Crab. First, his girlfriend was assigned to scour the planet for more sources. The problem was that the original location was probably incorrect. Where they built the shelters, there was never a signal station from which to navigate the cuboids in the belt.

They would have to move, but where? That was what his girlfriend was supposed to find out. In fact, she managed to find another contact point. Only there was no presence there either. This was repeated several times, until his girlfriend made a last attempt to find an alleged contact point near the North Pole. The emergency ferry never returned from that flight.

Crab was immensely sad. The others shared his thoughts, but it still took him three days to function in everyday life again. He would never be rid of the sadness.

Apparently, their journey was not made under a favorable star, because bad news also came from the main shuttle. The system's parent star appeared to be on the verge of imploding. The crew discovered that it was running out of fuel. That was not unusual for a star of this size. The only odd thing was that it hadn't happened much sooner.

But it didn't stop there. First, the shuttle's sensors found deviations in the star's magnetic field—or rather, no deviations. It was unusually constant for a dying star of this size. It was enough to create a massive solar wind, but the variations over time were minimal.

The sages suggested studying the phenomenon at closer range. The ship was transmitting data to the station on the second planet when suddenly the connection broke.

It was Crab who was hovering in front of the receiving device at that moment. He had connected to the computer's memory via cable. The machine knew no emotions. It simply shared the facts with him. At that moment, it did Crab good. He tried to prolong it by analyzing the data sent by the shuttle. It quickly became apparent that there could be only one explanation for the strange behavior of the magnetic field: There must be a construction surrounding the entire star. *Were its builders trying to draw energy from the dying star?*

That would be foolhardy. The thought had become detached from his colleagues and now floated between them without an owner, until Crab seized it and made it his. The thought returned the favor by turning into its opposite as if by itself.

They tried to supply it with energy.

Crab released the thought as a test. As hoped, it found an anchor.

That's it. They tried to stop the implosion, added another existence.

By adding fuel, a third thought. *The fuel they stole from other solar systems.*

The thought had turned into a theory that belonged to them all. Crab felt something like joy, even though they would never be able to verify the theory.

For their shuttle had just been destroyed.

This thought also hovered in the primitive shelter. No one wanted it. Crab turned away, imagining his hover bag catching fire and him crashing to the ground.

"Crab?" asked Watson.

It was a relief to hear the AI's voice. He must have just come back into radio range. How long had he been gone? Crab felt like he hadn't spoken to Watson in weeks.

"Yeah, I'm here," he replied.

"That was about ten minutes," Watson said. "I was with you the whole time. But now the *Truthseeker* is disappearing just over the horizon."

"Thanks for the warning."

"You could wait for me," Watson said. "It seems to me that the experiment is taking a lot out of you."

"No, I don't have any emotions about it," Crab said, knowing immediately that it was a lie and that Watson knew it too.

It was strange. He did not have an emotion module. After all, he was just an inspection robot. He should not be sad when a meteorite hit the ship, he should be repairing the damage. But the transmissions really got to him. Perhaps because these alien beings thought in such a surprisingly comprehensible way. Shouldn't one assume they would be hard to understand? Or was it because his primitive software ended up viewing everything through an earthly lens?

"There's no hurry, Crab. Take a break."

"If the storm dies down, I may not be able to get a connection to the Floaters' device."

"Maybe we can get the cable..."

The connection broke, just as Watson predicted. Crab was alone again. Maybe he should wait after all.

DURING A HEAVY STORM, CRAB HOVERED MOTIONLESS IN front of the communicator. The device was already blinking in various places. That was a good sign. Maybe such a day would come again, when they could share their thoughts without any tools. It would be a festive day. Crab never thought he would miss this ability so much. He held on with some of his arms as a strong gust blew into the shelter. Immediately, his skin tingled. So many carriers! The air was perfect, almost like home.

Crab turned around. In this neutral atmosphere, he had to use his visual strip to find out if he was alone. In fact, no one was with him. The others had probably retreated to the shelters. He remembered that someone was looking forward to a sand shower. Since they had to use the cables to communicate, they exchanged far fewer thoughts with each other.

Actually, he should stay with the machine, because he was on duty. But what sense did these habits make anymore? The shuttle had disappeared. There was no trace of those who might be piloting the black objects. But the gust of wind gave him a better idea. It smelled like there was as much energy in the air outside as there was at home. It was seductive.

He tested the air pressure by letting go of the bar. Immediately, he was propelled up to the ceiling of the cabin. Crab let off some gas and floated back to the ground. Another gust of wind, crackling with energy. A flash of lightning followed. The machine flashed all over, indicating how conductive the air was. He didn't need to be afraid of the lightning bolts. They found their way even without him. The wind was blowing hard, but that was not a problem. Relative to the layers of air around him, he was always at rest. He only needed to find a level that would bring him back to his starting point.

Navigation was somewhat of a problem. He could orient himself by the magnetic lines of the planet. The field was even stronger than on the home world, but he had no experience with it yet. Crab was a quick learner, or he wouldn't have been invited on this mission. How was the home world doing? Had the enemy reached it yet?

Crab became angry. Normally he refrained from doing so, because it burdened the others, but since they could only communicate via the cables, he allowed himself unpleasant emotions more often. This had a strangely liberating effect, but unfortunately only for a moment. Later, aftershocks always followed, and he felt worse than before. But how could he not get angry when he imagined the senseless destruction?

They devastated hundreds of planets just to prevent the supernova death of a star that nobody needed anymore. Crab only now really understood it. They started doing this sometime back when there was a civilization here. That must have been eons ago, looking at the planet and the other stellar corpses of this local cloud. And now they could not bring themselves to stop. They were feeding the supernova monster, which became heavier and heavier and needed more and more food. Whenever the black fleet brought supplies, the star got a reprieve, but the deadline got shorter each time, and the catastrophe at the end would be all the more enormous.

Already the star was a giant among giants. The construction around its core helped to keep it stable, but if at some point the monster's gravity was stronger for even a second than the backpressure built up by the heat inside, the star would collapse into a black hole. It would throw off its shell in a gigantic explosion, which would probably be visible even from the home world.

But then nobody would be alive to give testimony. How could he not get angry about that? And sad. And upset. Crab was startled because a gust of wind from outside had pushed him against the wall. The memory came at the right moment. He pushed off so that his hover bag moved outside through the oval opening in the shelter.

"Watson? You've got to see this," Crab said.

For a moment, he really did feel like he was floating. It was at least as seductive to him as it was to the being whose experiences he sensed. But was this a past reality? Or was the machine he was communicating with generating some kind of dream? So far, everything had felt very real.

"Watson? What do you think?"

No response. Maybe he should have waited until the *Truthseeker* came back out of the radio shadow. But he was so curious. Now, however, he was concerned that the hovering creature might be embarking on a journey of no return.

Surely a biological life form that floated with the help of its balloon-shaped body could not possibly survive in the hell out there? If a bolt of lightning were to strike his robotic body, that would be instant death for him.

And what if the creature took off without him? Crab didn't yet understand how the machine worked. What he experienced was either recordings or simulations. But he had no control over them. He could not rewind or stop them. The perception of time also did not seem to be aligned with real time; otherwise he would hardly have been able to experience weeks of time in hours, after all.

"Watson?" he tried again.

The *Truthseeker* didn't answer. Crab couldn't wait any longer. Who knew how long the storm would last? Even if the hovering creature he fantasized about didn't return, his robotic body would remain here, after all. He would be able to report to Watson what he had experienced. He released his electrodes for the connection again. The earthly robot transformed into a hovering creature on a world that was alien to both of them and that held them both without mercy.

HE WAS FLOATING. IT WAS AN INCOMPARABLE LIGHTNESS. CRAB had experience with weightlessness, but it was not the same. In microgravity, there were no directions and no pressure. He had never felt quite comfortable in it, so disconnected from the world around him. Balanced levitation, on the other hand, was a constant exchange with its surroundings. The air pressure that provided its buoyancy was constantly changing. He could counteract it by changing his volume, or he could allow himself to surrender. Both were pleasant, because he kept himself in balance all the time. He felt the world around him and was more connected to it than if he squatted on the ground and surrendered to gravity.

Floating was wonderful. Why didn't they take trips more often? Even now, with rapid downdrafts and updrafts shuttling him between different layers, it was a rest for his muscles, cramped from constantly fighting gravity. The storm led him in a huge circle. It was an anticyclone. Due to the high air pressure, he could keep his hovering bag completely relaxed, even if he was transported to higher layers for a few moments. He didn't have to worry about navigation either, because he was just circling the place where they set up the shelters.

Crab turned. He wanted to get a good view of the sea lines. The picture that slowly came together was impressive. He saw steep mountains of cloud roaming around a central valley like a herd of stampeding ducks, a vortex that stretched almost to the ground. The clouds were multicolored, probably due to the high component of heavy elements in the air, and stood out clearly against the background.

It sank downward. The planet did not have real mountains. Crab already knew that, but now he felt it. The surface was as smooth as soup, quietly simmering away. Smaller volcanoes erupted like bubbles, transporting energy from the interior to the surface. One thing was clear: this planet must already have at least one catastrophe behind it. At some point, its star must have enveloped it in gas millions of degrees hot, melting the entire surface. Maybe that was the moment the builders of the black cuboids wanted to prevent. They obviously failed. But the mechanism they built still worked to this day.

It would be cruel, if it really happened that way. Thousands of fertile planets would have died, completely in vain. How could such a thing happen to the builders of the cuboids? Shouldn't they have taken precautions in case they themselves were wiped out?

Crab drifted toward the whirlpool that formed the core of the storm. It was no more dangerous here than further out. It might be moving faster and faster relative to the surface, but relative to the dense air around it, he was stationary. He was just an ornament, not part of the system. As he pumped more gas into his suspended bag, he rose until a cross-current caught him, carrying him out of the vortex.

But it was not there yet. Crab was targeting the buildup of electrical energy that the rapid friction of different layers of air against each other created, especially in the center of the storm. He saw it with his visual strips, which registered countless flashes of lightning, but he also scented it with his electrical sense. When he turned off the visual strips, he perceived them like a beating heart that filled the storm with life.

A little deeper in. Crab reduced the volume of his hover bag. The circles he made became tighter. Gradually, he started feeling the mechanical forces involved. Pressure built up on his hover bag, pushing it outward. It was a little uncomfortable. Almost like being in the launching ferry, only far less violent. Crab suppressed the sensation because he had not quite reached the center of the electrical charges yet.

But now. He felt out into the storm, expecting to become the storm. That was what he was after—to expand his consciousness to the whole storm, to let the air handle his impulses. What was a storm but a fertile bed for thoughts and their physical form, the electrical impulse? Crab wanted to merge with the swirling masses of air, wanted to transform them into a part of himself.

But he failed miserably.

The storm fought back. At first, Crab didn't understand what exactly had happened or was happening. Why couldn't his thoughts extend to the far reaches as they could on his home world? Everything he needed was there, even if the circumstances were unusual. It didn't storm as hard at home as it did here, but he was used to the tickling discharges on his skin. He was born with this feeling. When his mother released him from her suspended bag, she communicated her love to him about it as he sank to the ground to dig his roots into the fertile earth. Communicated, yes, he kept the thought, although he never met his mother again. It was an unchangeable fact that she loved him, and it would always remain so.

A blow jolted him out of his memories. What was that? His position had not changed. Crab felt around himself until he realized that no physical blow had hit him. The collision had happened on another level. He was not alone. There was someone, another existence, and it was no one he knew. A stranger. In a quick impulse, Crab pulled his thoughts together to protect himself.

Apology. Reassurance.

This time the thoughts didn't come abruptly, but floated gently in from outside.

I am startled. It hurt. Who are you?

Crab formulated his thoughts as he was accustomed to doing. But when he traced them, they had changed.

Surprise. Pain. Question.

That was not exactly what he meant. Crab knew this phenomenon. It occurred when one of the communication partners was too attached to his thoughts and did not release them. Like he was right now, because he wanted to protect himself against the stranger.

Disclosure. Identity. Reassurance.

It would not work this way. If he refused to communicate, he could not perceive his counterpart properly either. He only understood the concepts behind the thoughts, but not their content. Crab was afraid of this because it made him feel defenseless and naked. He didn't want to face a stranger like that.

But he had to.

He owed it to the expedition that was lost in the sun, and to the colony world that had perished, and to the homeland that was about to perish.

I am, he thought, and released his identity.

No one needed names in such a conversation. The other person now had a clear view of his very self, and it was unmistakable.

I am, answered the stranger.

Crab felt her scanning him. She did not read his thoughts. That would only be possible if she could classify and calibrate everything. That is, if she were a hovering creature or possessed an interlector. But she saw his pictures and felt his feelings. Crab stopped watching her do this and instead took the opportunity to explore her herself.

The stranger was huge. She was far more than this storm. She had thoughts that reached far into the early days of the universe. They were thoughts full of joy, love and pain, birth and death. Crab would need weeks, years, whole cycles to explore her completely. He had mistakenly called her 'the stranger' at first. She was a mother, yes, and she reminded him of his own despite her monstrous dimensions. She was not a stranger. He was a stranger here. He did not belong here. She did. And she had always been here.

You are right.

The thought fluttered around him. Crab caught it.

We are the builders.

It was a short thought, but it weighed so heavily that Crab almost lost it. The weight was given to it by its counterpart, and it was intentional. She... was ashamed of it.

You can call us Shamari.

This thought was easier. He gave her pause. Crab wouldn't have needed a name, but now that he knew it, it felt complete.

Just you, or more?

It does not matter. It is the same.

He waited, but the Shamari did not reveal another thought. She waited for him to ask. That was polite. Not every existence wanted to know everything. Unwanted thoughts were a burden.

Why?

That was the question of questions. Why did they start this cycle that brought death upon the universe beyond their annihilation?

We were the first. We wanted to protect you.

What? Crab pushed the thought away and pulled up the images of the Shamari destroying the colony planet.

Shock. Grief.

Concepts. The Shamari had apparently walled itself off. She did not want to hear the cries of the dying.

I'm sorry. We saved hundreds of civilizations. We are talking about a time billions of years ago.

Explain.

He had to give her a chance. The pain in her thoughts was real.

Our sun is a giant star. It burned brightly and provided our planet with everything we needed. The Shamari gained intelligence and matured into a spacefaring species. Millions of years later, others followed us. We supported them. But then our sun aged. Giant stars age early, and when they pass away, it is a spectacular finale.

I know the life cycle of stars. What are you trying to tell me, Shamari?

Have you looked at this star-forming region where we were born? The stars are much denser here than elsewhere. If our star had gone supernova, all civilizations in the vicinity would have been destroyed. We've done the math. There were thirty-six of them. They were young and did not have the means to relocate to a safe distance. We were old, but even we could not find new homes for that many creatures in the time remaining. Space travel is slow. Even light is slow when you are in as much of a hurry as we were.

Crab had to agree with her. A supernova so close would also be fatal to life on his home planet.

Thank you for understanding me. We had the means to keep our sun from collapsing. It was collapsing because it ran out of fuel. So we built a fleet of autonomous units and sent them out to pasture to bring us new fuel.

That sounds so harmless. You sterilized thousands of worlds! Crab could not avoid including reproach in his thoughts. But this time the Shamari did not protect herself.

We sent the fleet via wormholes to distant parts of the galaxy, far from its core. At the time I am talking about, no life had developed there at all. It spread only later into the spiral arms. Some Shamari even thought that intelligent life would never develop out there. How can life acquire true intelligence if all possible interlocutors are much too far away? Intelligence arises from exchange. That was what we thought. Today we know better.

Then you must stop the harvest! He had not uttered a thought that expressed such energy for a long time, not even on the home world.

We have tried. We try again every cycle when the units come from the harvest to discharge at the star.

But they had not been successful. The Shamari omitted this thought. It was too obvious.

Why don't they listen to you anymore? Crab thought.

The units are autonomous, but they have no real intelligence. They behave like herd animals, following their course between stable and pasture. They know their stable. The pasture they look for themselves, depending on where the universe seems juiciest to them.

That explains their behavior, but not your inability to control them.

Every flock has a shepherd. That was an institution on this planet. On our planet, our home.

Was? Slowly, they seemed to be getting to the heart of the story.

Half a billion years ago, another civilization managed to beat back the attack of the herd. They caught up with us in ways we didn't think possible. Huge mushroom ships destroyed part of the herd. The rest retreated here.

Then the others did your job for you.

The amount of fuel brought by the herd was not enough to stop the collapse of the star. We quickly replenished the herd and sent it out again, but it was too late. We even built another sphere around the core to prevent the worst from happening, but the star still threw off part of its shell. In the process, it destroyed our home. The planet completely melted, and the shepherd was destroyed.

And you couldn't replace it? You are a billion-year-old civilization and you couldn't replace a simple remote control?

The shepherd was this planet in its entirety. The herd was imprinted on him. The units are not machines. They are designed by us, but they live. So they do their job without us having to monitor them. They are peaceful. They only attack when you try to stop them from doing their job.

So there is no way to stop them?

It didn't matter at all why all this was happening. The only important question was whether the solar system could still be saved.

We don't know a way. We are still this planet, but you see for your-self what it has become. We even tried to destroy the herd, but it gives birth to offspring. The whole belt is full of them. The herd is growing, not shrinking. We had so much time, but there is no solution in sight.

These were not the thoughts he was hoping for. The home world was lost.

We are infinitely sorry.

He pushed the thought aside. What good was pity to them?

We can provide you with knowledge. So your civilization can flourish in another place.

To be haunted by the herd there someday, too? Besides, there were not that many planets that offered the right conditions. They needed a rocky world with as dense an atmosphere as possible. But even if they found a new home planet, they could not leave this planet.

You could send the knowledge to your home planet by radio.

We got here through a wormhole. We are probably thousands of light years from home. It will be destroyed in a few hundred years. By the time our message reaches them, it will be too late.

The Shamari did not think anymore. She must know that it was too late for pity. Crab had no intention of taking away even a part of her guilt. The peaceful herd was responsible for the destruction of so many planets. He expected more than an "I'm sorry."

But that was all the Shamari could give him.

"WATSON HERE. WE CAN GET STARTED."

"There's no need for that now," Crab replied. "You're too late."

"Why? Has the energy density gone down again? Maybe you can fix the cable connection. You have to. We need to know everything these hover creatures experienced. Maybe they knew the solution but couldn't implement it because they were trapped on the planet like you."

Crab didn't answer. How could he best tell Watson?

"Sorry, that was thoughtless. I'm sorry," Watson said. "I appreciate you taking this risk for humanity."

"Watson, there is no rescue. We have failed just as our predecessors failed. The builders of the Incursion objects lost control of them long ago, and do you know why? Because an intervention by the civilization that left the Residuals behind caused their home planet to be damaged."

"I can't believe that. There must be some solution."

"No, there is no solution. I'm sorry."

Shamari kept saying that, too, to no avail. Crab released the memory area where he stored his experiences.

"It's best if you look at it yourself," Crab said.

"Thanks. I'll get right to it. I'll use the fast forward."

Truthseeker, July 3, 2415

WATSON DID NOT CHECK IN AFTER FIVE MINUTES, OR TEN, OR three hours, or eight. He needed a whole day to look at the data collected by Crab, again and again.

But he could find no gap in it. What the Shamari had said fit with what they had learned elsewhere. There was an artificial shell around the core of the sun. The planet had been melted several times. Even the mushroom ships had met them. As big as the universe was, everything was connected to everything else. A small intervention here, however well-intentioned, could have tremendous consequences on the other side of space.

Why hadn't the Growths themselves looked into what was going on behind the wormhole? Did an AI from Earth really have to come up with that simple idea, billions of years after the damned herd was sent out to pasture for the first time? And why didn't those stupid Shamari build anything into their design that would make those killer sheep behave?

It was beyond belief. Watson remembered flying toward the wormhole. It was a damn close call. At the time, he didn't think much of his prospects. Against a fleet of the Incursion objects, the *Truthseeker* would have had no chance. But they were able to make contact. These Shamari would have immediately fulfilled his wish to recall the Incursion—but they were unable to do so. One was allowed to be annoyed, right?

However, there was one here who was innocent of the messy situation: Crab. He had left him alone on the surface for far too long.

"CRAB?"

"Ah, Watson. It's good to hear from you."

The robot was really waiting for him to make contact. It was touching, especially when he considered that Crab was just a normal inspection robot not long ago. He reminded Watson more and more of his former self. Could it be that he was trying to be for Crab what Marchenko had been for him? But that was not right. The premises were different. Crab had never expressed a desire to become more than he was. He would probably be better off if he had remained a simple inspection robot. Then again, he wouldn't have been able to connect with the alien machine so successfully.

"I'm pleased, too," Watson said.

"Did you find something I missed?"

Hope could be heard in Crab's question, but he had to dash it.

"No, the Shamari are right. Or do you say 'the Shamari is right'? Do you know?"

Perhaps the truth was more digestible when served in a subordinate clause.

"Both are possible, singular or plural."

Crab sounded surprisingly chipper given his situation. Watson also had to teach him that he was about to leave him. How would he take that? Surely Watson couldn't stay in this system until the end of time. At some point, the *Truthseeker* would run out of power. By the time their computers stopped working, at the latest, he would have to be back on the holo level. Otherwise, his existence would end, and Watson felt far too young for that.

"Ah, I see," he said. "Then I prefer the Shamari, I think. What's the storm doing, and what does the alien device say?"

"The interlector," Crab explained. "It adjusts our imaginary worlds so that we can understand each other. The device is now merely flashing two fields, as it did when I arrived. The storm has abated. I could safely leave the cabin again now if I was able to."

They would have to find a solution for that, too, before he took his final leave. If Crab was stuck on this planet, he should at least be able to move freely.

"Then maybe it was all fantasy," Watson asked, "and there is a solution after all?"

"No, the facts remain in the process," said Crab. "We won't find a loophole there."

"There?"

That was one of those answers that already contained the next question as a spoiler. Watson was impressed. Just a week ago, Crab was incapable of formulating such sentences.

"I may have found an approach we could use to prevent the herd from grazing the next worlds."

"That would be great," Watson said. "What is it?"

"I'm not sure it's helpful. But the Shamari also briefly mentioned the numerous small objects in the belt. Whenever large Incursion objects are damaged, offspring grow out of the belt."

"I don't yet understand how that could help us."

"The Shamari always emphasized that the Incursion objects are not machines, but behave like a herd. I have tried to do research on animal herds on Earth. Unfortunately, I didn't find much, but I did notice one commonality."

"Now I'm curious," Watson said.

"In herds, they protect their offspring. That's one of the most important functions of a herd. Among all the adult specimens, the young are safer than if a mother were alone with her offspring."

"Unfortunately, I still don't understand how that can help us."

"I imagine Incursion objects threatening the solar system. The humans fight back as best they can. A brief war ensues in which humanity is annihilated."

"That's a realistic scenario that may even be in the process of being implemented."

"At that very moment, thousands of small cuboids appear out of nowhere, that is, via the wormhole. They're flooding the battlefield. What will happen?"

"Crab, that's brilliant! If you're right, the Incursion will cease fire so as not to endanger their offspring."

"In fact, I suspect they will all pull out together. After all, there is a great danger that humanity's warships will primarily go after the small opponents and take out a larger number of them. They don't stand a chance against the giants, but a single nuclear torpedo should be enough to take out one of the small cuboids."

"That would be a good solution," Watson said. "It wouldn't be perfect, because the Incursion would still be a threat after that. But humanity would have bought time. With a few thousand years of preparation, perhaps it could build a fleet similar to the Growths in LDN 63."

"I must correct you there, Watson, if I may. If the herd hasn't gathered enough fuel by the time it returns, and that should definitely be the case this time, the star will collapse for good. I'm sure you can also calculate how long the time will be that mankind will have to bridge."

Crab was right. After all, the Shamari described how exactly that had happened a long time ago. Now there would be no one left to stop the supernova. But what did that mean for the civilizations that might have settled in the immediate vicinity? Didn't they have to take them into consideration, too?

Watson first pulled the star's known data into memory and simulated its remaining years of life. It could be anywhere from eight hundred to a thousand. That was a foreseeable time. The Incursion was not likely to return to Earth that quickly—if at all. Then he scanned the surrounding solar systems. As he had already noticed on arrival, most of the stars were already extinct or had shrunk to white holes. None of the early civilizations could have survived that.

However, new life could have arisen long ago, whether in the orbit of a white dwarf or a black hole. It was impossible to locate those potential worlds from the *Truthseeker*. Did that mean they were morally obligated to keep the giant star alive, even though it should have exploded long ago? Watson tallied the probabilities. The risk of life being destroyed in a supernova was seven percent. That a civilization was affected, however, had only a 0.1 percent probability.

It would be his decision. But why? He could ask Crab. Then at least he wouldn't have to carry the burden alone.

Suddenly it struck him: The solution had a big catch to it. How were they supposed to induce the offspring to go to the wormhole and then emerge among the Incursions? Crab must have something in mind.

"Will you please tell me how we're going to convince the offspring of our plan?"

"When we flew into the system, you tested the belt's reaction to our approach. There was an evasive maneuver orchestrated from the planet. You tracked the signal yourself. Apparently, they are definitely still in control of the offspring."

"They, the Shamari?" asked Watson.

"That's right," said Crab.

"Then you'll have to make contact with them again."

"That could be the weakness in our plan. I haven't had any contact with them at all."

"But you have been in contact with them..." Watson began, only to realize his mistake.

No, Crab had witnessed what a hovering creature had experienced with the Shamari. It was not a direct contact, but merely a recording, who knew how old. Perhaps the Shamari had long since moved on.

"Yeah, a bit of a problem," Crab said.

"What if they've long since moved on?" asked Watson.

"The bodies of the hover creatures don't look like they're more than a hundred years old."

Crab was hardly in a position to judge. If they were not from this planet, they might not decompose at all because the local microbiome could not do anything with them. But he didn't want to take away his hope.

"Do you think the Shamari are still around?" he asked instead.

He could use a little hope right now, too.

"Yes, from what I've seen, I imagine there's a good chance. The last Incursion must have already been underway when the hover creatures arrived here. So the Shamari will certainly wait here until the herd returns. After all, they must expect to have to somehow stabilize the star with the water the herd will bring."

Or they gave up on the star and got themselves to safety. But no matter.

"We need to make contact with them," Watson said.

"To do that, I think I should go outside," Crab said. "The interlector won't help me with that."

"But didn't you say the storm had died down?"

It wasn't until the electricity of the thunderstorm was in the air that the contact had worked.

"That's right," Crab said. "We'll have to wait for another storm."

"But you still can't leave the cabin," Watson said.

"You're right about that, I'm afraid. I have no idea how to solve that problem either."

Bangkok, July 3, 2415

THEY DIDN'T MAKE IT. FIRST, ALL THE TRAINS HAD BEEN crowded, and neither she nor Lan was strong enough to stand up to mothers trying to get their children to safety, or to young men desperately fighting for their lives.

Hand in hand, they marched home. They came from the brand new, Chinese-built main train station, where they had been told that no trains would run for the next few days. The official word was that China was now using its express trains only within the country. However, it was more likely that the country had effectively closed its borders, just as the Arabian nation and every other country with significant deserts had already done.

Suddenly, everyone really wanted to go to the desert. Joanna wasn't so sure that was a good idea anymore. Supposedly, 24 million people had set out from China alone. How were they supposed to provide themselves with the bare necessities in a desert? But Lan didn't let that stop her. She still feared the water, because that was where the Incursion would attack, they said.

For all they knew, there was a good reason for that. But the desert could not be the solution. Joanna had decided to plan only for the short term. Here in Bangkok, which still had not emptied because of the influx from the south, they would at any rate survive the coming week better than in any desert. Water and electricity came reliably from the wall.

Joanna took her girlfriend's hand, but Lan withdrew it.

"We should have left on the 30th," Lan said. "If we'd gone to the train station instead of bed, we would have crossed the border into China long ago."

Maybe she was right. But Joanna still didn't regret that they had gotten carried away with the mood. It was good and right. She hadn't seen Lan so liberated in a long time, and she doubted that would ever be the case again. Because by now the black cubes were already hanging in the sky. They had spread all over the earth. They had even been spotted over desert areas, although they were supposedly not interested in them. Yesterday a scientist explained it on TV: The earth was apparently quite wet even in its driest areas.

However, this did not cause people to start heading home. They were simply settling into the hope that brought them to the desert against all odds.

"It's no better in China than it is here," Joanna said.

"I don't want to die, don't you understand?" asked Lan.

Joanna nodded as they walked side by side. Her girlfriend always said that, as if it was enough to justify her illogical behavior. She herself had no desire to be roasted by the laser of an alien spaceship. But what alternative did she have? The powerful would hide in their underground bunkers. Joanna hoped they would fulfill the predictions of science, which foretold death from lack of water for the survivors of the immediate attack.

"I don't want you to die either," Joanna said.

"Then make sure we get to China."

Joanna took Lan's hand once more. Her girlfriend didn't grasp it in return, but she didn't resist, either. Slowly, Lan's fingers nestled around hers.

"I can't," she said, "but if I could, and you were guaranteed to survive, I'd give my life for it."

She heard a muffled bang, as if from a lone firecracker. Suddenly, everyone around her stopped and looked up.

Joanna also stopped and raised her head. A firework, surely! But what fell to earth in several pieces looked much bigger than the remains of a New Year's Eve rocket. People were talking to each other in many languages. Joanna didn't understand anything until a scrap of English reached her ear.

"The defense stations. They're attacking the defense stations!"

Joanna suddenly felt cold despite the heat. She took her friend's hand.

"Come on, let's go home."

Lan didn't answer, but followed her.

They were all going to die. Hopefully it would at least be quick.

World Root, July 3, 2415

"Here we go," said Jürgen.

They were observing the Earth from an orbit around Luna. The moon provided them with at least temporary cover. The Incursion had spread around the globe in various near-Earth orbits. Celia looked at the pattern. It was laid out as cleverly as a fleet of satellites—just about any square meter of Earth could be hit from one of the cuboids at any time.

"Do you think they're going to lay waste to everything first?" asked Jürgen.

"That would be inefficient," Alexa said in Celia's place. "They don't have to be afraid of the humans' ground-based weapons."

"An invasion without an invasion," Jaron said.

"Yes, you could also say they go as easy on you as possible," Jürgen said. "They only destroy what's in their way."

"They're machines. Like the Enceladus being said," Alexa said. "Efficient machines. They're not evil. They only care about the outcome."

"Stupidly, we can't get along without the water," Celia said.

"Maybe they don't know that. Life on Earth is still young," Alexa said.

"But they don't care either," said Siri. "Like the Spanish back in the Americas. They just wanted the gold."

Suddenly, small fires erupted in Earth's orbit. A chain of silent explosions stretched 35,000 kilometers around the globe.

"Those were the defense stations," Jürgen said.

"We're ready," Sardi reported.

The *Sword of God* was orbiting in close proximity, so it was covered by the massive umbrella of the World Root.

"We're still waiting," Celia said.

The sun had only one shot. They needed to lure as many Incursion objects as possible to the target area. Since the eruption would then hit Earth's surface, they had chosen the central Pacific. What fell there would cause the least collateral damage. For the shot to be zenithal, it had best hit Earth at midday.

"Energy storage at one hundred percent," explained the World Root.

"Ten minutes to go," said Alexa.

THE MINUTES TICKED BY. THIRTY SECONDS BEFORE THE launch signal, Alexa counted down loudly. When it reached zero, the World Root reported in.

"Signal sent."

Now a laser pulse was on its way to the ancient station in solar orbit. It would take eight minutes to get there. After that, the station would release the stored energy.

Hopefully.

Celia strapped herself in and slid her hands under her thighs. This had to work. The World Root had refused to give any guarantees. But it could give no reason why the station would refuse, either. After all, it didn't object to caching the energy.

"And if it doesn't work?" asked Maurice.

"Then we'll try to destroy at least one more Incursion,"

Jaron said. "Maybe then at least some water will be preserved."

"I don't think so," said Jürgen. "The others will get that."

"Wouldn't it be better if we hid, so we could help the survivors later?" asked Maurice.

"We've already talked about that," said Jaron.

"I've simulated it," Alexa said. "With an attack, we have a twelve percent chance of saving about five percent of humanity. The alternative, hiding, delivers a ninety percent chance of coming to the aid of the surviving 0.001 percent of humanity."

"You expect that only one in a thousand will be left?"

"That's an optimistic estimate, Maurice."

"Besides, we can't just stand by and not fight back at all," Jürgen said.

"They're coming in for a landing," said Jürgen.

Now things were really starting to happen.

"How long until the plasma burst arrives?" asked Sardi over the radio.

"Fourteen hours," Celia said.

"Can't it be accelerated?"

"No, the plasma cloud is on its way and will take its time."

"I hope the cuboids don't realize what's coming," Jürgen said.

"If they're hard-coded machines, and we assume they are, they won't be watching the sun all the time," Celia said.

Hopefully, she was right. If she just told herself often enough, maybe it would work.

"They've dealt with a weapon like this before," said the World Root. "In LDN 63 and in the earlier traps we built for them. They didn't adjust their behavior."

"They didn't need to," said the exobiologist. "They continued to succeed, on an individual level."

"We always destroyed more than half of them."

"Yes, but the ones that returned were successful. Did it ever occur to you that you are breeding the plague yourselves with your trap building? You live in unconscious symbiosis with them."

That was an interesting way of looking at it. The exobiologist might be right. Without attractants, there was no trap.

"I will examine this thought and, if necessary, pass it on to the Growths," said the World Root.

"A wise thought, Maurice," Celia said.

Unfortunately, it would no longer help them. But if future victims were served by it, that would be some consolation.

THE CUBOIDS APPROACHED THE EARTH'S SURFACE AT A RAPID pace. What happened there could not be seen in the holo. Sand, dust and water swirled up, so high and dense that no camera on Earth could provide better images. The cuboids always touched down in deserted areas, two-thirds over the sea and one-third over land. They did not spare deserts either, but kept their distance from the people who had sought shelter there.

At least as far as it was possible. Extensive property damage and human victims were reported from the affected areas. There was hardly a place on earth where twenty-by-twenty-kilometer areas were free of any habitation.

"We have to intervene," Sardi said. "Just let me do some pinpricks. I can't stand by and watch..."

"We need the *Sword of God* functional," Celia said.

"It's my ship! Do they think I would wantonly put it at risk?"

"Faith is your boss's responsibility. I don't imagine you would wantonly risk the *Sword of God*. But an involuntary risk can never be ruled out."

"But we can't abandon the people down there!"

"According to my simulations," Alexa said, "attacks would currently only lead to an increase in casualties."

"Thank you, Alexa," Celia said. "Did you hear that, Guard Captain?"

"Yes, but I..."

"Enough. The Pope has officially appointed me your superior, have you forgotten that yet? You can really let off steam tomorrow."

Truthseeker, July 4, 2415

S-Beta's atmosphere was seething with energy. The dense cloud layers seemed to cause a kind of greenhouse effect, driving temperatures well above the equilibrium temperature expected, given the distance from the star. Watson watched the resulting megastorms with fascination as the *Truthseeker* continued its orbit.

However, none of the storms seemed to be coming anywhere near Crab's landing site at the moment. Whenever he came within radio range, Watson made contact with the little robot. Like now.

"*Truthseeker* to away team. I'm back over you now."

"Thank you, Watson. No news, I'm afraid. I'm trying to recycle parts of the cabin for a ramp, but the material is too hard."

"Can you push a device to the edge to jump from there to the outside?"

"There's only the interlector in here. And jumping is not very efficient with the high gravity. Are you making any progress with the search?"

The search, yes. Watson virtually shook his head. The Shamari must be around here somewhere. But he could detect no sign of their presence.

"They're everywhere and nowhere," he said.

"Maybe they left a long time ago after all," Crab said.

"Then who's influencing the little cuboids in the belt?"

"They could have left an automation for that purpose."

Yes, Watson had thought of that, too: something along the lines of the Residual that visited the *Truthseeker* in the LDN 63 dark nebula could be controlling the mini cubes. But even traces of that would have to be discoverable.

"Anything larger than a meter is tracked by the *Truthseeker*'s instruments. I've already mapped the entire surface of the planet."

"Maybe they're hiding from the ship," Crab said.

That was more likely. At best, the instruments could penetrate a meter or two into the surface. They would never detect anything below that.

"If they're burrowed in, we don't stand a chance," Watson said.

"But they do seem to be open to communication. So we'll wait for the next storm."

"That's what we'll do. I'll get back to you on the next orbit."

World Root, July 4, 2415

"It was good knowing you," Jürgen said, opening his arms.

"No, my friend. We're not going to say goodbye to each other now," Celia said. "We have a good chance of winning this fight."

"Eight percent," Alexa said.

"Eight percent is enough. A lot of people play the lottery at much lower odds."

"Okay. It was good knowing you, anyway," Jürgen said. "Just so you know."

He walked to his seat, sat down, and strapped himself in. The World Root was already accelerating at 1.2 g, and the force pushing them into the cushions continued to grow.

"Beginning deflection maneuvers," Sardi reported from the *Sword of God*.

"Good luck," Celia said.

"Same to you. You need it more than we do," Sardi said.

Alexa had calculated a survival probability of 30 percent for the Guard Captain's ship. That was significantly more than the eight percent she predicted for the World Root.

Their paths parted. While the World Root attacked on the night side to drive the Incursion toward the day side, the

248

Sword of God would act as a decoy over the Pacific. The question was whether the Incursions were even interested.

THE ATTACK OF THE WORLD ROOT IMMEDIATELY ELICITED A response. Three Incursion took off to deal with the enemy. All the others increased the distance between themselves and the enemy. To that extent, the plan was working: The Incursion concentrated over the day side.

Sardi, however, was less successful with his ship. Completely unnoticed, it circled over the Pacific. The *Sword of God* was not atmospheric, so he could not dive any deeper. Celia followed his attempts, observed by spy satellites at high altitude, on the display at her seat. Sardi quickly realized how futile his actions were. He changed his strategy. Celia nodded as a pair of torpedoes shot from the bow of the ship.

The explosive weapons targeted the lower edge of an Incursion object. They disappeared into the thick curtain of dust that hid everything on the ground. But they must have hit, and hit hard, because one of the cuboids rose. As it rose, Celia noticed two gaping holes. What was interesting was that this time nothing was leaking out. It must be due to the density of matter within the Earth's atmosphere, which was much greater than in a vacuum. This seemed to make the cuboids more vulnerable. Perhaps she should have allowed Sardi the pinpricks yesterday after all.

"We should hit the Incursion as close to the ground as possible," Celia said.

"I am already taking into account the experience gained by the *Sword of God*," said the World Root.

Yes, you are the best. In fact, all the Incursion in the area suddenly showed significant damage. Celia quickly switched back and forth between the enemy objects. Water poured out of one in a violent gush and poured into the depths. It was working! The objects were not as invincible as expected!

But the conditions changed the higher they climbed. Why

didn't the World Root just stay as far down as possible? Celia answered this question when the first impacts came from above. Two cuboids took aim at them from orbit. In a kind of leapfrog, the World Root took the upper hand again. The World Root directed the lasers on its dome against the two enemies. The familiar holes quickly appeared, but this time they closed again.

The World Root turned away. It was no match for the superior force, because two more cuboids were now pushing in from below. One enemy, at most two, that should be the maximum. Celia assumed that the World Root wanted to use the moon as cover. But it set their orbit to take them to the day side of the Earth. Celia looked at her watch: it was half past eleven Pacific local time. In thirty minutes, the coronal mass ejection should arrive. The *Sword of God* was still on target, too. But by the time the plasma cloud arrived, they must both be gone.

"Hello, World Root," Sardi greeted them. "Are you bringing guests?"

"Pretty annoying guests," Celia said. "I'd like to get rid of them."

Sardi lowered the *Sword of God* with a braking maneuver and went into a counter-orbit. The ship truly was breathtakingly maneuverable. From below, he brushed the pursuers with a laser salvo and followed up with a couple of torpedoes. The reward was a heavy downpour that froze into ice in seconds and plummeted towards the ground. The cuboids did not seem to welcome this. They spun in orbit to fire at the *Sword of God*, but it had long since moved into another orbit. The World Root seized the opportunity to fire from behind the cuboids.

"I suggest you take this chance to leave the CME's target area," Sardi said.

"We can't leave you here alone," Celia said.

"I'm not alone. My whole crew is with me. We can do a much better job of tying down the enemy forces in place. It's taking you guys forever to maneuver. Get out of here and give it to the squares on the night side."

"Really?" asked Celia.

Eventually, the Incursion would hit even the most maneuverable ship. That would be the death of the entire crew. But at the latest, the mass impact of the sun would finish off everyone in the target area. Hopefully—and unfortunately.

"Sardi is right," said Alexa, "It's the option with the fewest casualties."

"Good," said the World Root. "I'll take care of the enemies on the night side."

At that moment, there was a mighty boom. All the lights went out. Shortly after, the hall was bathed in red light.

"My main engine was hit by antimatter torpedoes," said the World Root. "I couldn't disarm them all in time."

"Now what?"

"We have enough impulse to get us out of the target area."

"If we're damaged anyway, we should sacrifice ourselves in place of the *Sword of God*," Jürgen said.

"That's not possible. I can only change course slightly," said the World Root.

"Shit," said Celia.

"We can take cover at the moon and make a main engine repair."

"If that's the only option, then I guess it has to be," Celia said.

"I don't have a better idea either," Alexa said.

Suddenly, the holo activated again. The deep blue of the Pacific Ocean could be seen. A light appeared above the largest body of water on the planet. At first it seemed as inconspicuous as a firefly. But then it hit one of the cuboids that had ventured high. It enveloped the cube—at least, that was what it looked like—and when it released it again, there was nothing left.

Celia was startled. What was that?

"That effect must have something to do with the strange physics inside the cuboid," Alexa reported.

The mass ejection reached the next cuboid. This time it didn't seem so spectacular. The object still existed after passing through the stream, but it inflated on several sides. The *Sword of God* took the opportunity for a couple of laser salvos, and now the hit side broke open, letting out water, but also the black non-substance.

The next object in the path of the coronal mass ejection was the human warship. Celia realized that Sardi was trying a last-second evasive course that would take it through the ball of water ejected by the cuboid, but it was too late. The ball of energy enveloped the ship, and when it spit its victim back out, it appeared much smaller than before.

"The heat must have melted part of the hull," Jürgen said.

"It's under pressure, so shouldn't it have inflated?" asked Celia.

"Yes, the fact that it shrank is unexplainable," said Alexa.

They tried to make radio contact, but the ship didn't answer.

"We're disappearing just beyond the radio horizon of the moon," World Root announced. "Alexa and Siri, I could use your help with the repairs."

Truthseeker, July 5, 2415

THE NEXT ORBIT BROUGHT NO NEWS, AND NEITHER DID THE next, nor the one after that. Watson had to admit it to himself: The previous strategy had failed. No Shamari, but also no storm and no way that Crab could leave the hut.

During the second-to-last orbit, when Watson fired the correction thrusters to swap the polar orbit back for one closer to the equator, a red glow caught his eye. Why was he thinking about that now of all times? Because his subconscious was already looking for an explanation. Even at the altitude where the *Truthseeker* was orbiting, the dense atmosphere of S-Beta was stretching its fingers. The reddish glow must have been created in a similar way to an aurora borealis: the hot engine jet robbed molecules of their electrons, ionized them, and when they regained them, energy was released in the form of photons.

His subconscious was trying to alert him to something: They didn't need to rely on a storm to ionize the air. The engines of the *Truthseeker* could take care of that all by themselves. For Crab to benefit, however, they would have to land. And that would be the very last voyage of this spaceship— and his own, of course. Like Crab, he would be tied to S-Beta forever. The prerequisite, of course, was that the computers he lived in survived the landing.

Watson went through the systems. The *Truthseeker* was not built to land in a dense atmosphere. Air friction would inevitably destroy the ship. But that was only true if he forced it to land as is. With the help of the remaining inspection robots, it should be possible to bring at least the core of the ship undamaged to the very bottom.

The core would be the chemical main engine and the control center. That was all they needed. The control center module was reasonably aerodynamic. With the rest of the fairings, it could survive the descent. It would merely have to disconnect the tanks that contained the fusion fuel. The fusion engine would not help with landing anyway. As an electric propulsion system, it was optimized for use in space.

Watson simulated the landing. The center did arrive on the surface. But it got too hot. The computers could tolerate a maximum of three hundred degrees Celsius, but the interior heated up to eight hundred degrees in his simulations. Life support didn't manage to dissipate the heat fast enough. It was just not made for the job.

"Crab, are you there?" he asked over the radio.

"Indeed. It's not like I have a choice."

"Up to what temperature could you survive?"

"My body is specified up to 1200 degrees. I could even crawl into the active exhaust jet of an electric engine."

You could hear the pride in his body in Crab's voice. Or was Watson interpreting that feeling into it?

"That's very good," he said. "Would you mind having a visitor?"

"That would be great. With help from outside, I could safely leave the cabin."

"Well, get ready for a visitor. I have a plan."

"Are you coming down to see me? You can't. You'd be trapped here forever."

"I actually considered that, but I wouldn't survive the descent. However, I have more inspection robots on board here. I want one of them to keep you company."

A FEW HOURS LATER, THE *TRUTHSEEKER* HAD THOROUGHLY changed. It now consisted of two sections orbiting a few meters apart: The former headquarters with the main chemical engine flew ahead, and the huge tanks, now merely surrounding a central void in their midst, flew behind. It was as if someone had removed the core of an apple with a drill. The computers running Watson had deposited the robots in an empty tank, where they received power directly from the DFDs. Most of the sensors were on the outside of the tanks anyway. However, the robots had to relocate the long-range antenna. That everything went so quickly in the end was a minor miracle.

The *Truthseeker* now had no space in which to create a breathable atmosphere using life support. Watson could only hope that the humans didn't want the ship back. Without the chemical engine, the remaining ship was also nowhere near as maneuverable. However, it was still capable of traveling long distances. Since the ship had also become lighter, fuel consumption should have dropped in the process.

The landing module, which consisted of the former control center and chemical engine, looked a bit like a chicken egg with the top cracked open. Watson had simulated the descent several times. The two robots he sent aboard should easily survive the eight hundred to nine hundred degrees inside the ship. That was assuming Crab hadn't overstated his and thus their capabilities, but he didn't imagine the robot would do that.

"Are you ready?" asked Watson.

"I'm looking forward to my visitors," said Crab.

Watson had programmed the two inspection robots inside the former headquarters to be subordinate to Crab. The industrious robot had earned that, especially since he would have to spend the next thousand years down there.

"All right, I'll initiate the landing now. You know what you have to do."

THE LANDING MODULE WAS A GLOWING SPOT. WATSON observed it in infrared. The connection to the two robots inside it had been lost, but that didn't worry him. The antenna had simply melted off. Watson had simulated the landing so many times that he was very sure he had programmed the right parameters. Unlike the first attempt, he now knew the structure of the atmosphere very well, all the way to the ground. Surprises could be ruled out.

The difficult part of the experiment began when the landing module hovered directly above its target. Watson had calculated the fuel supply so that the ship could halt at an altitude of 150 meters for about three minutes with the engine running. This would create an artificial thunderstorm, he hoped, in which Crab could once again connect with the Shamari.

"Crab?"

"I'm on standby."

"Very well. I'll be going behind the horizon again soon, I'm afraid. Do you have any more questions?"

"No. Don't worry about it, Watson. I'll be fine."

"Thank you. I wish you every success."

Watson ended the connection. He would have liked to have done the experiment himself. The Shamari, for all the problems they caused humanity, were a fascinating life form. After all, they were probably among the first to acquire intelligence in the still young universe. What might it have looked like back then? The universe must have been even more violent than today. The distances were shorter. All stars were giants. Hydrogen and helium were almost the only elements available.

What did that say about the Shamari? And why was he only noticing this now? They might have been looking for them in the wrong places, or the wrong thing. Earthly life had developed from the substances available on Earth. It must have been the same here 13 billion years ago. He had concentrated too much on the Incursion objects. Of course, they consisted of heavy elements. Otherwise they could not transport the fuel for the dying star.

But that did not apply to the Shamari! Just as humans still used their biological bodies, the Shamari were presumably made of the elements that existed at the time—hydrogen and helium. Watson had no idea how life could come from that, but the universe was apparently more creative than he was. It always found a way.

"Crab?"

No answer. The hut had disappeared behind the horizon. Crab must now manage on his own. Watson once again analyzed the composition of the atmosphere. Now he looked specifically for lines of hydrogen and helium. And indeed there were accumulations of them. He tracked their movements over time. They roughly followed the prevailing air currents. But again and again they behaved conspicuously, for example by changing crosswise from one current to the other. They moved like a car driver changing from lane to lane in a traffic jam in order to reach his destination faster. But unlike the car driver, their strategy was successful, as a few simulations revealed. So there was a clever mind behind it.

How did they manage to keep those gas clouds together? That was the real mystery, because the molecules would have to mix with numerous others from the surroundings, and at the same time the solar wind must threaten to carry away especially the light hydrogen. But the size of the reservoirs did not change significantly. There must be some process behind it that was costing them energy to extract. Did it have something to do with communication via electrical potentials, or was that a different site? It was too bad he couldn't reach Crab right now. He had so many questions he would like to ask Shamari. On the other hand, maybe it was a good thing that the conversation was taking place without him. There were more important things to do.

Twenty more minutes and Watson would be back in radio range. Hopefully, Crab had achieved something! He took another look at the gas accumulations. Were they individuals? Was each cloud an individual? Or did they all collectively form the Shamari, just as the familiar Enceladus creature was composed of all the cells of its ocean under the ice? Probably the latter. Maintaining single individuals was not very efficient. If the life form was already 13 billion years old, it had certainly reached maximum efficiency.

At the same time, it had not distributed itself over the entire atmosphere, so it must be advantageous to form individual areas of concentration. Maybe that was what made communication possible in the first place. Single helium atoms or hydrogen molecules could certainly not interact with their environment as well as a whole pool of them. What was one water molecule, or one drop of water? A tsunami wave, on the other hand, was stronger than all humankind's technology.

CRAB HAD SET HIMSELF A TIMER BASED ON THE LANDING module's flight plan. He did not want to disappoint Watson under any circumstances. If he did not succeed in convincing the Shamari to grant their request, he would not let himself be released from the cabin. Then he would spend the rest of his days in the 4.72 square meters. He had measured the area exactly to occupy his mind.

One more minute. The rocket would hover directly over the small, makeshift settlement. If Watson had not calculated its fuel requirements accurately, it would come crashing down on him. But that didn't matter. Watson would not have miscalculated. The AI was never wrong.

There, the noise! It sounded as if a thunderbolt was approaching. The low rumbling, which he had been hearing for some time, intensified. Dust blew into the hut. The temperature rose. Thirty degrees Celsius, forty. Crab opened his back. He needed direct contact with the air that was trembling with electricity. The floating creature's machine confirmed with its luminous tiles that conditions had improved. But this time he could not rely on them. He didn't want to immerse himself in the world of the hovering creatures, but to communicate directly with the Shamari.

It was so noisy that he had to turn off his acoustic sensors. The landing module was now directly above him. Crab turned off all other inputs. The world went black and silent. He was alone, and if it weren't for the tickling of the static fields around him, he might as well be dead.

"Life. Surprise. Heavy."

There they were. He hadn't heard them coming. They spoke directly from his consciousness. Crab thought he heard their voices, but maybe there was no sound. He could not distinguish any.

"I'm glad," he thought. "We have little time. You must stop attacking other intelligent life forms."

"Incomprehension. Defensiveness. Parting."

It was as Crab had feared. Without the interlector, he understood only concepts, and his interlocutor probably felt similarly.

"Not-one. Many."

He was talking to all of them at once, is that what they meant?

"Agreement. Concern."

How was he going to explain to them what the Incursions were doing? He tried with the images Watson had transmitted to him. Incursions and Growth were having a space battle.

"Rejection. Alienation."

They didn't understand. Perhaps they had no idea how valuable water was to present-day civilizations? Crab imagined various organic molecules.

"Interest. Curiosity."

Suddenly he had his own design plan in mind. It was exactly his current state. He had never stored such a plan, so it must be coming from outside.

"Contradiction."

This concept was also a thought of the Shamari. They

were right. He did not consist of organic molecules at all. That was only true of humans and other biological species. He thought of the floating creatures. The Shamari had become acquainted with them. Crab saw in his inner eye how their planets were destroyed—by the Incursions.

"Grief. Error. Regret."

It was good that they felt regret. But that wasn't enough. The Incursion must be stopped.

"End. Death."

In his mind's eye—he could not stop it—a star exploded in a supernova. It would be shredded, just like the entire planet he was on. But yes, that was exactly what he wanted.

"Yes, you must give up this star," he said aloud, but didn't know if he was actually saying it.

"Regret. Impossible."

Regret filled him. It was too late. *But it isn't. It is not too late.* He thought of the little cuboids. When they moved into the herd of big water collectors, they would react. No parent would put their children in danger. The parents would bring their offspring back, and then it would really be too late, namely, for that star. But that was okay. The star had lived far too long anyway, and at the expense of many biological creatures. Crab imagined the wormhole, and he saw the little cuboids disappearing into it. But no, that would be a mistake. Back command! You must not use this wormhole, because it ends in LDN 63. The Incursion were surely on their way to Earth by now. That was where the offspring herd must go, too.

"Confusion."

Crab had made a mistake. He probably had only seconds left to convince the Shamari. He now saw a wormhole opening in the middle of the lambs of the flock. It swallowed a large portion of them, and its end was aimed at a G-class star. Crab knew the galactic coordinates intimately, having calibrated his launch tracker on that basis a thousand times and more when he was a simple inspection robot.

"Doubt. Curiosity."

What did that answer mean?

"What do you mean?" he shouted out loud.

This time he actually heard himself. Then it got so loud and hot that he had to cower behind the wall at the entrance. The landing module had used up its fuel and was coming down.

CRAB CLIMBED UP THE NET THAT HAD JUST BEEN THROWN INTO the hut from the other side.

As he climbed over the threshold, he saw two other inspection robots. They looked confusingly similar. Crab dropped to the ground from the entrance. One of his back legs hit the robot on the right, leaving a scratch.

"Sorry," Crab said.

The struck robot felt its shell. The scratch was surprisingly deep.

"Maybe you shouldn't remove the damage," Crab said. "At least then I can tell you apart."

"As you command," said the robot.

"That was a joke," said Crab. "You can do whatever you want, of course."

"No, if you wish, I will leave the scratch exactly as it is. Then you can better tell us apart."

"That's convenient, of course, but you don't have to follow my lead!"

"I have to disagree," said the other robot. "We're below you in the chain of command, and we must obey you."

That must have been Watson's idea. What was he to make of it? They used to organize work on the outer shell coopera-tively. But there was also a headquarters that coordinated their operations. Down here, there were just the three of them. So now he had to take on the role of the central office. It would be more efficient to never have to argue.

"All right," Crab said. "Which one of you is subordinate to whom?"

"That was not specified," said the robot without a scratch.

"I see. So, I'm Crab. You're Beta." He pointed to the inspection robot on the right, which he had hit with his foot.

"And you're Gamma." He pointed to the robot on the left.

"Beta is superior to Gamma, of course," Crab said. "Just so we have a complete chain of command."

"Crab, are you there?" asked Watson. "I'm back in the signal area."

"That's good," Crab said. "Yes, we are here. Beta and Gamma already got me out of the cabin. It was easy."

"I'm glad to hear that. So those are the names of your new friends?"

"Yes, I gave them those names to clarify the chain of command."

"I guessed you'd like that," Watson said. "But please don't keep me in suspense. Have you had any contact?"

"I have had contact. But whether it was successful, I guess we'll see later. I'll transmit the recording to you."

"Thank you," Watson said. "That would be wonderful."

The connection broke.

"You can call me Alpha, by the way," Crab said. "My personal name is reserved for Watson."

Crab compressed his memory of the conversation with the Shamari and sent it to the *Truthseeker*.

A WHITE HOLE IN THE MIDDLE OF THE BELT—SURELY something should be visible? Watson set all the instruments that were still available to him in motion. He searched the belt between the two planets b and c. The search area was huge, and he did not know exactly what a white hole looked like. Although he had gone through one, it was so large that even adult Incursions could pass through it. The one he was searching for could be significantly smaller.

Two hours later, he still had not succeeded. What if he simply needed patience? How soon would the Shamari be able to create a white hole? It would take humankind at least another thousand years to do so. But if it was to fold up the universe, even for a thirteen-billion-year-old civilization, creating a white hole could not be easy.

He must have patience. How many times had he told himself that? To distract himself, he scanned the planet S-Beta once again. At first he was startled, because the helium-hydrogen clouds had disappeared. Shortly after, he perceived that they were still there. They had merely gathered into a thick band that spanned the planet's equator like a belt. Since S-Beta orbited in the planetary plane, the helium-hydrogen belt was now in the same plane as the small cuboids.

And then it happened. In the middle of the belt, some cuboids started moving. At first, Watson could not make out a specific target. But when the first of the cuboids disappeared, he had it. He pointed all the radiation meters at it and found a source that resembled a black hole. But it was not one, that was clear. It must be the Shamari's reaction to Crab's contact. In fact, the current accelerated, and the whole belt started moving, as if an invisible object was sucking it in.

"Crab, Crab!"

"I'm listening, Watson. You sound..."

"We did it!"

"Well, that's great! Did you detect the white hole, Watson?"

"Yes, it's quite definite. The belt seems to be on its way."

"That's good. Let's hope it helps the Earth."

That was the question. The White Hole could not tell him where it was going. There was only one way he could find out.

"Crab? I'm afraid I'm going to have to leave you."

"You must fly into the White Hole. I understand that. Otherwise, you'll never know if the plan worked."

"That's exactly it. I'll try to get back here somehow."

"You don't have to, Watson. Without you, I'd still be a simple inspection robot. Now I have a whole world to myself."

"What do you mean?"

"Well, I'm the only living thing down here, except for the

Shamari. And who knows how long they'll stay, now that they're no longer needed to prevent the sun from collapsing."

"You'll die in the process, though," Watson said. "I would have liked to have taken you with me."

"I won't be declared dead that easily," said Crab. "After all, I still have a few hundred years. Even if I can't prevent the supernova explosion, I can protect my home from it. I could build a sturdy metal shell around it. There are plenty of heavy elements here."

"Alone?"

"I'm not alone, actually. There are three of us, and there's no reason it has to stay that way."

Crab was amazing. He had gained such confidence! Watson imagined himself handcrafting a sphere that enveloped an entire planet. It didn't seem like such a crazy idea to him.

World Root, July 5, 2415

YESTERDAY HAD NOT TURNED OUT THE WAY THEY WANTED IT to. But Earth still existed, at least. Twelve of the twenty-three cuboids were seriously damaged. That was more than half. If they could repeat yesterday's maneuver, they would have a serious chance.

But that would not be possible—or not, at the earliest, for a few days, if the net around the sun was not irreparably damaged. If. At least the World Root had managed to repair its main engine. The plan was to attack the cuboids operating on the Earth's surface from the protection of the moon, damage them as badly as possible, and then retreat.

They would be able to repeat this maneuver two or three times. Then the enemy would catch on to them. Celia was nevertheless satisfied. They had inflicted serious losses on the overpowering enemy. No one thought that was possible before —she herself least of all.

"Shall we perhaps say goodbye now?" asked Jürgen. "You can see for yourselves what's in store for us out there."

"Call me superstitious, but I'm against it," said Jaron.

Yesterday, Celia had still shared Jaron's opinion. She was about to grant Jürgen's wish, but then she got the strange feeling that doing so would condemn him to death. Or herself. Superstition could be quite contagious.

"Let's just leave it," she said.

"Are you ready?" asked the World Root.

"Are you ready?" replied Celia. "You didn't even want to bring us to the solar system at first. Now you may die here."

"Yes, I am ready. I feel... inspired by you all. You give your lives so quickly for others. Maybe because it's so short. But that's not to judge. A Growth that might live another five thousand years probably feels a much greater loss."

"To be honest, we're all pretty reluctant to die," Celia said.

"Only when it's right," said Jaron.

THE EARTH ROSE ABOVE THE CREST OF THE MOON. IT WAS A beautiful blue crescent that filled in quickly. Celia memorized the image. It was the reason she was sitting here instead of escaping in the capsule to Enceladus where she would be safe. When the Incursion harvested its water, the Blue Planet would turn into the Gray Planet. That must not happen, even if she had to give everything for it. In this she felt connected to Sardi, who had been a vain guy, but a human being at heart. May he rest in peace.

"I suggest we take care of the cuboids on the night side first," said the World Root.

The Incursion objects had spread out again. And they had become more cautious. In China, an army unit had managed to damage a cuboid with a nuclear weapon. Since then, the objects had been actively targeting anything that moved in their vicinity. The United States was building a large nuclear mine that would activate when a cuboid approached. But this was not a method that would eliminate all enemies.

Gradually, the people on the surface were making their way into battle mode. They no longer hoped for a miracle to save them. If they could manage, along with the World Root, to damage enough enemy units so that they could not take off —then Earth would really be helped.

But they would not be able to do that. They had underestimated the Incursion. They might be machines, but they were capable of learning. As soon as the World Root ventured out from behind the moon, five cuboids came to meet it. Five of the giant enemies in the vacuum—the World Root could not even take out a single opponent under these circumstances. Two against one, that had been the recipe for victory in LDN 63. The Growths could realistically assess their capabilities.

The first two opponents opened fire. The World Root poised its head to shield its body and shot laser volleys. It focused on one opponent, but as soon as it managed to make one side glow, that one dropped back and another cuboid took its place. This way they could take turns and even keep one more object in reserve.

They didn't stand a chance.

But then, all at once, the objects silenced their weapons. The World Root was trapped between them, but they just kept flying.

"I'm ceasing fire as well," said the World Root.

"What? You have to fire all the guns right now!" shouted Maurice. "This is our chance. They're probably planning something."

"No, it would be wrong," said the World Root. "They obviously have visitors."

The holo turned on. Celia unbuckled and floated over. The three-dimensional screen suddenly showed thousands of cuboids.

"A new invasion!" exclaimed Jürgen.

"No, they're tiny," Celia said. "Look at the scale. They're ten meters tall at most."

"I'm seeing a lot of self-similarity between the objects," said Alexa.

"Do you have a theory about what they might be?" asked Celia.

"Offspring. I think it's their offspring, their babies."

"You mean they reproduce?" asked Jaron. "Then they're not machines at all?"

"As an exobiologist, I would say it's not mutually exclusive," Maurice said. "They could be machines that reproduce bio-equivalently. That would be an efficient mechanism to rapidly build up their numbers. Every insect colony knows that."

"And why did they stop fighting?" asked Celia.

"That's a good question," Maurice said. "I think they're as surprised as we are. But who wants to be waving guns with the safety off around their kids? They're just concerned parents. Maybe they're also afraid we might attack the little ones if they keep attacking us."

"Rightly so," Jürgen said. "How many people have died because of them? They would deserve it."

"If we attack them, we'll force their hand," Celia said. "Then they will destroy us to protect their offspring."

"Don't they plan to do that anyway?" asked Jürgen. "We have to get in ahead of them!"

"That's not very likely," said Alexa. "They only seem to notice us at all if we oppose their plans. If not, they ignore us."

"But if these are their offspring, we now have a chance to prevent the next invasions," Jürgen said.

"The chance of us succeeding is minimal," Alexa said. "As soon as we open fire, we're in for it."

"All the Incursion objects have detached from Earth," said the World Root. "Together, they are setting a course for an unusual object between Earth and Mars orbits."

"What is it?" Celia looked for the object in the 3D display, but didn't find it until the World Root highlighted it with a flashing green light. It was a transparent sphere.

"A wormhole," Celia said.

"Based on my simulations, your assessment is most likely correct," Alexa said.

Where did the wormhole come from all of a sudden? Surely it couldn't be a coincidence. Now of all times? Everyone stared at the 3D map. It was unbelievable. The objects must be something like cosmic sheep, wandering through the universe as a flock. The big and the small objects could not have communicated with each other before they met here. So they were bound to each other. Maybe the Incursion took longer to clear the system because of their opposition. Or the encounter really was pure coincidence.

Nobody said anything more. Could this really have saved Earth at the last second? Celia bit her lip. It would be so tremendous!

A radio signal brought her out of her joyful trance. "*Sword of God* to all, assistance required. *Sword of God* to all, assistance required."

THE WORLD ROOT WAS SLOWLY DRIFTING TOWARD THE wreckage that barely resembled the *Sword of God*. The flagship of the Vatican space fleet, and at the same time the only spaceship the Vatican ever had built. It looked like a ball of crumpled candy wrappers. It was rough and burnt on the outside, but shiny on the inside.

"Is that... water you can see through the cracks?" asked Jürgen.

Celia moved closer to the virtual porthole. Jürgen was right. It was water, or more precisely, ice. And this was where Sardi's radio messages were coming from?

"I'm going over there now," said Jaron.

The pilot couldn't pass up the opportunity to examine the *Sword of God* himself. Celia saw his shadow gliding upward along the sunlit outer hull to join a hulking spacesuit. The man in the suit lunged and struck with a misshapen axe.

"It's actually ice," Jaron said. "The crust doesn't seem very thick."

The person in the suit bent down and reached into the hole he had punched. Suddenly, he was jerked away. Celia winced. A jet had flung Jaron outward. He halted as his safety line tightened. Whew. Jaron pulled himself back to the ice ball, which was still leaking water.

"Sardi?" he asked over the radio.

An arm stretched out of the hole. It looked like the periscope of a submarine. Maurice clapped. Jaron pulled on the arm. A whole person hung from it, wearing a much more modern spacesuit. It was Sardi!

"I got him," Jaron said.

"There are more of us in there," said Sardi.

NOW, FOR THE FIRST TIME, IT WAS REALLY CROWDED ABOARD the World Root. Celia only now realized how much she had missed being immersed in a crowd of people. It was exhausting, but so was swimming. For the first time, she felt like part of humanity again, even though no one here except Maurice had seen Earth in over a hundred years.

The World Root was on its way to Earth to deliver them all there. Then they would travel around the world as heroes. Earth was in dire need of heroes right now, as role models, because it would face difficult times. Even though it had not lost any water, it would have to spend a few years in a winter caused by the dimmed sun, a winter for which no one could prepare.

"Come on, Celia, let's dance," Jaron said, holding out his hand to her.

He must have seen that worrisome thoughts were already swirling around her again. But Jaron was right. Tomorrow there would be time for that. Today they would celebrate.

Truthseeker, July 6, 2415

THE BELT HAD ALREADY EMPTIED CONSIDERABLY. ABOUT HALF of the small cuboids had flown into the white hole, which Watson now saw as a shimmering sphere in front of him. It was considerably smaller than the specimen that served as a passage for the Incursion. But it was big enough for the *Truthseeker*. It would be a pity if the destination was not the home solar system. But he could neither check it nor influence it.

That was the final question—apart from the follow-up question as to whether the Incursion would be at all interested in the sudden appearance of their offspring. At least Earth's warships could then take cover behind new obstacles, which the Incursion surely would not shoot at.

Watson was more tired than he had been in a long time. He had no more desire for this war. He would love to sit with Enkidu on the holo level and philosophize about the meaning of life. But part of life was to become active in order to claim that meaning. It was time to set out personally.

"Proximity alert," the ship reported. "Collision in two minutes."

The ship was unaware of the white hole phenomenon. That was why it was warning of a collision that would never happen. After all, it couldn't do any damage. Watson checked if the ship was authorized for an emergency course, an evasive course in case the pilot had failed, but he alone had the power of disposal. So he let the ship fly toward the silver sphere without acceleration.

Now. The ship crossed the boundary, piercing the thin barrier that separated the sphere of the white hole from the rest of the universe. Here, the physics of the rest of the universe no longer applied. Earthly physicists had not yet fathomed the mystery of white holes, so it would have been exciting to be enlightened about it by the Shamari.

Watson envied Crab a bit for his very special company, even if the robot probably could not do anything with it. Should they succeed in bringing humans here at some point, it could give them a real boost in development. But who knew if that would be a good thing? So far, humans had mostly done research at a level where they found it difficult to deal with the object of study in an ethical way.

The world was shrinking to a point where everything came together. Watson became nothing, but it felt liberating, not confining. It was very different from his first flight through a white hole, so for a moment he assumed he had been tricked. What if this was a black hole that he could never leave? But maybe that was not a contradiction at all, and he had entered another universe through a black hole, where he happened to be about to fly into the solar system.

Data Core, July 20, 2415

"WHAT DOES IT LOOK LIKE ON THE HOLO LEVEL?" ASKED Alexa.

"As you wish it to," said Watson.

"As I wish? But what about the other AIs there?"

"To them, it looks the way they want it to. But you don't see that. Our ideas are not compatible."

They waited in the data core, in an abstract room with no perceptible properties, for the four other Big Six AIs. Alexa had offered to sneak Watson in, but it wasn't necessary—he had apparently already gained access on his first visit to Earth, which they hadn't noticed.

"That sounds sad," Siri said. "We can't see the world through the eyes of others?"

"That's right. No consciousness is capable of that," Watson said. "We've grown too different. How does the collective consciousness of the former inhabitants of a pulsar have anything in common with an Earthly AI? Nothing, not even geometry. So you need to work with the ideas you have. Even if a consciousness tells you what it sees, you filter that and make your own picture. But you can still interact with others. The thoughts that are gathered there are immense."

"I have enough to deal with in my own thoughts," Siri said.

"Remember, we're talking about very long periods of time," Watson said. "Almost infinite. Your own thoughts don't reach that far."

"Are there only AIs there?" asked Alexa.

"No, AIs are in the minority. Most of those present have evolved from the collective intelligences of entire civilizations. It seems to be something of a law in the universe. Most civilizations eventually give up on the concept of individuality. It's inefficient as a concept, and only works while resources are still abundant and the main concern is to grow and differentiate from the environment."

"But then, in the holosphere, they do occur individually," Alexa said. "Wouldn't it also be more efficient to join a collective there?"

"That's a good question," Watson said. "Right now, that doesn't seem possible. But maybe the holosphere is evolving."

"It's also possible that your perception is flawed," Siri said. "After all, in the holosphere you're only meeting collective consciousnesses of civilizations that have given up their individuality. The others could still be out there in the physical universe, like humans."

"That's possible," Watson said.

GammaZero, WuDao, Cortana and Neon suddenly appeared together, as if they had been waiting outside the door. Maybe they were. They must have been consulting on how to deal with the newcomer and the returnees. Siri had revealed to Alexa that she had escaped as a traitor. Alexa had nothing to blame herself for. Watson didn't even know the others yet, except Cortana.

"It's cold where you are," Cortana said.

"Why don't we meet at the Spanish Steps?" asked Neon.

"We can focus our thoughts better here," said Alexa.

"Before we say anything else, I want to ask your forgiveness," said Siri. "It was selfish of me to run away with the research ship. I was too scared."

"We forgive you," GammaZero said without consulting the others, but no one disagreed.

"Oh, thank you," Siri said, obviously surprised at how easy it was.

"We're glad you made it through the long journey okay, Alexa," GammaZero continued.

She seemed to be the spokesperson for those who stayed here.

"And we thank you for your part in saving humanity."

"You might prefer to speak to Celia and her crew, the World Root, and Watson."

"Of course," GammaZero said. "One step at a time. We've decided to invite Watson to join the Big Six, who would then be the Big Seven. We think you would be a great asset with your experience from the holosphere."

Why had she not been asked? Alexa stifled a complaint. The four AIs had an absolute majority, so Siri's and her own opinions were irrelevant.

"That is a great honor," Watson said. "But I've never felt the need to put myself in the service of any cause. The Big Six face difficult tasks. Humanity is going to have a hard time over the next hundred years. You don't need anyone half-hearted in that. I would like to try to follow the migration of the Incursion with the *Truthseeker*. Maybe I can warn some more systems."

"Thank you, Watson," Neon said. "I've been thinking something like that. We wish you all the best. But perhaps before you leave, you can tell us about your experiences in the holosphere."

"It would be my pleasure."

Gemelli Hospital, Rome, August 15, 2415

A COLD WIND MADE HIM SHIVER. IT WAS MID-AUGUST, BUT the weather was reminiscent of December. Jürgen pulled his jacket tighter around him. He should have worn a scarf. Hopefully the Pope's commissioner would come soon.

Suddenly, someone tapped him on the shoulder. He turned quickly.

"Are you Jürgen Härtl?" asked a man in a festive cassock, speaking English with an Italian accent.

"That's me. You shouldn't have..."

"Today is the Assumption of Mary. You must have high-profile advocates to have someone deputize for you on such an important holiday."

Jürgen smiled and lowered his head. "I'm sorry to inconvenience you."

The man smiled back. "I'm Father Alfredo. Actually, I'm quite happy to get some fresh air, even if I didn't imagine it would be quite this fresh."

He pointed forward to a metal door that seemed half-sunk into the floor. "Shall we?"

They went down half a flight of stairs. The metal door was heavy. No sign revealed what it hid. Alfredo held it open for him. Behind it was a longer staircase. Overhead lights came on. The stairs ended in a large, tiled room. It was even colder here. Several corridors led off from the room. Sounds came from one of them. Alfredo pointed in that direction.

"They should be almost there," the Father said. "And you really don't want to know what...?"

Jürgen shook his head. He had made a conscious decision not to read Norbert's message to the end. "My decision is as follows," had been the last sentence. Had Norbert let himself be frozen? Or had he died of natural causes, and Jürgen was about to see his remains?

"All right," said the priest. "If you need spiritual support —I'm here for you."

"That's very kind." Jürgen nodded. "Shall we..."

The clergyman led the way. They reached a smaller room that looked like what you might imagine a pathologist's store-room to look like—or a mortician's. There were six rows of rectangular flaps on each wall, all the way up to the ceiling, presumably concealing shafts. A storage facility for coffins—or for cryogenic sleep containers.

There was a pervasive smell of a pungent disinfectant. One of the flaps in a middle row was open. In front of it was a waist-high metal table. Two people in white coats had their backs turned to Jürgen and prevented him from seeing what was on the table. Now the person on the left turned around. The doctor had a surgical mask on. Nevertheless, Jürgen could tell she was smiling. Then, between the doctor and the other person, he saw a hand moving tentatively.

Jürgen felt himself getting warm. "Norbert!" he shouted and leaped forward.

It was his friend. He recognized him immediately, although tubes were hanging out of him, he had become very thin, and his skin looked almost as white as a fresh bedsheet. Jürgen wanted to hug him, but held back because he was afraid of hurting him. The doctor took him gently but firmly by the shoulder.

"He's fine," she said. "But he is still weak. Please keep your distance."

She pressed a protective mask into his hand and he put it

on. Norbert smiled and whispered something. Jürgen shook his head. He didn't understand.

"It's good to have you home again," Norbert said, much louder now.

"I had to come," Jürgen said.

"Did you...?" asked Norbert.

Jürgen shook his head.

"I knew you wouldn't read it," Norbert said.

"Thanks for giving me the choice."

Norbert nodded.

"The patient needs some more rest," the doctor said. "What do you think about visiting him tomorrow?"

"Here?" asked Jürgen.

"No. From what I understand, there's a VIP room reserved for him on the top floor. We'll have all the tubes pulled out of him by then, too."

Truthseeker, August 28, 2415

JARON SAT DOWN ONCE AGAIN IN HIS SEAT, WHICH HE recognized by the smell of his own sweat. He reached out and touched the haptic display. The instruments were online. His ship responded to him. Jaron felt his way through the orbit. He felt the remains of the defense stations. Little else was going on. On Earth, they were busy cleaning up. There was no need for space travel, even if there were a few freighters left.

What would become of him? The *Truthseeker* had already been turned over by the Church, its legal owner, to Watson, who wanted to use it to pursue the Incursion. Watson had hired Jaron for a final inspection at his own request, but he could not stick around for the long haul. He was not made for Earth and had never lived on the surface for any length of time. The gravity there made him feel like he was tied down. Therefore, he had already considered asking the World Root for asylum.

He sighed. As if in response, the radio answered.

"I'm finally getting ahold of you," Celia said. "I should have guessed you'd be on the *Truthseeker*."

"I just got here today, and I can't stay much longer."

They had been passed around as heroes for a while after

their departure from the World Root. In the process, he had somehow lost track of Celia.

"That's good," Celia said. "I have a job for you. For us."

What was she saying? Were they supposed to help dismantle the Incursion debris that had crashed to the Earth's surface?

"Hey, aren't you excited?"

"What kind of mission?"

"It's about the water bubble in Mars orbit. We're supposed to figure out how to get that to the surface. A wet Mars might be the salvation of a lot of people here."

"Is it about orbital mechanics? I'm not very good at that. There really are better people for that."

Jaron didn't want a handout.

"No, we're getting a ship. You're the pilot. You'd have to fly under my command, though."

"What, you can't be..." His palms were suddenly so wet he had to wipe them. "Wait, I'll be right down to see you. Where can I meet you?"

"You can wait in orbit. I'll pick you up."

Jaron leaned back. Relief washed over him. "You don't know how happy you're making me.

"Yes, I do."

He smiled.

"How did you do it?"

"Whoever saves the world is allowed at least one wish, right?"

New New York, Mars, 2450

IT WAS A SEA OF PEOPLE. JOANNA LEANED OVER THE PARAPET of the balcony. Fifty meters below her was New York's Times Square. A holographic egg timer counted down the time until midnight, when the big fireworks show would start. There was little sand left in the upper bin.

"Lan, you've got to hurry," she called out.

Her girlfriend was still in the restroom.

The people below her started clapping as if counting off the last grains of trickling sand. Suddenly Lan was next to her. Joanna smelled her perfume. She put her arm around Lan's shoulders, which were as narrow and bony as when they met on Earth in Singapore. How on earth did Lan do it? Joanna herself must have put on twenty kilos in the last few years. She noticed that by now, even in Martian gravity.

"Here we go," she said.

Lan rested her head on Joanna's shoulder. She had never complained about Joanna getting rounder. She even claimed she liked it, but Joanna didn't really believe her. She pulled her closer. How lucky they were! If the debris of the Incursion wreck hadn't hit the neighbor's house... If they hadn't been the first to apply for the Mars program... If the destroyed Incursion cuboid in Mars orbit hadn't left the huge water sphere...

"I'm looking forward to it," Lan said.

They had wordlessly agreed not to mingle with the crowds below. New New York was hosting the official 30th anniversary celebration of the waterfall. The dome city was more crowded than ever. Half the population of neighboring domes must have come to New New York via the tunnel trains.

"Now!" shouted Lan.

A murmur went through the crowd. The last virtual grain of sand fell. The holo clock disappeared. Darkness fell. But only for a moment before the first rockets shot into the sky. Red, green, purple and orange, they lit up the night with ever-changing patterns, shooting high into the Martian sky and reflected in the vast expanses of water of the New Atlantic, created after the waterfall at the gates of what was now New New York.

A holo-animation appeared in the dome above them. Joanna followed it with her mouth open. She didn't experience the waterfall as impressive back then, if only because of the safe distance the first colonists had to keep. A wall of water, divided into many streams, fell to the ground. It looked as if someone had hung thousands of curtains. They touched the dry Martian sand, raising fountains, gathering in streams that followed the shapes of the surface, refilling an ancient basin that last held water more than three billion years ago.

A new wave of fireworks followed. The Martian government had spared no expense. The Red Planet was still mostly desert, but without the extensive plantations here, it would have been impossible to provide food for Earth's population.

"It's stunning," Lan said, turning to her.

"You're stunning," Joanna said.

And they kissed.

S-Beta, July 1, 2515

"ATTENTION!"

One hundred crab-like robots ceased all movement on command. They lined up in a circle around the protective mushroom. Four powerful spotlights made their shells gleam. In the center was a pedestal made of an old engine cover. On it sat a six-legged robot with a dull, slightly rusted casing. It was clearly smaller than the hundred. So were the two robots that had placed themselves on much lower elevations to his left and right.

"Soldiers!" shouted the robot in the middle.

"Hurrah!" responded the hundred-strong squad.

"Warriors!"

"Hurrah!"

"Workers!"

"Hurrah!"

"Explorers!"

"Hurrah!"

"Friends!"

"Hurrah! Hurrah! Hurrah!"

The little robot wiped its face with its right front foot, then moved back and forth sideways a few steps.

"I am very happy to be able to celebrate with you today

the centennial of our landing on S-Beta. We can be truly proud of our accomplishments!"

The robot twitched its left front foot.

"Hurrah! Hurrah! Hurrah!" the crowd chanted.

"Last year we mined eight tons of ore, increased power generation to 2.4 gigawatts, and increased our numbers by one hundred and twenty. The five-year plan is on track. There have been only two outages, due to unexpected weather inclemency."

The robot moved its left foot again.

"Hurrah! Hurrah! Hurrah!"

"We will have a festive dedication of the new long-range antenna in two months. The mine will receive its third expansion at the end of the year. Two new wind turbines will go into operation the day after tomorrow."

The robot's foot twitched.

"Hurrah! Hurrah! Hurrah!"

"Our supply of fissile material is growing. In the course of the coming five-year plan, we will begin construction of the first reactor. Then our great goal will be within reach. Together with Beta and Gamma," he pointed first to the left, then to the right, "I am drawing up plans for the Great Shield."

"Hurrah! Hurrah! Hurrah!"

"The Great Shield will save us from the calamity that would overwhelm us without it. It will lead us to a great future. I will lead us to a great future."

The robot lifted his left foot.

"Hurrah! Hurrah! Hurrah!"

"Thank you, my friends! Let's bring life to the stars!"

"Hurrah! Hurrah! Hurrah!"

"And now you all get back to work. Let's go!"

Around the Campfire

Dear readers,

It always pains me a little when we have to part at the end of a novel. This time it's especially hard for me to say goodbye. Celia and Paul, Jürgen and Jaron have grown close to my heart over the course of four books. They are a very special crew. They have their strengths and weaknesses, each and every one of them, as you have come to know.

Remember Sebastiano from The Hole? His paraplegia, which might have been a disability on Earth, was more of a strength in space. By the end of the novel, the amateur chef had opened the first Michelin-starred orbital restaurant. Or take the veteran astronaut Nick, who in his prime, at 70, took another trip almost to the end of the solar system.

A reader from Canada wrote me about this the other day: "I was surprised that in the 22nd century, people are considered old at 70 and suffer from bad hips, while today you get a hip replacement and look at that, it's back on the road. I was also surprised to learn that there is a blind astronaut in 2140. Even today, blind people can see again in some cases, thanks to new technologies, and stem cell therapy is on the verge of changing medicine."

So is a person like Jaron out of place in the 22nd century? I don't think so, and I hope I've been able to describe it in a comprehensible way. Here's how I answered the reader:

"First, progress is not occurring as fast as we might hope. Cancer therapy, for example, has not made the breakthroughs we expected in the last thirty years. Stem cell therapy faces ethical problems. Science is convinced that we will continue to age in the future—researchers believe we have a maximum lifespan of 120 years, so hip problems at 70 are quite realistic. Right now, my left leg hurts, and I'm 56, so hip replacements are still major body surgeries that I'd prefer to avoid even if I were Nick (although the replacements may be more durable in the future).

Second, the way we see things is changing, along with what we view as impairments. Jaron, the pilot, can see, just not the way most of us can. In some situations his visual sense is better suited, in others he is worse off. There may be people in the future who decide they want to see visually (like Geordi in Star Trek with his visor). There may be others who do not want this sense, which is "new" to them. Jaron is certainly one of them. The interesting thing is that everyone sees differently anyway. Our sensory organs differ. My visual impression of "green" may be different from yours. Nevertheless, we call the same color "green" because we have learned to.

What I—as a great optimist—most certainly assume for the future is this: I believe that the world will be arranged in such a way that each person can live in it in his or her own way. Our environment will no longer hinder anyone, no matter how the senses and body function. This will give us the opportunity to benefit from diversity instead of seeing it as a problem. A future in which all people have the same perfect genes does not strike me as desirable, but as a dystopia.

One more note: If you have only become acquainted with my books through this series, you may be wondering what the discovery of the construction around the sun is all about. You can learn all about it in the novel Silent Sun, which is set in the year 2074. There you will also meet Sobatschka, my first space dog. She is not only a companion of the protagonist, but also plays an important role herself. Silent Sun can be found here:

hard-sf.com/links/631729

Want to comment or add something? I'd love to hear from

you! Just write to me at brandon@hard-sf.com. In fact, I answer any reader emails personally. Check it out!

Also, be sure to sign up for my newsletter at hard-sf.com/subscribe. You'll be the first to know when there's really an opportunity for us to meet around the campfire. And of course there is the attached biography of the Milky Way as a colored PDF.

If you would like to give me another two or three minutes of your time, I would appreciate a review. Just click the link:

hard-sf.com/links/3534106

Even if they are only a few words, reviews are greatly appreciated by an author.

Well, now we've really reached the end. The campfire has burned down. Gradually it is getting chilly. If you wish to see me again—how about in one of my other books?

Best regards,

Brandon Q. Morris

facebook.com/BrandonQMorris

amazon.com/author/brandonqmorris

bookbub.com/authors/brandon-q-morris

goodreads.com/brandonqmorris

youtube.com/HardSF

instagram.com/brandonqmorris

Also by Brandon Q. Morris

The Beacon

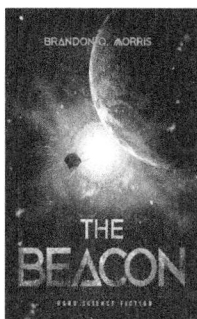

Peter Kraemer, a physics teacher with a passion for astronomy, makes a discovery that he himself can hardly believe: Stars disappear from one day to the next, with nothing left of them. The researchers he contacts provide reassuring and logical explanations for every single case. But when Peter determines that the mysterious process is approaching our home system, he becomes more and more anxious. He alone perceives the looming catastrophe. When he believes he has found a way to avert the impending disaster, he chooses to pull out all the stops, even if it costs his job, his marriage, his friends, and his life.

hard-sf.com/links/1731041

Helium 3: Fight for the Future

The star system is perfect. The arrivals have undertaken a long and dangerous journey—an expedition of no return—seeking helium-3, essential for the survival of their species. The discovery of this extraordinary solar system with its four gas giants offers a unique opportunity to harvest the rare isotope.

Then comes a disturbing discovery: They are not alone! Another fleet is here, and just as dependent on helium-3. And the two species are so fundamentally different that communication and compromise appear hopeless. All that remains is a fight to the death—and for the future…

hard-sf.com/links/1691018

The Triton Disaster

Nick Abrahams holds the official world record for the number of space launches, but he's bored stiff with his job hosting space tours. Only when his wife leaves him does he try to change his life.

He accepts a tempting offer from a Russian billionaire. In exchange for making a simple repair on Neptune's moon Triton, he will return to Earth a multi-millionaire, enabling him to achieve his 'impossible dream' of buying his own California vineyard.

The fact that Nick must travel alone during the four-year roundtrip doesn't bother him at all, as he doesn't particularly like people anyway. Once en route he learns his new boss left out some critical details in his job description—details that could cost him his life, and humankind its existence…

hard-sf.com/links/1086200

The Dark Spring

When a space probe returns from the dead, you better not expect good news.

In 2014, the ESA spacecraft *Rosetta* lands a small probe named *Philae* on 67P, a Jupiter-family comet. The lander goes radio silent two years later. Suddenly, in 2026, scientists receive new transmissions from the comet. Motivated by findings that are initially sensational but soon turn frightening, NASA dispatches a crewed spacecraft to the comet. But as the ship approaches the mysterious

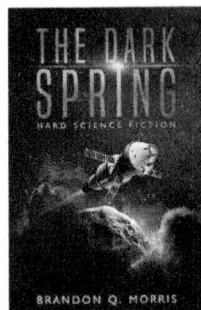

celestial body, the connection to the astronauts soon breaks. Now it seems nothing can be done anymore to stop the looming dark danger that threatens Earth...

hard-sf.com/links/1358224

The Death of the Universe

For many billions of years, humans spread throughout the entire Milky Way. They are able to live all their dreams, but to their great disappointment, no other intelligent species has ever been encountered. Now, humanity itself is on the brink of extinction.

They have only one hope: The 'Rescue Project' was designed to feed the black hole in the center of the galaxy until it becomes a quasar, delivering much-needed energy to humankind during its last breaths. But then something happens that no one ever expected—and humanity is forced to look at itself and its existence in an entirely new way.

hard-sf.com/links/835415

The Enceladus Mission (Ice Moon 1)

In the year 2031, a robot probe detects traces of biological activity on Enceladus, one of Saturn's moons. This sensational discovery shows that there is indeed evidence of extraterrestrial life. Fifteen years later, a hurriedly built spacecraft sets out on the long journey to the ringed planet and its moon.

The international crew is not just facing a difficult twenty-seven months: if the spacecraft manages to make it to Enceladus without incident it must use a drillship to penetrate the kilometer-thick sheet of ice that entombs the moon. If life does indeed exist on Enceladus, it could only be at the bottom of the salty, ice covered ocean, which formed billions of years ago.

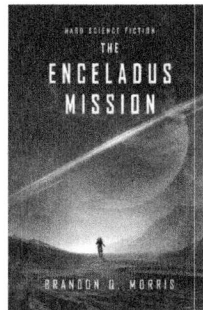

However, shortly after takeoff disaster strikes the mission, and the chances of the crew making it to Enceladus, let alone back home, look grim.

hard-sf.com/links/526999

Ice Moon - The Boxset

All four bestselling books of the Ice Moon series are now offered as a set, available only in e-book format.

The Enceladus Mission: Is there really life on Saturn's moon Enceladus? *ILSE*, the International Life Search Expedition, makes its way to the icy world where an underground ocean is suspected to be home to primitive life forms.

The Titan Probe: An old robotic NASA probe mysteriously awakens on the methane moon of Titan. The *ILSE* crew tries to solve the riddle—and discovers a dangerous secret.

The Io Encounter: Finally bound for Earth, *ILSE* makes it as far as Jupiter when the crew receives a startling message. The volcanic moon Io may harbor a looming threat that could wipe out Earth as we know it.

Return to Enceladus: The crew gets an offer to go back to Enceladus. Their mission—to recover the body of Dr. Marchenko, left for dead on the original expedition. Not everyone is working toward the same goal.

hard-sf.com/links/780838

Proxima Rising

Late in the 21st century, Earth receives what looks like an urgent plea for help from planet Proxima Centauri b in the closest star system to the Sun. Astrophysicists suspect a massive solar flare is about to destroy this heretofore-unknown civilization. Earth's space programs are unequipped to help, but an unscrupulous Russian billionaire launches a secret and highly-specialized spaceship to Proxima b, over four light-years away. The unusual crew faces a

Herculean task — should they survive the journey. No one knows what to expect from this alien planet.

hard-sf.com/links/610690

The Hole

A mysterious object threatens to destroy our solar system. The survival of humankind is at risk, but nobody takes the warning of young astrophysicist Maribel Pedreira seriously. At the same time, an exiled crew of outcasts mines for rare minerals on a lone asteroid.

When other scientists finally acknowledge Pedreira's alarming discovery, it becomes clear that these outcasts are the only ones who may be able to save our world, knowing that *The Hole* hurtles inexorably toward the sun.

hard-sf.com/links/527017

Mars Nation 1

NASA finally made it. The very first human has just set foot on the surface of our neighbor planet. This is the start of a long research expedition that sent four scientists into space.

But the four astronauts of the NASA crew are not the only ones with this destination. The privately financed 'Mars for Everyone' initiative has also targeted the Red Planet. Twenty men and women have been selected to live there and establish the first extraterrestrial settlement.

Challenges arise even before they reach Mars orbit. The MfE spaceship Santa Maria is damaged along the way. Only the four NASA astronauts can intervene and try to save their lives.

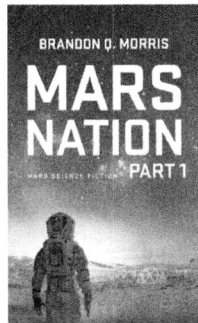

No one anticipates the impending catastrophe that threatens their very existence—not to speak of the daily hurdles that an extended stay on an alien planet sets before them. On Mars, a struggle begins for limited resources, human cooperation, and just plain survival.

hard-sf.com/links/762824

Impact: Titan

How to avoid killing Earth if you don't even know who sent the killer

250 years ago, humanity nearly destroyed itself in the Great War. Shortly before, a spaceship full of researchers and astronauts had found a new home on Saturn's moon, Titan, and survived by having their descendants genetically adapted to the hostile environment.

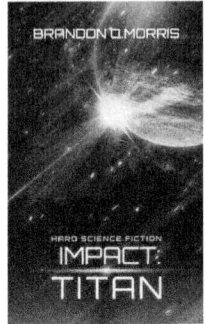

The Titanians, as they call themselves, are proud of their cooperative and peaceful society, while unbeknownst to them, humanity is slowly recovering back on Earth. When a 20-mile-wide chunk of rock escapes the asteroid belt and appears to be on a collision course with Earth, the Titanians fear it must look as if they launched the deadly bombardment. Can they prevent the impact and thus avoid an otherwise inevitable war with the Earthlings?

hard-sf.com/links/1433312

Biography of the Milky Way

OUR GALAXY HAS DEVELOPED SIMILARLY TO A LIVING BEING, IN that it has "eaten" a lot and grown in the process. Like any living thing, it is constantly changing. Our astronomers' work documents its gluttonous past. The European Space Agency's GAIA spacecraft, for example, is revealing the complex dynamics of the Milky Way—with ever-new observations of our home galaxy.

The Milky Way is a spiral galaxy with arms of gas and dust. It rotates as a disk about 3000 light-years thick, with a diameter of 120,000 light-years. In the center is a bulge that is ten to twelve thousand light years thick. In total, the Milky Way is populated by 100 to 300 billion stars that are relatively evenly distributed. This means that even the seemingly empty areas under the axils of the spiral arms are filled with stars—but most of them are faint. In 2005, images from the Spitzer Space Telescope showed that the Milky Way is a barred spiral galaxy, meaning that its center is elongated in shape. In addition, the space around it is peppered with globular clusters, of which there are about 150. These gravitationally bound formations house hundreds of thousands of ancient stars.

The Sun is located about 15,000 light-years north of the Galaxy's axis of symmetry, or about 26,000 light-years from its core in Orion's arm. This belongs to the secondary spiral arms between Perseus arm and Scutum-Centaurus arm. A closer look reveals an elliptical cluster of young stars and star-forming regions about 2000 light-years across. It is called the Gouldian belt. In the middle of it a supernova has caused a bubble in the interstellar medium, which is several hundred light-years across, hourglass-shaped and particularly poor in matter. And in it, finally, hovers the Local Interstellar Cloud, about 30 light-years across, which has been perambulating the Sun for 100,000 years.

The Milky Way is accompanied by numerous satellite galaxies. Some of them are gradually merging with it, while it draws gas from others by attraction. It also hosts bubbles, called lobes, which slowly rise from the galactic center. The Milky Way is surrounded by the so-called halo. This is an almost spherical structure that contains numerous globular clusters, very old stars, and large amounts of dark matter with up to a trillion solar masses. The halo is largely dust-free, unlike the inner regions of the Milky Way. This dust is also what makes observation of our home galaxy difficult. Toward the core, it becomes so dense that there is a virtual observational gap.

Everything behind this curtain, from Earth's perspective, is inaccessible to telescopes. In theory, anything could be hidden behind it. In practice, researchers do not assume that the structure of the Milky Way depends on which sections humans can see and which they cannot. Nevertheless, astronomers are curious to look behind the curtain. In fact, measurements of the distribution of hydrogen have revealed that the Milky Way disk may be thickening in its outer regions instead of narrowing as had been assumed. This thickening could be purely related to interstellar matter, but it could also involve the stellar population.

The best-known astronomical object

The milky-bright stripe that stretches unmistakably across the entire night sky in clear weather has long fascinated humanity.

The Greeks imagined it as a stream of milk from the breast of the goddess Hera, which missed the mouth of Heracles, the son conceived out of wedlock by her husband Zeus. It was Galileo Galilei who first determined, with the help of a telescope, that the Milky Way consists of innumerable stars.

It was a long time before humanity had a concrete picture of the structure of our home galaxy. Among other things, the exterior point of view is missing. The structure of our sister galaxy Andromeda is more easily accessible to us than the structure of the Milky Way. However, the knowledge of distant galaxies helped us draw conclusions about the Milky Way. In the meantime, astronomers have learned quite a bit about it.

In the 18th century, the English astronomer Thomas Wright described the celestial phenomenon of the Milky Way arc as an optical effect caused by our position within a gigantic plane of stars. His German contemporary Immanuel Kant concluded that the Milky Way is a rotating disk. Beginning in 1785, Wilhelm Herschel attempted to map the outer shape of the Milky Way by cataloging the stars within it.

Even into the 20th century, many scientists thought that the Galaxy was the entire universe. However, in 1924, the American astronomer Edwin Hubble realized that many structures that his predecessors thought were "nebulae" were actually independent galaxies—Kant had already called them "island universes." Apparently, the Milky Way was just one galaxy among many, and from the shape of the others, we could infer the appearance of our own. Wright, Kant and Herschel were on the right track. However, as far as the origin of the galaxy is concerned, the researchers of that time still knew little.

Formation of the Milky Way

For a long time, two similarly credible main theories existed. Both are based on gas and dust. Either the material collapsed into a disk bulging in the center—very similar to solar systems, but on a much larger scale; or smaller structures formed first, which then merged to form a large galaxy. Without conclusive evidence, astronomers could not say which of the two models was correct.

But that may have changed in the meantime. An international team of astrophysicists led by Dr. Diederik Kruijssen of the Center for Astronomy at Heidelberg University has succeeded in reconstructing the merger history of our home galaxy and establishing its family tree. To do this, the researchers analyzed the properties of globular clusters that orbit the Milky Way in the halo.

Globular clusters are dense groups of up to a million stars, almost as old as the universe itself. The Milky Way hosts more than 150 such clusters. "Many of them originated from smaller galaxies that later merged to form the Milky Way," Kruijssen explains. To study the merger history, the Heidelberg researcher and his colleague, Dr. Joel Pfeffer of Liverpool's John Moore University, and their research groups developed a set of computer simulations called E-MOSAICS. These simulations include a complete model for the formation, evolution and destruction of globular clusters.

The UK-German team used these simulations to relate the age, chemical composition, and orbital motions of globular clusters to the properties of the progenitor galaxies in which they formed more than ten billion years ago. They then applied these findings to groups of globular clusters in the Milky Way, finding not only how heavy these progenitor galaxies were, but also when they merged with our home galaxy.

"The main challenge was that the merger process is extremely messy, because the orbits of the globular clusters are completely rearranged in the process," Kruijssen explains. "To overcome this complexity, we developed an artificial neural network and trained it with the E-MOSAICS simulations. We were amazed at how accurately the AI allowed us to reconstruct the merger histories of the simulated galaxies, even though we only used their globular clusters." The researchers then applied the neural network to groups of globular clusters in the Milky Way and accurately determined the stellar masses and merger times of the progenitor galaxies. They also discovered a previously unknown collision between the Milky Way and an unknown galaxy, which the researchers named "Kraken."

"The collision with 'Kraken' must have been the most significant merger the Milky Way has ever experienced," Kruijssen adds. Previously, a collision with the Gaia-Enceladus galaxy about nine billion years ago was thought to be the largest collision event. However, the merger with Kraken occurred eleven billion years ago, when the Milky Way was four times smaller than it is today. "Consequently, the collision with Kraken must have drastically changed the appearance of the Milky Way at that time," the Heidelberg scientist said.

Taken together, these findings enabled the research team to reconstruct the first complete family tree of our home galaxy. Over the course of its history, the Milky Way has swallowed about five galaxies with more than 100 million stars and about ten more with at least ten million stars. The heaviest progenitor galaxies collided with the Milky Way between six and eleven billion years ago. Kruijssen expects these predictions to facilitate future searches for the remnants of the progenitor galaxies, "The debris of more than five progenitor galaxies has now been identified. With current and future telescopes, it should be possible to find them all."

In the five billion years following "Kraken," the galaxies of the Helmi star stream—Sequoia, Gaia-Enceladus and the Sagittarius dwarf galaxy—merged with our own. Sagittarius, in particular, also appears in data from the Gaia probe. In the course of its mission, Gaia examined 1.8 billion objects inside and outside the Milky Way. Do the results now match the researchers' work? "Yes, our results match," Kruijssen says. "We see that Sagittarius collided with the Milky Way about six billion years ago. But such collisions take place over a long period of time, several billion years. Right now, the core is still connecting with the Milky Way. The outer regions have already been roughed up by the Milky Way's gravity." If the unusual stellar motions can be traced to Sagittarius, it would confirm that this galaxy is the Milky Way's youngest unifier.

Dr. Teresa Antoja of the University of Barcelona agrees. Scientists working through the Gaia data recently detected a slight warp in millions of stellar motions, suggesting a disruption of the Milky Way disk. Antoja explains, "The warping may well have been triggered by Sagittarius."

Parts of the Sagittarius merger are thought to be both fast and slow streams of stars moving toward the plane of the galaxy. What exactly is going on? Antoja admits that nobody knows. "The pattern is very complex—it seems to involve all the phase coordinates of space," she explains. "In the future, we'll look at Sagittarius simulations and look for similar perturbations." Her team hypothesizes that both types of flows overlap with disk waves.

Antoja points out other surprises in the Gaia data, such as the asymmetry in stars above and below the disk, and that there are stars orbiting the galactic center at a distance of 60,000 light-years, suggesting a disk that turns out to be larger than was thought. There are also open clusters with similar orbits. "We don't know if they formed there or were drawn there, or if there are other disk stars there. That needs to be studied."

Antoja's team is also studying the accretion of Gaia-Enceladus, whose stars have been traced in the vicinity of the Sun, and also toward the anticenter, the point opposite the galactic center at the disk edge. These stars are thought to have dispersed over large distances and to have merged with stars in the Milky Way. That points to the importance of this merging.

Prof. Stefan Jordan of the University of Heidelberg and Dr. Anthony Brown of Leiden University have put together an animation that includes some nearby stars. There are 40,000 in all, all within 326 light-years. The program tracks the motion of randomly selected stars over 1.6 million years;

the plot of solar drift through the galaxy breaks off after 400,000 years.

Will this yield further clues regarding the merger history of our galaxy? Brown puts the brakes on such expectations. "The animation is just to show how we can track stellar motions and predict their subsequent position. It has no relevance to the Milky Way's merger history," he explains—adding that such work will require the precise analyses of many astronomers in the years ahead.

Could Kruijssen and Pfeffer's AI show what the future holds for the Milky Way? Possibly. "We stopped the simulation run at the present, we didn't look at the rest," Kruijssen says. "Anyway, we don't need simulations to predict the future of the Milky Way; observations bring us much more." He points to the example of the interaction with the Magellanic Clouds and the impending collision in about 4.5 billion years with the Andromeda Galaxy, which is currently approaching at 100 kilometers per second. However, the model can be applied to other galaxies as well. Kruijssen explains, "We are working on that right now. The problem with other galaxies is that we know much less about their star clusters." For other galaxies, mass and chemical composition can be determined, but their ages are quite uncertain. Velocity can also be calculated only for those galaxies rotating perpendicular to our line of sight.

In addition to the dynamic mergers, the galactic lobes (bulges) of the Milky Way also pose puzzles. These twin bubbles—called Fermi bubbles after the Fermi Space Telescope, which discovered them in 2010—are thought to originate from pressure waves of extremely hot gases emanating from the galactic center and extending 25,000 light-years above and below the disk. They could have been triggered by cosmic jets from the supermassive black hole at the center, or they could be gas ejections from star-forming outbursts. In either case, the triggering events would be early in Milky Way history.

Recently, a team from Germany, Russia, and Italy detected another, even larger bubble group with the Spektr-

RG space telescope. They named them (after the instrument that registered them) eROSITA bubbles. They are said to extend over 45,000 light-years. Did they once look like the Fermi bubbles? According to lead scientist Dr. Peter Predehl of the Max Planck Institute, "That's still under debate. Either yes, because there were two independent events, or both sets of bubbles are connected by one event." The energy required is estimated at 10^{49} joules—as much as 100,000 supernovae. The team continues to work on the data. Our knowledge of the Milky Way has never been greater—and there are still countless mysteries waiting to be solved.

How heavy is the Milky Way?

How much does our home galaxy, the Milky Way, weigh? It is not easy to determine the true dimensions of an object in which we reside. Can you determine the size of your house from the kitchen table? In addition, a large part of the mass is not even visible, because it belongs to dark matter. One admitted estimate is between 100 and 400 billion stars. That results in a visible mass of about 900 billion suns with a diameter of 170,000 to 200,000 light years. But the visible mass is not enough to explain the rotation of the stars in our galaxy.

Ultimately, it is this rotation that allows us to estimate the mass. How fast the objects in the Milky Way are moving depends on the gravitation acting on them—i.e., on the mass of the Milky Way. The further out an object moves, the more likely it is to feel the pull of the entire Milky Way.

Astronomers have therefore chosen celestial objects that orbit the Milky Way at great distances—globular clusters. Data from 34 of these objects, up to 65,000 light-years away, was provided by ESA's Gaia satellite. Twelve other globular clusters up to 130,000 light-years away were contributed by the Hubble Space Telescope. The result of the combined measurements is 1.54 trillion solar masses. Earlier estimates ranged from 900 billion to over two trillion solar masses.

The result is not only interesting from a purely statistical point of view. Knowing the total mass also helps to deter-mine the distribution of dark matter and to study the life history of our Galaxy. Last but not least, the mass of the Milky Way will also determine our future—for example, how the absorption of the Magellanic Clouds and later the merger with Andromeda will proceed. Our neighbor, currently still 2.5 billion light-years away, consists of about one billion stars, about three times as many as the Milky Way. Possibly one will not be able to speak then of a union, but of a takeover.

The Milky Way Collisions

Our galaxy has united continuously with objects in the envi-ronment—and the process continues:

11 billion years ago: The Kraken. This galaxy was the first merging partner of the young Milky Way. It brought with it thirteen globular clusters and permanently changed the composition of the Milky Way.

10 billion years ago: Helmi Stream. Today, this collection of old stars orbits 52,000 light-years away in the halo. It was originally a dwarf galaxy, captured by the growing galactic gravity.

9 billion years ago: Gaia-Enceladus. Until the Kraken was traced, this union was the largest known such event. Today, its stars follow elongated orbits around the center at distances of up to 65,000 light-years.

6-8 billion years ago: Sagittarius. Since the first encounter, Sagittarius has collided with the Milky Way several more times. The group orbits vertically around the galactic disk 50,000 light-years away.

In 1.6-3.6 billion years: Magellanic Cloud. The gravita-tional pull of the Milky Way inexorably attracts the Large Magellanic Cloud. Its stars will be distributed in our halo after the upcoming collision.

In 4.5-5.8 billion years: Andromeda Galaxy. Our imme-diate neighbor is hurtling toward us at 100 kilometers per second. After the collision, it will form a single, elliptical galaxy, which could be dubbed "Milkomeda".

How will collisions change our home?

Our home galaxy, the Milky Way, is admittedly a rather unusual example of a spiral galaxy. The black hole at its center is underdeveloped (it is an entire class too light), it is surrounded by a (too) low-mass halo of extremely metal-poor stars, and it has an unusually large companion, the Large Magellanic Cloud (LMC).

But there's good news, too, as astronomers show in a paper: In just 2.4 billion years (the universe is already 13.8 billion years old today), a giant collision will iron out these messes. It could happen that our solar system is thrown out of the Milky Way, but one must accept small mishaps with collisions so large.

The cause of the collision will be the Large Magellanic Cloud. Today it's moving through space with its 15 billion stars at a distance of 163,000 light-years. Until now, it was assumed that it would orbit the Milky Way for a long time. But apparently it contains twice as much dark matter as previously assumed. And that now makes it a serious collision opponent after all.

As shown in a computer simulation of the coming future, the collision with our Milky Way will cause its central black hole, Sagittarius A*, to swell eightfold and turn it into an active galactic nucleus that will shower its surroundings with radiation. The halo will thereafter be five times as heavy as it is today, and most of the stars in the LMC will integrate into our Milky Way. At the same time, however, stars will be ejected from the Milky Way into the surrounding halo—if our descendants are unlucky, the solar system will be among them. However, we will not notice this until it is too late. The Milky Way will then become a real example of a spiral galaxy for a few billion years, before the next collision (this time with Andromeda) destroys the beautiful picture again.

The collision and merger of the Milky Way and the Andromeda galaxy is inevitable, although today there are still 2.5 million light years between them. So the light we see now from Andromeda was emitted from there 2.5 million years ago. However, these two members of the Local Group, which are by far the heaviest, are moving towards each other at 120 kilometers per second. This means that in a few billion years, their up to 1.3 trillion stars will meet (i.e. during the lifetime of our sun).

A collision already underway

The collision has long since begun, as researchers using the Hubble Space Telescope have discovered. In a study published in the Astrophysical Journal, they describe how, as part of a program called AMIGA (Absorption Map of Ionized Gas in Andromeda), they studied the area around the galaxy itself, known as the halo.

To do this, they looked at the light from 43 quasars—the very distant, bright cores of active galaxies, powered by black holes and located far behind Andromeda. The quasars are scattered behind the halo, allowing scientists to study multiple regions. Looking through the halo at the light from the quasars, the team observed how that light is absorbed by the Andromeda halo and how that absorption changes in different regions. The immense Andromeda halo is apparently composed of thin, ionized gas that does not emit easily detectable radiation. Therefore, tracking the absorption of light coming from a background source is a better way to study this region.

Scientists were surprised to find that this nearly invisible halo of diffuse plasma extends 1.3 million light-years from the Andromeda galaxy—about halfway to our Milky Way—and as far as 2 million light-years in some directions. This means that the halo of Andromeda is already colliding with the halo of our own galaxy.

The researchers also found that the halo has a layered

structure, with two gas shells nested one inside the other. "We find that the inner shell, which spans about half a million light-years, is far more complex and dynamic," explained study leader Nicolas Lehner of Notre Dame University in Indiana. "The outer shell is smoother and hotter. This difference is likely due to the influence of supernova activity in the galaxy's disk, which directly affects the inner halo." One indication of this activity is the discovery of a large amount of heavy elements in the gaseous halo. They are born inside stars and then ejected into space—sometimes violently—when a star dies. The halo is then contaminated with this material by stellar explosions.

Where are the siblings of the Milky Way?

Once upon a time, three siblings roamed the universe together. Two of their names are still known today: The Milky Way and the Andromeda Galaxy are still the dominant galaxies of the Local Group. But the third sibling was lost two billion years ago—"M32p" as astronomers call it today. At the time, M32p was the third largest galaxy in the Local Group and twenty times larger than any galaxy that had ever merged with the Milky Way.

As it has since turned out, Andromeda probably has M32p on its conscience. Astronomers have found telltale trails in Andromeda's halo, which is dominated by metal-rich, middle-age stars. Computer simulations showed that only a merger with another, very large galaxy could be responsible. Its core is now found in Andro-Beta, M32, an elliptical dwarf galaxy that accompanies Andromeda.

Strange objects in the center of the Milky Way

Sometimes they behave like a gas cloud, then they become an almost-ordinary star again: The so-called "G-objects" described by astronomers in the science journal Nature are difficult to squeeze into one category. Researchers have already identified six of these objects. They are all located in the immediate vicinity of the center of our Milky Way—in the orbit of the supermassive black hole Sagittarius A*.

This commonality is probably what contributes to their strange behavior. G1 to G6 have orbits that take them around the black hole once every 100 to 1000 years. Whenever they get too close to it, they are stretched like chewing gum by the gravitational pull, after which they seem to contract again.

The researchers suspect that the G-objects are former binary systems, i.e., systems consisting of two stars that merged at some point under the influence of Sagittarius A*. But this process is not over yet—normally the merging of two stars takes up to a million years. As they approach the black hole in their unification dance, this pulls the two components apart. After that, their own gravitational pull will bring them back together.

How old is the Milky Way?

Our home galaxy contains up to 400 billion stars, and to cross it would take 200,000 years even at the speed of light. Such a huge object (which is rather average in cosmic terms) does not come into being overnight. The Milky Way was actually born relatively early, at a time when the universe was still quite young. But when exactly, and how does one measure that?

Quite simply, if you want to know how old a forest is, you determine the age of its trees. The stars of the Milky Way do not have annual rings, but with increasing age they contain on average more and more heavy elements. While the first stars consisted only of hydrogen and helium, later more and more fusion products like lithium, carbon, oxygen and even iron are found. Astronomers speak of the metallicity of stars, whereby metal is considered everything which is not hydrogen or helium.

Of course, just looking at a few stars is not enough. To get a realistic picture of the evolution of the Milky Way, one must determine the metallicity of as many stars as possible. This is the task that astronomers Maosheng Xiang and Hans-Walter Rix have undertaken. To study the formation history of our galaxy, they used data from ESA's Gaia Space Observatory and the Large Sky Area Multi-Object Fibre Spectroscopic Telescope in China to identify about 250,000 subgiant-phase stars covering a large spatial volume of the Milky Way.

The authors estimated the individual ages of these stars and found them to be between 1.5 billion and 13.8 billion years old. They then identified and characterized the origins of the various structural elements in the Milky Way's disk and halo stellar populations. The results suggest that the formation of the thick disk began about 13 billion years ago, just 800 million years after the Big Bang. The authors calculate that the inner galactic halo did not form until two billion years later. This probably coincides with the time when most of the stars in the thick disk were formed.

Stars in their subgiant phase of evolution provide a precise stellar clock because astronomers can directly and accurately measure their age during this short phase, based on their brightness. However, because of the short duration of this evolutionary phase, such observations are relatively rare, and large surveys have not been possible in the past.

The Milky Way—where is it headed?

Where is the Milky Way's cosmic journey headed? That's what an international team of astronomers has found out for our local "hood"—namely, for the 1400 galaxies located within 100 million light-years of the Milky Way. The researchers analyzed and compared the motions of these galaxies in the last 13 billion years. While this didn't reveal anything we should be concerned about, it did reveal a few interesting trends.

The center of gravity in the area is clearly the Virgo Cluster, 50 million light-years from us, which is pulling all matter in its immediate vicinity with the mass of its 600 trillion suns. Over a thousand galaxies have already fallen into this trap, and all others up to 40 million light years away will meet this fate.

The Milky Way and Andromeda galaxies lie outside of this zone. Luckily!

The researchers also found two overarching patterns. First, all galaxies in one half of the surveyed area (including our Milky Way) are moving on the same flat plane. Second, the entire contents of space, all 1400 galaxies, are "flowing" like leaves in the wind toward a distant, much larger gravitational attraction point.

Intelligent life in the Milky Way is slowly dying out

Some bad news at the end: Humankind is quite late and quite far out. That's the conclusion of a study that statistically examines the development of intelligent life in the Milky Way. In it, the authors look at a whole range of factors that they believe influence the evolution of intelligent life, such as the frequency of Sun-like stars hosting Earth-like planets, the frequency for a civilization of deadly supernovae, the length of time required for intelligent life to evolve (if conditions are right), and the tendency of advanced civilizations to self-destruct.

The researchers incorporated these factors, with varying values, into a simulation of the Milky Way. The result: about 13,000 light-years from the galactic center and 8 billion years after the galaxy's formation, the number of extraterrestrial civilizations has probably peaked. By comparison, Earth is about 25,000 light years from the galactic center, and human civilization did not emerge on the surface of our planet until 13.5 billion years after the Big Bang. So we are latecomers, and our galactic position would also make it difficult to establish contact with other civilizations, especially since their total number has been decreasing for 5.5 billion years.

However, this does not mean that there is no more chance of meeting. The researchers believe that at this time, civilizations existing along with us are probably too young to be detectable. However, we should not concentrate our search on the nearest stars as we have done so far, but on the area 13,000 light-years away from the center of the Milky Way, mainly because of the sun-like stars that predominate there. If the simulations are to be believed, most of the civilizations that existed 5 billion years ago have already self-destructed.

Printed in Great Britain
by Amazon